THE SELKIRK STRIP

The Selkirk Strip
A Post-Imperial Tale

FERDINAND MOUNT

faber and faber

This edition first published in 2010
by Faber and Faber Ltd
Bloomsbury House, 74–77 Great Russell Street
London WC1B 3DA

A CIP record for this book is available from the British Library

ISBN 978–0–571–26053–9

for

M. J. M.

Ah, God! One sniff of England –
　　To greet our flesh and blood –
To hear the traffic slurring
　　Once more through London mud!
Our towns of wasted honour –
　　Our streets of lost delight!
How stands the old Lord Warden?
　　Are Dover's cliffs still white?

Kipling. The Broken Men. 1902

There's no breathing done in England now;
Hearts have failed from Surbiton to Slough.
　　Dead as doornails, dead as mutton –
　　Cobham, Chorleywood and Sutton –
History bereaves the rotten bough.

T. F. Sturgis. Dead Ground. 1936

Grateful thanks to Mr William Sturgis and the Executors of the Sturgis Estate for permission to quote from 'Dead Ground' from *The Shorter Lyrics of T. F. Sturgis* (London 1939) and 'Closing Time' from *Delenda – the suppressed verse of T. F. Sturgis* (New York 1977).

Excerpts from the Crupper Papers are taken from the *Diaries and Letters of William Crupper*, ed. E. Cotton, Cambridge (forthcoming).

CHAPTER 1

I stand barefoot on the doorstep, taking in the milk, householder, husband, parent, man in pyjamas. The milk bottles chink as I bend to gather them up. They leave pale rings on the cold stone. How white my toes look on the stone, like the flesh of boiled fish. I think of my father's long feet striding across the wet grass on summer mornings in my childhood. Two bottles in each hand, the fifth bottle tucked into my armpit deathly cold against my chest through the thin pyjama, the milk-bringer, flushed a little breathless, resumes the upright position, male pasteurised and bottled, otherwise closely resembling the many-breasted Diana of the Ephesians.

The morning is chill and still with a touch of damp. There is dew on the lemka bush by the flaking black railings. The dumb parked cars are wet with it. The man in the raincoat who looks like a chicken walks past with averted gaze, trying not to catch sight of me in my loose-tied, low-slung pyjamas. Good morning, good morning. There is terror in his 'Good morning'. I can kill him with my smile. One day, he knows, I shall engage him in conversation and his happiness will be over. All day long in his office he will remember my bared teeth and my blue and white pyjama bottoms.

These are the precious moments of a North London dawn, the stale breath in the cold air, the rub of stubble on the chin, the cold toes on the lip of the step, a sharp sensation of the world's otherness, never quite the same after getting dressed.

The lemka bush — a dwarf cousin of the now mighty tree brought back to Kew as a seedling by Lemprière and Kay in 1884 and named in their honour by the curator (the Mogana people called it simply 'the bitter tree') — shudders as the sparrows bob at its bright orange berries. 'Of upright habit, sturdy evergreen',

1

would that as much could be said of me. I have a trembling knee, presaging cartilage trouble or so my doctor says, and a trembling heart. On the other hand, I earn £18,996 a year, which is at the top of the scale for a 42-year-old assistant secretary in the Civil Service. On the other hand again, Riley-Jones, who joined the same day as me, is an Under-Secretary already. My shoulders are hunched, but pleasantly so, and my sense of smell has gone. I have a dry wit and a dry skin. Both are getting drier.

My wife is tall. She has a long back and a warm blushing smile which you will remember from the missing pre-molar. She comes from an academic family which would scorn cosmetic dentistry, having no more idea of tooth care than the men you see yanking teeth out with pliers in a haroosh of blood in films about Morocco.

The Dudgeon-Stewarts have a flirtatious relationship with gentility. In fact, to call them an academic family is to take them at their own present valuation. Their great-grandparents were brass-founders and teabrokers. Their grandparents went into the Church and the Indian Civil Service. It is only the parental generation who are mostly to be seen, fathers and mothers alike, pedalling along the Backs and down Rawlinson Road on blossom-heavy May mornings. Nellie, Nell, Eleanor – she answers to all three – was, I believe, named after the brass-founder's nurserymaid who survived to be the oldest of retainers. Or was she named after her mother's terrier which had been named after the nurserymaid? A kind of confident shimmer surrounds Nellie's family so that when she describes them the precise facts tend to slip my memory.

Nellie goes in for shawls and cardigans and cousins and old-fashioned turns of speech. The spirit of a waspish Victorian aunt hovers over her. 'Limbs' is just the word to describe her arms and legs so long and round and bulby, as slow as her mind is quick.

Her cousins, many of them, exhaling the clammy hauteur of English Roman Catholicism (although mostly lacking the deviousness of that embattled sect), descend upon us singly, preceded by complicated letters written in fine script with Greek 'e's. They do not use the telephone. They come to London to draw bucketfuls from the inexhaustible well of culture, splashing themselves all over with Exhibitions as vulgar persons dowse themselves in aftershave. They too go in for shawls and long cardigans, regardless of fashion. They dress with a certain fringey magnificence. They live to a great age, smoking strange brands of cigarettes (sometimes through amber cigarette-holders), eating and drinking greedily without getting fat, careless of their persons. Cholesterol dares not linger in their veins.

One of Nellie's cousins – Aidan I think it was – once wrote a history of mortgages. The publishers he sent it to said they thought the book had only limited appeal, or so Nellie reported in that tone of mild wonder with which she greeted news of any worldly setback experienced by her relations. Later, he sent it to us. The publisher was right. Mort gage – dead wage. There are eight and a half years to go on ours. I keep count of such things.

Gazing idly down the street, I catch sight of the local hippie – no, we no longer use that word, we are not to be caught with second-hand slang about our person – the local free person sauntering up it. Rob Bunsen's elder son by his first marriage, a comely, irritating youth with clear blue eyes. We are the dead-waged. He is the unwaged. He is kind to us, he does not patronise, but he cannot help letting us know that he is a traveller, of the non-commercial kind. My son, Rob said, not without a smidgeon of pride, is like the Almighty in the Old Testament. In the disappearing rain forest, there he is. In the manmade dust bowl, there he is. In the melting ice cap, you can't miss the little bugger. Woe unto ye my people that you have made an abomination of the earth, that's Marco's line, he has a terrific time. I think he's really just a romantic at heart, his stepmother Janey said, but he's got to have a reason for going all that way. Janey is right. No use telling him that if you get too close to the blue mountains on the horizon all you see is slag and scree. Being there is what matters, or rather not being here.

'Where you off to this time, Marco?'

'Sketchleys and then Java,' he answers, swinging his dirty bush jacket over his shoulder with a kindly smile.

We are locked in fidelity, my wife and I, faithful to each other and to our limitations. She is a population historian by trade, if trade it be, and can tell you the average family size in Great

Crupper between 1450 and 1470, if you like, or the rate of pre-nuptial conceptions and, what's more, that they were running at a significantly higher rate than in Little Crupper, where the influence of the De Garsingtons may have affected standards of local moral-ity, since they formally controlled access to the chapel of ease. You mean, I said, that, if you were in trouble, the De Garsingtons would prevent you from marrying in the parish. Broadly yes, Nellie said. Don't broadly me, I said, it was only an idle enquiry, I am not supervising your thesis, I have better things to do. I wish I knew what you do all day long in your office, she said.

You see how much good we do in the world, Nellie and I, how generations yet unborn will thank us. There is, I am sure, a philosophy or religion somewhere which teaches us the virtue, even the beauty, of contemplating our own uselessness. Perhaps it is Christianity – a curious faith which I never quite got the hang of. Belief I never found much of a problem. It was enthusiasm which I found so hard to simulate. But don't you believe in the Virgin Birth, Cotton? Yes, sir, I just don't find it very interesting. How can one recapture the indifference of youth, that dreamy self-absorption as bland and endless as a blue summer sky? Now on the verge of middle age – over the verge perhaps, I sometimes feel the tyres bumping – I find myself gripped by strange crazes, sometimes fleeting sometimes lasting, for things once auto-matically scorned; paper flowers, rugby football, coloured bath-room tiles, and religious broadcasts. The sight of a robin on a spade or a child at prep sets me whimpering. Weak lachrymal ducts like all the Cottons, my father used to say, wiping his eyes after playing 'Il mio tesoro' with Heddle Nash soaring over the crackle of the blue Decca 78.

Down the street comes the sound of jogging, the slip-slop of flat Adidas feet hitting uneven pavement. And round the gentle bend in the railings comes Liz Littlejohn with her grey tracksuit and her proud high wobble. She runs as though escaping from a gang of Italian bottom-pinchers. Flushed, indignant-looking, twisting her flanks away from greedy hands. A shoulder-strap has risen up to her damp neck, flicking against the stray curls of her wild brown hair.

'Hi, Gus,' she calls.

'Hi,' I call back, although I deprecate the use of fake American. In the Civil Service, several of my colleagues have taken to saying 'Ciao', a still more ludicrous attempt to indicate sophistication and knowledge of foreign parts. I feel pedantry coming upon me like the falling of soft rain in the West. You scarcely notice it at first, then you rather like its caress, and suddenly you notice you are wet through. My proper name is Aldous.

Anyway, Liz has no business hi-ing. She has no title to the blithe. Her awkwardness with slang, her mistimed chuckling ohh, halfway through someone's anecdote, the way she pats you on your upper arm just at the moment when you don't need comforting − all undermine her desperate efforts to be laid back when nature has, cruelly but firmly, laid her so far forward. The weight of her attention bows down the slightest encounter. She cannot buy a bar of chocolate without making everyone else in the shop feel gay and frivolous. 'That's right, is it, it's the Topic bars which have the nuts in them, but not the Picnic? And which is the one *without* the coconut?' she will say, pointing carefully at each of the items in question like an actor in a mediaeval mystery play pointing at a fragment of the True Cross, and so on until you can feel the woman behind the counter wanting to say: what the hell, they're only chocolate bars, why should I care, I wanted to be a ballet dancer − except that if she did Liz would say: oh really, that *is* a pity, wouldn't your parents let you, but I expect you're better off not being because it's such a hard life, isn't it? And this seriousness, this attentiveness, is all the more crippling because it seems so drenched in kind-heartedness, so that even when she is talking about different kinds of chocolate bar, you are aware of charitable impulses buzzing around inside her and liable at any moment to stream out and swarm around your head so that you can't think properly.

I do not think Liz is vain or even ambitious. True, no woman who jogs, even in a track-suit which looks like a Klondike miner's underwear, can be quite unconcerned with self. Yet she does such things less out of self-love than a sense of obligation. To what or whom, you may ask? Not God, or convention or posterity. It is a kind of formless sense of obligation which covers everything she does, like the soft white ash from a distant volcano erupting. Religion and ideology may have collapsed, but in Liz the collapse seems to have left untouched the sense of the serious. Far from everything being permitted now that God has died, nothing is permitted without some kind of licence. There is no free zone for nonchalance. I sometimes think Liz may be a new type in the history of the human race.

There was a time, which I cannot help remembering now and then, when all that serious energy seemed like gaiety to me. 'Just wait while I have a bath,' she would call down the stairs from the attic bathroom. And I would sit on the bed with the Mexican bedcover and talk to her friend Janey while I listened to the taps running overhead and her bare feet moving from room to room. When I pass in Camden Town the shop which sells Mexican clothes – all violent reds and yellows – I still think of her feet on the attic boards. But even then she was not really carefree; she discarded boyfriends quickly, not in a hectic pursuit of pleasure but because she was after a serious relationship, one which could be weighed in the hand; I scarcely registered on her scales. which was just as well since evenings with her were wearing. The best of it was in the waiting on the bed with the Mexican bedcover, talking awkwardly to her friend Janey, now Rob Bunsen's second wife. Janey is still her friend and lives round the corner; Liz sets store by friends, all the more so now that she has been married for years (they have no children – this fact to be kept in brackets and not to be allowed to hitch itself to a 'but'). There is a reverence, a relish about the way she says the word – 'friends' – just marked by the way she faintly rolls the 'r'. She imagines the people she knows as a set, a crowd, a gang, although none of the rest of us see ourselves like that at all. But when she looks round at us as we sit down at her table – which we do quite often since she entertains with energy too – she'll say something like 'isn't it nice we're all here again?' – drawing a great circle round us with the 'all'.

As she dodges round the low-branched limes at the end of the street, she bumps into an immensely tall and thin man in a duffel coat coming round the corner. The man takes a step backwards and makes a courtly gesture of apology. He walks up the street towards me with long uncertain strides like someone testing the ice. Under the navy-blue, open-toggled coat I can see a gingerish tweed jacket, an old-fashioned viyella check shirt and a clubby tie – all this like a schoolmaster, perhaps one who had formerly been a soldier, except that on his feet he has gymshoes of a blue which had once been bright. His face is long and mournful, an Easter Island god's with horn-rimmed spectacles added. He is carrying a large suitcase.

When he came level with our house, he stopped and turned to face me, with feet neatly together.

'Good morning,' he called.

I was taken aback by him planted there in front of me at the bottom of our steps. His voice, light tenor, rather rasping, seemed to be calling for my attention from a greater distance, as if I had been pruning roses the other side of a hedge.

'Good morning.' I hitched up my pyjamas as he climbed the four steps to reach our doorstep.

'You must be Cousin Gus.'

'Ah, you're ... '

'I am Alan Breck Stewart, your first cousin by marriage, at least once removed as you can see by my old grey head' – which he wagged in a slow parody of senility.

'We thought you were coming for tea,' I said feebly.

'I travelled down by the sleeper. We finished clearing up earlier than I had expected.'

Smiles exchanged, mine nervous his welcoming, as though our roles had been reversed. His teeth were long and plaquey yellow round the gums, but there was something unexpectedly pleasant and relaxing about his smile, like a patch of sunlight passing across a cliff face. All the same, he had caught me off guard. I was not prepared for entertaining. Ours is not an open house. We have people in only after an agony of forethought. And I was still chasing half-remembered facts through the morning mind-fog: the death of Nellie's old cousin Catriona Stewart, the mother of the man in front of me, Nellie's letter of condolence written with some

7

difficulty because of the miserly and ill-tempered character of the deceased, Alan's reply inviting himself to tea on his way home to Italy – Rome, I think – after he had been north to clear up the house in North Berwick.

'Come in,' I said, but he was already half-way into the hall, squeezing past me with a grim urgency as if about to tackle a gunman holed up on the bedroom floor.

'Is anybody there?' he called.

'What?' Nell called back, in that slow contralto which thrilled me from the first (no, not contralto, that suggests warble and show, it is more of a soft, reposeful moan, suggestive of exhausted passion – however, enough of that).

'It's me, Cousin Alan.'

Nellie's head came into view at the top of the basement stairs, long, thoughtful, large-eyed with her flurried mane of enhanced mouse.

'Oh, *hullo.*'

She remained standing half-way up the stairs with her usual physical irresolution, only her head and shoulders being visible above ground level. Her self-proclaimed cousin bent to shake her hand, stooping as if greeting a child. At the same instant, she resumed her progress up the stairs. Her ascending forehead banged against the side of his descending jaw.

'Ah, the Stewart embrace, bone on bone,' he said, putting an arm round her, with a clumsiness no less conspicuous, when she had attained the landing.

'The best you ever got was a mouthful of hair,' Nellie replied.

He now held her at arm's length, in the manner of a couple about to begin a country dance they did not know too well, gingerly yet comradely. I could see she was already touched, even warmed by the glow of family reminiscence, the shared recollection which stressed, quite correctly, the awkwardness of her family when faced with the need for physical contact, in public at any rate.

Smoke began to fill the stairway. The fumes of burning toast brought her back to earth.

'The children will be suffocating. Come downstairs.'

The three of us descended the stairs with Alan in the middle looking back up at me with a grin which was somehow complicitous, as though we were up to something together which not everyone knew about.

'And this must be Thomas, and you of course are Elspeth.'

'How clever of you to know their names.'

'When you wrote about Mother, you told me all about them,' Alan said, not without a touch of reproach.

I watched my wife slowly pick the burnt toast up out of the toaster and try to put it in the pedal bin. On the first attempt, she mistimed the pedal so that the toast landed on the green plastic lid and slid onto the floor. Alan, hovering beside her, swiftly bent down from his great height and flicked it into the bin.

'Mum's spastic,' Thomas said.

'Totally spacky,' Elspeth said.

'I am sorry. It is a most inconvenient time to arrive.'

'Oh no. You must stay the night. I do hope you can,' Nellie said.

'Well, I do have some things to finish off in London.'

'Do stay please.'

'For ever and ever Amen,' Elspeth said, picking up, as she often did, that rather chanting way Nell repeated a plea.

'Yes, do,' I said, a laggard chorus.

'You are kind. I would like to renew a few old friendships before I go back. Mother's death has knocked me off balance a bit. And that house. I never slept a wink in it.'

'It must have been awful,' Nell said.

'She was a difficult woman. I expect you remember that. Nobody could tolerate her for long, least of all me.'

Alan put his hand over his face and began to sob. When he raised his head from his hand, his face was wet with tears.

'Oh, *poor* Alan,' Nell said. She leant across and rested her hand on his left shoulder. With a grand gesture, his right hand swept across his chest to clasp her fingers, which he held for several moments while the children furtively finished off their cereal, eyes peeping over the parapet spoon. Then he released her and patted Thomas's head, a thing Thomas normally resented but now did

9

not appear to mind. 'I expect it's time for school,' Alan said. 'You must not allow me to wallow in sentiment. There is work to be done.' He gave a peculiar cough, rasping and jerky yet also light, like someone imitating a two-stroke engine failing to start.

'You need time to get your breath back,' I said.

He looked at me with the quick half-suspicious, half-gratified look which elderly bachelors give me when I have said something unexpectedly warm. A somewhat cool and detached temperament, it said in my last Civil Service annual assessment, that curious exercise which each year tempts our superiors to put out their shiny little novelist's antennae. Even in the Civil Service, a cold fish is not thought appetising. And yet I am always surprised by judgments of this sort, for I imagine that I have schooled myself to act warmer than I feel. Myself, I find genuine coldness in others quite comfortable. What seems to me creepy is the pretence of coldness, the assumed frigidity of the artist or the would-be leader of men who pretends to be a man from nowhere without affections or relations, in order to be able to stand outside and beyond the rest of us.

Thomas and Elspeth, late fruit of these tepid loins, began to quarrel in an undertone.

'That is *not* your ruler.'

'Why's it in my satchel then?'

Alan turned towards them, tucking his head down and to one side.

'Oh dear,' he said in mock despair, not without a hint of menace. Something, whether his recent agitation or a growing irritation with the children, seemed to push him into a higher register. Coming from this lanky figure with his decayed military bearing, such a tone sounded put on. This detour into shrillness prodded me into thinking more realistically about what we had taken on.

'We aren't much practised at house-guests,' I said, 'but the spare room needs using.'

'Don't worry, don't worry. I can shake down pretty well anywhere.'

His long fingers clasped the coffee cup, his square-cut fingernails pressing the earthenware like wan little trowels. Close up, he seemed no longer quite so robust.

'Polly Parrott used to have a flat near here. Did you ever come across Polly?'

'He was a friend of my father's.'

'Was he? I only knew him in his Red phase. A very wild young man. Then, like so many of us, he defected to Rome and eventually, I believe, landed up in the *Reemy*.' The Royal Electrical and Mechanical Engineers was made to sound like a sect given to exotic practices.

'I think he was a sapper, in fact.' As I uttered this flat rebuke, it occurred to me how I had spoken in the same tones to my father, restraining his flights of fancy with the same smack of fact. Those dim, unhappy days had been lived through, survived even on those terms. Often, in later years from my mid-thirties onwards, I have recognised fellow sufferers from a dismal period in their twenties. For us those years, far from being a time of adventure and discovery, were a time of unspeakable latency and withdrawal, of long walks in interesting cemeteries and solitary sports, indoor and outdoor. We are to be recognized now by a general air of relief that those times at least are behind us.

Alan put his coffee cup down in its saucer, pushed his chair back, and came to stand beside me looking up out of the window.

'Ah, the London *area*. On hot nights in Rome, in my little oven, I often think of areas I have known.'

'Do you?' I said.

'Somehow, the area is always the heart of a London house. Housemaids kiss on the area steps. The dreaded lodger lurks behind the net curtains. That is where it all happens, or did in my day. There was a basement in Belsize Park with a little glass porch to keep the rain off where the most extraordinary things went on.'

'Don't extraordinary things go on in Rome?' Nellie said, turning down the collar of Thomas's blazer as he stood sullenly at the foot of the stairs. Her normal recessive purity had deserted her.

'Too few, my dear, too few. I live like a hermit, translating the most bizarre medical treatises into Italian and translating the dreariest commercial nonsense into English. I simply no longer have the energy for any of that side of life.'

11

The confession, like so many of its sort, brazenly suggested the opposite. To exaggerate the effect of the advancing years is one way of resisting them.

'The neighbours? Are they interesting? Do you see much of them?'

'Well,' said Nellie, 'there are the Littlejohns. We're going there for supper this evening. They're the ones we know best. You must come. I'm sure they'd love to have you.'

'You must brief me.' Alan said. 'Are they intelligent? How much does he earn? What does she do?'

'Hector's an oil analyst. Thirty thousand a year, I should guess. And Liz teaches remedial dance.'

'They must be very talented.' As so often, I could not tell how far, if at all, he meant to be ironic.

'And children?'

'None, I'm afraid,' Nellie said. 'Liz has tubes trouble.'

'That is sad.'

'She's not exactly pretty, really. Rather blobby, but vivacious.'

Melancholy crept over me. These brief sketches were too facile, like the portraits executed by pavement artists with dead eyes, who sourly scratch conventional types in the crude colours that show up best on the unhelpful pavement.

'You passed her in the street,' I said.

'Oh yes. The sweaty woman. I shall do my best with her,' Alan said.

'I'm sure you will,' I said.

'I'm not an asset at dinner parties. I have no small talk. In Rome I never go out. There is an extremely convenient little shop near my flat where I buy pasta.'

'Ah. That's good.'

Thomas, my son, stood on the bottom step of the basement stairs, his arm crooked around the thick white newel-post with its bulbous floral carving – the period feature which, the estate agent claimed, quite made the kitchen. Eight years old, round-cheeked, floppy-haired, gap-toothed, contentious child, more nervous, less strong than he looked. His sister, Elspeth, a year younger, despatched upstairs to get her hairslides, tried to push him aside. They

12

swore at each other in fierce, hoarse voices, repeating the same monotonous swear words. I was aware of Alan stiffening at my side. Either the brown-skinned *bambini* to which he was accustomed swore not at all, or the Italian words sounded sweeter.

All the same, he had that ease with children which can be detected from the moment an adult comes into a room. It was not a question of treating children on equal terms but rather a matter of tone, almost like a musical instruction, graceful, relaxed, unforcing and unforced — the opposite of the inquisitive, intrusive style which immediately jars on children. Despite this gift, it was plain that children were for him not quite part of life in its largest sense. Even to compare their status with that of a cherished dog or cat was not quite accurate, for the pet could be woven into plans, its whims, habits and diseases could be made much of, could even come to dominate a life or a conversation. But children were different, more self-willed, more a serious undertaking and yet in the end more elusive and unrewarding. In life as in art, they were best seen and not heard.

As Thomas and Elspeth tussled at the foot of the stairs, how poignant, yet how unspeakable they seemed. The tendency of art to exclude children is one of the things that makes the middle-aged lose faith in art, or rather it is because artists use children only as playthings and obstacles to grown-up plans that we begin to suspect that art is merely an excuse to get out of the house and that the artist flees family life not because it is false and shallow but because it is too overwhelmingly real. The artist likes to remember himself as a child — shy, put-upon, painfully sensitive. He does not like to think of himself as the parent which now and then willy-nilly he becomes. Yet how strange it is, this artist's world, populated by solitary men-children. How unlike this spacious, moony universe is to the intense, crowded world with its regular heave and jostle.

'Shut up,' I shouted at the children.

'He started it.'

'She kicked me.'

It is easy to see why childhood had to be rigorously excluded from the Iliad or the sagas. Even Western films never show children quarrelling, at most a cute and wry moral is pointed by children going bang bang you're dead in the dusty street. But the real rage of children, the real biting and kicking and swearing cannot be shown in art for fear of making Achilles and Wyatt Earp seem like poor child-substitutes. Children are the artist's rivals. No, it is worse than that. For the artist has stopped growing and started to decay and his comforting little fabrications about the reality of memory wither under the child's cold gaze. Art is such a poor imitation of childhood, its passions paler, its reveries staler.

'Hurry *up*,' Nellie said, shooing them up the stairs. 'Have you been yet?'

'Oh, mum.'

'My mother,' Alan said with that abruptness with which people signal that adult life is to be resumed, 'was a curious woman much given to analysing the state of my bowels.'

'Mothers tend to be like that.'

'She took it to extremes. Not only did she keep a chart of my marks at school, she also kept this other chart of my bowel movements, but as she was frightened of the servant seeing it, she did not spell out what was being charted. It would just say Monday 7th March Good a.m., or Poor a.m. It was horrible.'

'Why didn't you always tell her it was good?'

'Well, I couldn't during the holidays because she refused to allow me to pull the plug so that she could inspect the result. If I did it while she was out, and then went again later in the day, having claimed a Good after breakfast, she immediately assumed I had a tummy upset and she would pour the most filthy medicine down me. I didn't dare to rebel until I was sent away to school when I pointed out that the master on duty would be reading the letter and would he really want to read all about my big-jobs blow by blow, so to speak. So we agreed that I could just put some innocuous general statement which would cover the week's per-formance – "My state of health has been good" or "I've been feeling a bit slow this week".'

I pictured the little boy with a long face and a mutinous expression writing home to an imperious woman smelling of lavender.

'The pity is that if she asked me now, my mother, I would be quite prepared to enter into such graphic detail. In later life I have come to take an interest in the body and its malfunctions. One never gets asked the right question at the right time in this life.'

His last words were nearly lost in the sound of Nellie beginning to wash up. She is not one for the cloacal. It is not that she thinks bodily functions are not to be spoken of, but they are not to be lingered on. In her mind the practicalities of adult life call for a certain briskness. And then I think she finds it shocking to realise not only that our elders go to the lavatory but also that their minds may brood upon the business. I had a friend who loved the poetry of T.F. Sturgis, and when the poet came to lecture at our forlorn academy, my friend, being mildly that way inclined, in adolescence at least, made eyes at Sturgis and secured an invitation to join his coterie for coffee afterwards. For two hours by the clock, without let or pause, Sturgis told lavatory jokes, some infantile, some complex and ingenious acrostics, some brutally homosexual but all remorselessly attached to the toilet. My friend never spoke of Sturgis or his poetry again.

CHAPTER 2

I shivered as I sat down at the Littlejohns' long kitchen table. Ah, chill the bloom on the quiche, and chill the empty heart, I said to myself, the rhythm dredged up from the words of some hymn we must have sung at school. My knees knocked together, barely brushed by the breeze from the blower heater at the far end of the vast knocked-through many-alcoved room. My gaze roamed over the gingham ruche, the lovely white neck, the tumble of hair. Liz was still bent over the work-surface, a muted gamboge formica, chopping fiercely at some blameless herb. Above her head, the coronation mugs twitched on the dresser, pine cruelly stripped, knot-holes preening. She turned and the blue gingham swirled as for a square-dance.

'There,' she said, 'it's not really a quiche, more a . . .

' . . . way of life,' Hector Littlejohn said, in the sad voice he used for jokes. He lived in a low key and played on it, tending to roll his soft round eyes, specialising in a range of dispiriting sounds – groans, sighs, wet indrawings of breath. He seemed to confide, to lead you into a world in which the best of pleasures was to watch yourself being disappointed or rather, since you had made no serious appointments, to enjoy the monotonous regularity with which life would have fallen short of your expectations if you had been foolish enough to have any. His head was cocked on one side, his mouth a little drawn up at one corner, a human wryneck. Living at this low pitch, he took little out of himself and slept badly, roaming the house in the small hours, swearing quietly, in search of back numbers of *Country Life*. By day, he was an investment analyst, specialising in oil stocks. He was younger than Liz by, I think, about seven years, and she was protective towards him, while he now and then showed the self-absorption, even the callousness, of a child. Liz worried that he did not stretch himself, that he was both overtired and not tired enough. And yet to see his long body curled along the sofa of an evening as he watched *Dallas* was to feel that he had taken no less trouble than the rest of us in inventing himself. A certain purity and good humour were required to keep him going and he had to ration his supplies. Yet this husbanding had itself quite a charm, since Hector invited you to share his vision of the world as an unbalanced and perilous place, like a window-cleaner's platform in a high wind, in which movement of any kind was likely to end in tears.

He liked puzzles and gadgets. The sitting room at Number 43 (for some reason, the Littlejohns' house was always known by its number while the Bunsens' house was known, humorously, as The Laurels) was hung with pictures of perspective puzzles. There were complicated executive toys on the shelves – confections of wires and pulleys and silvery clicking balls. Hector kept the one called Newton's cradle, designed to demonstrate the laws of motion, on a little low table by the side of his chair, reaching out now and then to keep the balls moving or vary their rhythm from a steady pendulum pace to an uneasy trot which made you feel that time was treading on your heels. Over the fireplace there hung a lithograph of a dove, in pink and yellow.

For the host's role Hector was not a natural. When called to take a coat or fill a glass, he would give a stagey little jump as if he was just a stand-in who kept on forgetting his duties, the real husband being away on business or dead. He would then, but only for a short time, overdo it, leaning over the table with out-thrust bottle to inquire 'would you like some more of this stuff?', at the same time squinting at the label with apparent surprise that anyone could have bought such indifferent wine. These impulses might not last long enough for him to cover all the guests, one or two at the far end of the table left fingering empty glasses. Hector would then slip back into his steamy lagoon of self-absorption, occasionally stung into speech by some mosquito droning across the surface of his mind.

I saw him looking at Alan Breck Stewart, who sat very upright next to Liz, eating his quiche with darting, precise movements of the fork, wide thin Easter-Island lips opening and shutting to receive the ochreous spongey morsels with machine-like regularity. Some mild apprehension rose within me; Hector was quite capable, in order to show off how fresh and unabashed was his way of looking at things, of asking why Alan ate his quiche like that, whether he had always done so, or whether he had picked up the habit in Rome. In the event, what Hector said was:

'Alan-Breck-Stewart. I've only just got it.'

'Ah. That does not surprise me. Few people read Stevenson these days, I should imagine. For which I am grateful. You could scarcely imagine how much I disliked *Kidnapped* as a child when I discovered what my mother had done to me. The last thing I wished was to be named after a wandering Jacobite. All I wanted at that time was to be very, very English.'

'But you are in fact Scottish?'

'Scarcely. My mother, it is true, was connected with Nellie's Stewarts, but my father was German.'

'Wasn't that awkward during the war?'

'My father had left Scotland long before the war.'

'Why did he leave?'

'I don't know. Why does anyone leave a country?'

'Is he still alive?'

'Probably not. I have had no news of him for thirty years or more.'

He drained his glass, which Hector instantly refilled with a flourish, as though rewarding a circus dog for performing its trick. The rasping melancholy in Alan's voice seemed to lessen as the evening wore on; he answered Hector's questions without reluctance; yet he still radiated unease. He sat so upright. The quiche-laden fork, held, I now noticed, in his left hand which partly explained the awkward look, returned to the trap-mouth like a mechanical grab, while his idle right arm seemed to twitch as though acting as a lightning conductor for nervous impulses which were otherwise suppressed. He continued to be an unsettling presence – certainly by comparison with the relaxed and relaxing inquisitiveness of his host.

'Can't stand the bloody Scots.' This was a routine, attention-getting rumble from the massive baggy presence of Rob Bunsen sitting at the end of the table. Rob was a columnist celebrated mainly, as he himself said, for still being around, 'like that chap who was asked what he did during the French Revolution and said "I survived". ' He was much loved, mostly because he made his friends and acquaintances feel so superior. Somehow in early life he had taken on the personality of the uncompromising, ungagg-able man of strong but comfortingly familiar views. He carried this personality around with him, using it like a heavy suitcase to clear a path but then parking it in a corner and being himself, insofar as there was a himself left to be. In repose, he became an amiable family man, his bearishness shifting rapidly from grizzly to koala, children ruffling his thick grey hair and climbing on the thick woolly jersey which he always wore under his tweed jacket, a precaution common among drinking men so that a group of three or four of them standing together in a room suggested a hard winter or an imminent power cut.

On nights when he was drunk and the red blotches flared around his nostrils, the Man-of-Strong-Views personality tended to be left on autopilot, so that he would growl on about Johnson and Boswell, the bad manners of barmen, the price of books, the stupidity of women and other standard topics, which on softer mornings after he would dismiss as 'the same old guff'. This seemed to be just such a night.

'Government hasn't the faintest bloody idea. Who wants the place? Took a bloody Scotsman to discover it. There's nothing bloody *there*. Bauxite – there's about as much bloody bauxite on that strip as there is in a Soho strip club.'

This tirade concerned the Selkirk Strip (more correctly called the Selkirk Mandated Territory), a misbegotten and largely forgotten piece of colonial territory between the jungle and the mountains, which had recently jumped into the news. I say forgotten, and yet it always lay only just below the horizon of our minds. The long curve of white sand where the breakers ended, the great jagged hills turning that strange iridescent grey-mauve in the sunset, those devastating tropical sunsets, whose bright gold and orange were so fiercely, irremediably swallowed up in the blackness of the night – how could we forget them? Nor could I forget the overwhelming scene with which Conrad begins *Coal*, the terrible story of shipwreck both moral and physical that takes its start with the grimy old tub, the *Nonchalance*, wallowing so cheerfully in Selkirk harbour. Graham Greene, I believe, as a young man used that queer desolate harbour as the setting for one of his earlier entertainments; his tramp steamer had called there on the way to Mogana, which was about to fall to Captain Roberts, 'Roberts the Liberator', the half-caste with an American accent who had once pushed garment racks on Seventh Avenue. Those were the days of high hopes in the region. There was indeed talk of bauxite, of gold even, and of parliaments and women's rights. Only Evelyn Waugh, writing from his cabin in the deeps beyond the thorny sandspit they called Victoria Island, dissented from these hopes: 'this is a dreadful place. The mosquitoes live longer than the natives who are mostly sodomites.'

'But we do have a responsibility to the people,' Liz said, clearing the plates.

'People, what people? Half of them work over the border and the other half are dying of bloody malnutrition.'

'That doesn't mean we aren't reponsible.'

'Oh yes, we're all bloody guilty,' said Rob in a mincing Hampstead voice.

An immense weariness suffused me. I stumbled to my feet to carry the serving dish over to the gleaming scullery alcove. As I put it down on the sink, Liz seized my arm in a state of high excitement.

'I must say your friend's incredibly randy. A fantastic groper. I'd only just sat down.'

'Oh,' I said.

'Right up my thigh,' she said.

'Ah.'

'You wouldn't think it.'

'No.'

'Not to look at him.'

'I'm sorry,' I said.

'It's not your fault,' she said with a smile as I followed her across

20

to the stove which was in another recess of this domestic control centre.

My gloom thickened. I did not like to think of the life-force still throbbing behind that weathered tufa. Even less was I cheered to learn that Alan Breck Stewart went for women as well or instead. In a quiet way, I had fancied my powers of diagnosis in that department, although, now I came to reflect, his campness of manner could well have been left over from a pre-war raffish past. There were echoes of old BBC voices.

'I worked in the Strip once,' said Alan, smiling at Liz as we came back to the table, she with the steaming coq au vin, I in tow with the vegetables.

'Were you in the Colonial Office?' Hector asked. Once fully wound up, Hector was capable of asking an infinite series of questions, ranging from the unpardonably intimate to the numbingly dull. This trait was curiously at odds with his otherwise retiring, taciturn manner; the putting of each question seemed to give him a minute electrical charge which could be gradually built up by constant repetition of the experience.

'No, when I returned to civvy street I became a humble functionary in the Food and Agriculture Organisation. They sent me all over the shop – India, Central America, Africa, before I finally tottered back to Rome.' He pronounced Africa with a faintly elongated 'A', as if it was a foreign word.

'Are you still working for them?' Hector asked.

'No, they put me out to grass years ago, thank God,' Alan said. These phrases which slipped off other people's tongues – 'civvy street', 'put me out to grass' – he enunciated stiffly with a faint intimation of irony, almost in inverted commas, or was it only an intonation which had crept upon him after years of living in Italy?

'They do themselves pretty well, you know, the famine wallahs. Thirty thousand a year tax free, first-class travel and a permanent bloody halo.'

'Rob,' said his wife Janey in a limp formal protest.

'We were rather more austere, I think, but I do recall one or two people of the sort you mention, especially in the sub-Sahara section, strangely enough.'

For a moment my attention wandered off to a vision of plump men in tropical suits getting out of helicopters, and flicking cigar ash onto skinny brown women squatting in the dust and pounding some tiny heap of grain. When I floated back, Janey was saying:

'Fanny's just written a story about a little girl who gets lost in the Sahara.' She herself wrote children's books, and illustrated them too. 'She wrote it to read to Undine, but the funny thing is that it's Jack who really loves it. Fanny's teacher said it was the best story out of all the kids in Fanny's year, not just her form.'

'How splendid,' I said.

'It's so funny, I didn't think Fanny was going to be the creative one. She's much more sort of down-to-earth, like Rob, but she loves writing stories now and it's funny, but the stories are awfully like my stories.'

'Which ones, the ones about the three Grubbleys or the ones about the hamster?'

'Well, sort of both really. But it's terribly embarrassing because the characters keep on going to the lavatory.'

'That's a sign of real literary talent,' I said. 'Great writers are always obsessed with the lavatory. Sturgis was.'

'Really, was he?'

'Surely his interest was not strictly lavatorial,' Alan Breck Stewart with a return of his earlier rasping manner, 'I remember – at least I think I remember – some verses of his which were quite current in my youth. Of course they could not be published at the time.'

'Oh, how exciting. Do recite them,' said Janey.

He folded his hands on the table and recited sitting up straight and wooden.

'The cops will be coming soon my dear.
Oh don't you wish that we were too?
Button up quickly now my dear,
It's closing time for me and you.

22

We're all of us pissing in the dark,
So shake your willy as you wee,
The cops are coming through the park;
It's closing time for you and me.'

Silence fell, or rather, for that is too gentle a phrase suggestive of
leaves and snowfall, silence struck the table. Even Rob's grunting
and Hec's faint sigh only emphasised the quiet, like the coughing
in the Two Minutes Silence on Remembrance Sunday.

'I think that's sweet,' Janey said.

'At least, thank God, they haven't published it, which must
make it about the only bloody thing they haven't published.'

'I think it's sad more than sweet,' Liz said.

'Yes it is, Liz, you're absolutely right.' Janey was always con-
ciliatory to women. To men she talked mostly about herself. This
distinction seemed somehow not exactly feminist, if anything the
reverse, although she irritated most men in the ways that feminists
do. The only exceptions were men who took pleasure in being
courtly and liked coping with women who were said to be difficult.

'It's not sad or sweet. It's a lot of homosexual bloody rubbish.
And don't for Christ's sake tell me it's typical Thirties either.'

'Well it is, duck,' Janey said.

'Of course it's typical bloody Thirties. That's not an excuse.'

Well, nor it was, but even Rob in his Johnsonian demotic could
not kick it out of the way. The plangency of the decade, the low
dishonest decade, decade of the locusts, was not so easily dismissed, nor the tinkling of half-heard bells which Sturgis managed so
well. The last decade in which a sense of guilt gave some point to
foreboding, in which life seemed to hold meaning and pattern,
even if of the grimmest kind – these images of a past we were all
too young to know, although Rob only just, still flickered and
haunted us.

'This is very good. Coq au vin, is it?' said Alan Breck Stewart.

'Yes, it's my old cock, I'm afraid,' said Liz. How pretty she
looked at times like that. Even the stalest of doubles-entendres
brought the roses back to her cheeks.

'Well, we can't get enough of it,' Rob said.

23

'Oh, Robbie,' Janey said.

'Why don't you write a bloody story about a cockerel who gets put into a bloody coq au vin?'

'Because I don't like cruel stories.'

'But children do.'

'Not all children. Undine and Jack get very frightened by jabberwocky things.'

'Did you know Sturgis?' I asked.

'Not well. I find him unreadable now.'

'Why?'

'So dated, don't you think?'

This was part of what I liked about Sturgis, but I felt that such a judgment would have appeared to include Alan Breck Stewart as another Thirties antique. People do not care to be assigned to a period. Yet the more I saw of him, the more strongly he seemed to bear the stamp of the decade, although he would, I imagined, have been only in his early twenties by the end of it.

'Were you a Communist?'

'Really, Hector darling,' Liz said. 'It's like saying are you now or have you ever been.'

'It's a perfectly reasonable question or was until Senator Mc-Carthy got going,' Alan said. 'After all, why on earth should one be ashamed of proclaiming one's political beliefs?'

'But if you're going to be punished for them, lose your job, get hounded out of your community.'

'In that case, you ought to go and live somewhere else, as Lenin did. You're not going to do much good for your cause being an undercover Communist.' Alan spoke with a brightening confidence as the argument progressed, like one accustomed to the cut-and-thrust of such arguments, and by contrast ill at ease with conversational rambles.

'But surely the whole bloody strategy of the CP is based on having some of your chaps underground, burrowing away in the trade unions and the Labour Party.'

'This is a myth perpetuated by housemaids' novelettes. Most so-called moles of that sort – I don't mean actual spies – are moles because that is what they want to be. They are sympathisers who do not feel committed enough to become full party members. But full party members and enough of them are essential for growth. If the American Communist Party had been larger, it would have had more influence and witch-hunts might have been more difficult.'

'Were you ever a full party member?' Typically, Hector was undeterred by the flow of the argument, indeed not much interested in it, having a taste only for information, or to be more precise for gossip.

'Oh, Hec,' Liz said, smiling at Alan.

'You just seemed to know a lot about it.'

'Like most rational people, I think Marx gave a good account of the world. But I never felt tempted to join the Communist Party. Naturally, like everyone else at the time I knew a lot of people who did join.'

'I don't think I know a lot of people who join anything much,' Liz said. 'It must have been a fascinating time. So much commitment. What was the last thing you joined, Gus? I expect you'll say you're not a joiner, but isn't that a cop-out? It's like saying you don't believe in marriage because it's just a piece of paper. Of course, I know you believe in *marriage*, I mean, you and Nell, it just works so brilliantly. I'm so pleased for you but somehow I always knew you'd find the right person, although you're so self-sufficient. Do have some more, there's lots more – well, perhaps it's just *because* you're self-sufficient that you always know what you need basically, whereas I've always taken a long time searching. Well, you saw me doing some of the searching, I was awfully muddled, wasn't I, do you remember Rashid, and Georges, Gorgeous Georges? I don't know why I'm like that. I do wish Hector would hand round the wine, Heck duck, we're dying of thirst up this end. My sister is quite different in that way. She married an awfully nice solicitor, when she was twenty. You've never met her, you wouldn't have, she lives in Staffordshire. But she joins things too, like me, but different things, the Women's Institute and women's lunch clubs and so on, she does a lot of good in, you know, an old-fashioned sort of way. I do think you have to try. Because, without do-gooders, the world would – no, you really must have some more, it's got to be finished – oh, I do hope Rob's all right, he looks a bit funny, don't you think he looks a bit funny?'

There had been no sound from Rob on my right since he had last spoken. Such silence was ominous, for his normal accompaniment of grunts and wheezes signified, if not agreement, at least tolerance of the way the conversation was going. I turned to look at him, fearing one of the great rages which people who lived in his shadow spoke of with anecdotal awe and precision, much as dwellers on the slopes of Vesuvius could put a date on the last big eruption.

His usually florid complexion, all red and mauve and raw sienna, had gone dead uniform white. His body stiffened, he leant forward, woolly jersey bosoming over his plate, and his mouth opened, for one split second bringing to mind one of Munch's pale screamers, before the jet, the plume, the cornucopia of sick arched nobly across the full width of the table. The chrysanthemums in the middle reeled under the impact as waves broke on the plates and cutlery of Janey and Hector on the other side of the table. Their chairs screeched on the quarry tiles as they attempted to flee, bumping into one another, cannoning into occasional tables, as the tidal wave swept over their canvas chairs of the sort used by film directors.

For a moment Rob sat still, surveying the space he had cleared in front of him. Then he rose, took Liz's hand as though about to lead her to the dance and was himself led, not without dignity, off to the bathroom. Indeed, the force and dignity of the event left me feeling somehow inadequate.

'I expect he's got a bug,' Liz said, returning with cloths and a mop.

'The mysteries of vomiting remain obscure to me,' said Alan turning to Hector with his pleasant relaxing smile. 'The muscular mechanics are relatively simple, but what is it that makes one person vomit at the slightest provocation, whereas others may abuse their digestions as much as they like? I myself have not vomited since the late 1940s.'

'I'm sure it must be a bug,' Liz said.

Alan continued to discuss vomiting, using phrases like 'the relaxed oesophagus'. Hector leant foward, nodding and frowning to conceal his pleasure at the whole event, any incident, whether comic or tragic, serving to take him out of himself and raise his spirits.

Rob's return startled us. He was back so soon and looking spruce. He was wearing a blue city suit and a blue striped shirt. He had brushed his hair and no longer wore a jersey under the jacket.

'That suit,' Hector said.

'Liz said you wouldn't mind.'

'Oh Robbie, you shouldn't have,' said Janey.

'It's quite all right really,' Hector said.

Worn by Rob, the suit appeared to be almost a costume. He might have been playing in a modern-dress production of some classic, a highland chief in *Macbeth*, say. He sat down in it awkwardly – no doubt because it was a tight fit.

'As I was saying when I was so rudely interrupted ... you remember Cassandra?'

'Cassandra?'

'The columnist in the *Daily Mirror*. It was how he started his first column after the war.'

'Yes, of course. My mind was wandering. I have been abroad so long that one forgets.'

'Well, it's bloody years since he died. But I thought you might remember him from before the war.'

'I remember very little that far back, I'm afraid,' Alan said, rather curtly. 'I prefer to keep my mind on the problems of the day.'

'Crikey,' grunted Rob, half to himself.

'I do agree,' said Liz, doling out the mousse with great shuddering dollops from the spoon. 'We all live in the past much too much. That's what wrong with this country.'

Hector sighed, restored with unnerving speed to his normal devitalised state. It was usually this provocative kind of remark which blasted great quarries of silence round Liz, and these silences which she desperately filled with the first thing that came into her head. That was how she had gained such a reputation for being featherbrained; in truth, she was suffering mainly from a sense of social obligation and from the fact that her husband did not share it. Hector seemed happy to listen to the silence fill the room until it became so quiet that you could hear the breeze from the kitchen jangle and swish the executive toys on the shelves.

But here there was no such silence, for Alan Breck Stewart responded readily to her brave offerings:

'Nostalgia is the simplest way to avoid thought,' he said.

'What about history?' I said. 'You have to think a bit to understand ...' I must have meant to complete the sentence with some stale phrase about why we were in the present situation, but I trailed away as once again I noticed Alan's right hand jiggling up and down while his left hand steadily spooned in the equally spongey morsels of mousse.

'History is merely an academic form of nostalgia. It has nothing to offer anyone who is serious.'

'But we're so frightened of being serious, I mean, that's the thing about the English, isn't it? We always make a joke of everything.'

'I happen to be Scots or rather half-Scots and half-German,' said Alan, showing his plaquey yellow teeth as he smiled. 'So I do not suffer from that particular complaint, nor, I like to think, from the obsession with class which I understand still afflicts this country.'

'Oh, you are lucky,' said Janey. 'The class thing is so awful.'

'It's rubbish about the Scots being classless, they're the worst snobs in the world, wittering on about bloody Bonny Prince Charlie.'

'But there isn't all that awful thing about accents and U and non-U.'

'Ever heard a Scotch duke talk with a Gorbals accent?' Rob said. He leant across the table, all pale and spruce in his borrowed suit, now the D.A. moving in for the kill.

'That's not the point, duck.'

'It is the bloody point.'

The bracken cutting across bare legs, the slap of wet tweed, the panting of breathless men in the heather, down below in the valley the crunch of soldiers' topboots on the stony road and the jangle of harness, the single musket shot in the keen damp Highland air. A far remove from the flat sheen of the polished wood, the flat bland colours of the lithographs clipped behind their perspex shields, and the flat glitter of the executive toys on the shelf units. Had any of us ever run for our lives? Would any of us ever have to? Alan Breck Stewart alone seemed to have the insecurity of the wandering Jacobite and, in a way which I could still scarcely glimpse, the hope of coming into his own.

We flatter ourselves by talking of each other as feeling insecure when we mean only being low-spirited or lonely. Insecurity implies a free spirit, a ranging of the seas, a bit of knocking about. To such a commitment to liberty not many of us could lay claim; we merely read the travel brochures.

The front-door bell rang, a piercing peal. Liz jumped up.

'I expect it's Jehovah's Witnesses,' she said.

She brought back a thin girl with dark eyes and long dark hair straggling and damp from the rain. There was a wet leaf in her hair from the decading lime trees outside.

'It's Thérèse,' said Liz. We could see it was Thérèse, another of Nell's countess Dudgeon cousins, taken on by Janey as mother's help a few months earlier, the best we could do for her. An awkward, brooding girl, so shy that it was a surprise to hear she longed to be an actress, and yet there was something about the way she spoke even when confessing failure to understand the washing machine that left an impression. She was not stagey or had not yet become so; her gestures — of hesitancy, unease, sulkiness — were often irritating, and yet it was not quite for that reason alone that their traces stayed in my memory, often coming to the fore at odd moments during the day.

'Oh, I am sorry, but the telephone isn't working and I couldn't get through, so I thought I'd better come round. It's Undine. She's all hot and flushed and her cough is awful and you said to — '

The telephone was lolling half off its cradle on one of the tables which had been bumped into. Hector put it back quickly but not before Janey had seen it.

'Rob, it's your fault,' said Janey, standing up instantly. 'If we had been having dinner miles away, Thérèse could never have phoned up — '

'But we aren't having dinner miles away. And anyway, Undie's always having coughs.'

'Don't call her Undie and it isn't just a cough, it's probably – '

'Pneumonia or lung cancer. Oh, don't be such a bloody – '

She walked swiftly round the table and took hold of Rob's jacket collar and pulled him to his feet, beating the side of his head fiercely with her other fist and forearm.

'Get up, get up,' she said.

'I'm sorry it had to end like this,' he said, turning to Liz, as he yielded to Janey. 'The Bunsen family hasn't done too well tonight.'

'What do you mean Bunsen *family*, it's you, you, you ... Oh, I'm sorry, Thérèse.'

As Janey had first abused Rob, Alan had stiffened. When she had raised her hand against him, his own had ceased its fumbling and flown up to his face, as though he too were warding off a blow. White and quiet he sat as the quarrel went on, seeming unable to move or say goodbye as the Bunsens swept out with Thérèse. As we settled back again, he rose abruptly, muttered 'please excuse me' and left the room.

We began to make ready to go. He returned pale and dignified, but still unable to get out more than a few words of thanks.

As the three of us stumbled down the street, across the main road and down our slumbrous avenue, Alan in the middle linked his arms with ours. At the first touch of his heavy woollen sleeve, I thought it a blithe and friendly gesture. But, as his arm dragged at my elbow and I sensed the lurching of his legs, I realised that he too was drunk. That was not surprising; he had first asked, awkwardly but firmly, for whisky at about half-past five that evening. Past midnight on a damp November night, his mother barely cold in the ground, parked on people he scarcely knew, who could blame him? But the drag of his arm lowered my spirits, and so did the sour, sick tang of his breath.

As we crossed the main road, rockets hurtled up from some nearby back garden. Green, rose and gold stars, scattered and few, climbed above the skyline, and faded into the night almost as they climbed. There were two days to go before Guy Fawkes. I thought of the Dudgeon-Stewarts down in Devon putting up the shutters so that they should not hear the noise from the village, according to Nell, dreading each year with growing intensity the celebration

30

of the triumph of heresy. As we reached the safety of the pavement, bangs and whooshes filled the sky behind us. I felt as if Nell and I were a couple of first world war other ranks, dragging a badly winged sub altern back from no-man's land.

'Ah, fireworks,' Alan said.

'Somebody jumped the gun for November the Fifth.'

'I enjoyed the evening,' he muttered, as if confessing to some shameful practice. 'It was pleasant to meet your friends.'

'I'm afraid it was a bit chaotic.'

'No, no. They were kind to have me. Very kind,' he mused, his mind already on something else. Our heels clopped loudly through the silent streets. He began to breathe a little jerkily. I wondered about his health.

'Tomorrow,' he said, 'I must recover my papers, really get down to it. Routine, that's the secret. Routine and a modicum of forethought. I believe they call it ergonomics nowadays.' He gave a husky cackle.

'I do hope Undine *is* all right,' Nellie said.

'It's probably just a virus,' I said.

'Yes indeed,' said Alan Breck Stewart.

By the time we had got inside the house, he had recovered a little and hung up his overcoat with care, straightening his jacket before attempting the stairs.

After showing him to the attic, I came down and sat on the bed. My limbs had turned to lead.

'Why is that man staying in this house?' I said.

'You asked him,' Nellie said.

As I lay in a foetal ball, searching for sleep, the Sturgis verses elbowed their way through my brain:

'The cops will be coming soon my dear,
Oh don't you wish that we were too.'

CHAPTER 3

Undine was not all right. Her fever rose. She had a temperature of 104. The doctor came. The neat, rather severe little girl – quite unlike Rob except for her fuzzy hair – was a crumpled damp bundle, moaning without words as her mother gazed down at her helplessly with Nellie at her side.

'Janey was desperate,' Nellie said, 'And then there was this knock at the door and there was Alan with a bunch of pink chrysanthemums.'

'How extraordinary.'

'Janey was very touched. I mean she'd only just met him. He said if she didn't get better soon he had a friend from university who was the best virus man in Harley Street.'

'I thought you couldn't do anything with viruses.'

'It's the thought. I think he's really much nicer than he seems. It's just living abroad by himself that makes him so offputting.'

'Living abroad's supposed to make people charming.'

'You *know*. Don't be so mean. He's only just lost his mother, after all.'

'Any moment now you'll be saying why don't I ever think of things like taking flowers round to Janey when her children are ill.'

'Well, you don't.'

'Oh, all right.'

Ian Riley-Jones was standing, bland sentinel, in front of me as I put the receiver down. I had not noticed the door open. He was a shimmerer of the Jeeves sort, materialising and dematerialising at will; like Jeeves too he was of a melancholy humour.

'Time for elevenses,' he said.

Along the cream corridor I followed him, feet thwacking the

cream lino like the sound of someone being slapped by a distant masseur. A sign at the double doors said Alert Green. The double doors whimpered as we came through into the central hall, feet now clanging on the stone floor and the open stairs which led down to the ground level across which other colleagues were now walking to their eleven o'clock meetings with the purposeful nonchalance of senior officials, unhurried, strolling, rejoicing in a clear conscience, a regular digestion and a full diary. In this great well, undecorated, windowless, yet not stuffy, I felt myself at the blank core of my life. We greeted a couple of treasury men heading over to the green baize door that was kept locked, the taller one gloomily swinging the heavy key he had collected from Sir Wilfred's office.

'You have the look of condemned men,' Riley-Jones said. 'It must be Star Chamber.'

'No, no, we've brought that ship limping home to port. It's Misc two-three-six. Maritime spillage.'

'Ah, these are murky waters.'

Our business was not enquired. The Central Operational Co-ordinating Unit for Policy Appraisal — Coh-coopa to its friends, Cockuppa to the rest of us — was already a legend in the service. I had in earlier years taken the minutes at a more modest committee, the Under-Secretaries Policy Analysis and Review Staff — in its day known as Yew-parze or Up-arse according to taste. But that was a small affair, compared with the baroque splendour of COCUPA.

'If I die here in Conference Room K,' Riley-Jones wrote on the note which he slid across the table to me, 'wh. seems increasingly probable, wd. you arrange for me to be cremated after a brief non-denominational service and have the ashes placed on this table in a simple urn of a design sanctioned by Estacode.'

'I don't think security wd. allow it,' I minuted in the margin of the paper.

'I shall take the matter up with the First Division Association. This seems to me a matter of conscience. I.R-J.'

'I disagree. It wd. be a disquieting precedent. Wd. staff agree? Pl. consult the Manpower and Personnel Office. A.L.C.'

Conference Room K was underground, reached by a long passage with three right-angled bends in it. After each bend there were whimpering fire doors. The cream walls were immensely thick. The cream ceilings were low. It was a last lair of government, impervious to terrorist blast or the changing of the seasons. It still had the air of a wartime ops room. On the wall behind us, there hung a map of the London area which cried out for little flags and a colonel with a billiard cue. The mahogany table in the middle was too big and rich for the room.

Here the edges of our hopes and fears were gently chamfered as we settled down to the day's agendum: The Use of Fire Engines in Non-Fire Emergencies; Puttock of the Home Office in the chair, owlish, boyish, zippy yet respectful, once a high-flyer, his wings now clipped somewhat. His speech melded old Whitehall mandarin with Harvard Business School demotic: 'Our masters in their wisdom have instructed us to embark on a new ballgame, but it is, I think, for us to mark out the ballpark. What precisely constitutes a Non-Fire Emergency? Flood, of course, hurricane, tidal wave no doubt, but do we go nuclear? Or would that be to trespass on the territory of the Civil Defence sub-committee?' As he spoke, his broad hand swept in ballpark-marking circles over the polished mahogany, a gesture aped from Sir Wilfred rather than any minister he might have served. We would no more have dreamed of copying our political masters than of imitating the way our dogs barked. Indeed, to us the two species seemed quite similar: loud, clumsy creatures with short sight but a remarkable sense of smell, so easily alarmed, so easily wooed.

'But we *are* the Civil Defence sub-committee,' Riley-Jones said.

'Personnel-wise undoubtedly. But we would, I think, be exceeding our brief if we failed to separate our two hats. No doubt we can find some *modus vivendi*.'

'Peaceful co-existence?'

'Right,' said Puttock. 'That at any rate is one type of question which properly falls to us. The committee may then wish to define "fire engine". Would we be right to restrict ourselves to the fire engine *stricto sensu*: four wheels, a ladder and a hose? Or should we go wider and comb both the public and private sectors for what has been termed Non-vehicular Firefighting Equipment? Previous correspondence suggests that this would,' he said, twitching a fat file at his elbow not without satisfaction, 'greatly complicate our task.'

'If we include the Niffies,' I said, 'we shall have to keep tabs on every canteen fire extinguisher in the country.'

'That *is* the downside,' Puttock said, 'but I beg you to take on board the possibility that, if we shun the Niffies, Ministers may draw attention to this gap and set up yet another working party. Such a group – and I need hardly mention that membership of it would again include most of us round this table – would find itself confronted with intolerable dilemmas in dealing with, say, informal firefighting equipment within civilian nuclear establishments. With the benefit of hindsight we might have done better to consider our present remit within the compass of our earlier work on The Use of Fire Engines in Emergencies. Which brings me to yet another curve ball: is it for us to set out for Ministers, or at least to adumbrate a distinction between Use, Deployment and Control?'

As the man from the Welsh Office cleared his throat, a messenger came in and whispered to me that my wife wanted me to ring her urgently. I rose, giving a solemn apologetic nod to Puttock, to indicate an engagement of some grandeur, and went out to the telephone in the passage.

'She's had to go to hospital, she's much worse,' Nellie said. 'Alan's taken her with Janey in our car, because she couldn't find Rob. I'm looking after Fanny and Jack.'

This intrusion of a life which knew itself to be real and said so, abruptly, offensively, did what it always did to me: irritated, depressed, humiliated, caught at my heart. I heard myself answering in the way I always answered, nettled, practical, superior.

'Haven't you tried the Feathers?'

'Janey says they won't serve him there any more. The office says he usually goes to the Crown now. But he wasn't there. He's not *anywhere*.'

'He must be somewhere.'

'Janey says she can never get hold of him in the middle of the morning. She thinks he's got a woman.'

'In the morning?'

'Oh, Gus, can't you come home?'

A clean, mild, milky day, sun on the yellow and brown leaves, only the faintest tremble of autumn in the air as I panted up the hill the back way from the Northern Line station. In quiet Slocock Lane off the High Road, parked on its own under the overhanging trees, a dirty white Volkswagen minibus with a NZ sticker on its rear quivered slightly as I approached. Through the steam of its windows, it was just possible to make out the brown blanket which had been rigged up all round to block out the view. Dozens of these antipodean wigwams were to be seen at night along the desolate stretches of the South Bank, revving up in the morning to chug into the compound of the National Car Park in order to avoid the traffic wardens coming on duty. But up here in the settled avenues of North London they were rare.

As I crossed the road to turn off up the mews which was the short cut to our street, the side door of the minibus opened. A burly man with fuzzy grey hair got out awkwardly, bending his head and finding the step with difficulty.

He stood on the pavement and stretched his arms, like a man in a bedroom shaking the sleep from his body. It was Rob Bunsen, although at first I was not sure because the low autumn sun gilded his outline, giving the brief illusion of a young and golden Bacchus. He growled a few words through the door. A beige trench coat was handed out to him by someone inside. I thought I heard a woman's voice, only a few words, low and perhaps chuckling. Then the door shut.

He did not move off as a man usually does when the door shuts behind him but stood there for a moment holding the coat in front of him with both hands like an unfamiliar object he did not know what to do with. Then he seemed to stir himself into getting on with life or at least making a show of it, put on the coat with a shrug, leaving the belt undone, and stumped off down the lane towards the main road and the station.

I began to hurry after him, then stopped and decided to wait a minute or two before retracing my steps, pretending to hope to bump into him, apparently by chance, at the station entrance. This interlude here in the quiet lane seemed another side of his life too private and strange to be broken into, even in this emergency. Yet I was ashamed of failing to beard him, knowing in my heart that I would miss him at the station.

The white minibus in the quiet lane was gently disquieting: romance, adventure, mobility lurking under the sycamore trees. At the end of the season, these minibuses were sold for seventy or eighty pounds to some local plumber or window-cleaner who needed a van, while the nomads would take off by plane or ship back home to Australia or New Zealand. This one seemed to have lingered beyond its time like a belated swallow; the November rain had already bedraggled the stickers from Oslo and Aix-en-Provence on the back of it.

The side door of the minibus opened again and out stepped a tall, dark-haired woman in a smart royal blue coat and skirt, the blue if anything a little too royal. She went round the minibus locking doors carefully, stared at her reflection in the rear window, tugged her coat straight and walked off briskly down the lane, the high heels of her old-fashioned black court shoes clicking in the silence.

In her neatness, she was as surprising an apparition as Rob Bunsen. I was prepared for some tousled girl in a sloppy jersey and jeans to tumble slowly out of the van and rub the sleep from her eyes. I did not hurry to catch Rob at the station and indeed I missed him.

'Oh, it must be his seccy,' Nellie said when I told her, and when I rang his office, having allowed him forty minutes start, a brisk New Zealand voice told me that Rob was in conference but she would tell him to go straight to the hospital.

'I remember now,' Nellie said. 'She's married to a radiologist at U. C. H., that man with huge eyebrows we met with the Bunsens last Christmas. They couldn't find a flat so they were living in this minibus. She was very funny about it.'

'Ah,' I said.

'Janey said she was sweet – and very helpful.'

'Poor old Rob,' I said.

'Why do you say poor old Rob? Why not poor old Janey or

poor old radiologist?'

'I don't know. I just felt poor old Rob.'

'That sounds like envy to me.'

'It wasn't meant to.'

'Of course it wasn't *meant* to.'

The old electricity filled the air, corroded batteries of lust and fear suddenly recharged, neglected emotional wiring beginning to fizz and short, and beyond the sparks the awareness of the invading dark.

'And don't say it's the male menopause.'

'Why not?'

'Because it's a horrible sort of phoney excuse. And Janey has had such a rough time anyway.'

'If only she wasn't so ...'

'I'm afraid she's easier to like when she's suffering. She's terrible with illness, she said, because people were always dying round her when she was a child — her mother and her elder sister — and her father retreated into himself and she was all by herself in this Army place in Malaya. She used to dream of family life with lots of brothers and sisters and presents.'

Janey sat like a queen on a little upright chair covered with garish embroidered flowers, once thought ugly, but now resonating charm surrounded by the stripped pine floor and the plain furniture. Her neat face was pale and still. The denim dungarees she wore made her look like the victim of the rural depression in an old photograph.

Squatting on the floor, his great gangling legs doubled under him, Alan Breck Stewart was talking to the middle Bunsen child, Jack, aged seven, who lolled in some comfort in an ordinary armchair. I could not help feeling that he and the child had swapped rightful places.

'And then,' he said, 'we built ships of ice. Huge great ships all made out of ice, so we could go round the North Pole and the Germans couldn't catch us.'

'But couldn't the Germans melt the ships before you got to the North Pole?'

'No, the ice was too thick.'

'But didn't the sailors freeze too?'

'Oh, the ships weren't all made of ice, just the outside. Inside, they were very comfortable.'

'Really? Did they really make ships out of ice?' Janey asked.

'Well, only prototypes. Churchill was immensely keen, but eventually the brass-hats managed to commandeer the scheme and squeezed us out. They couldn't cope with the challenge to the conventional thinking that ships had to be made out of steel. It would have revolutionised the convoy system.'

'You actually helped to make the ships?'

'Yes, I was in Mountbatten's circus for a time, with Zuckerman and the rest. An amusing bunch, but totally unsystematic.' His knees cracked as he rearranged them. Jack, bored with the conversation, got up from the chair and went across to switch on the television, quietly, having lost all sense of company. A fair-haired young man was standing on a green mound, gesticulating vigorously; probably a programme on archaeology; Jack seemed to feel no need of the sound.

'It's time to ring the hospital. I'll go upstairs. Will you come with me, Nell?' Janey said.

The room was cold for a November mid-day. The daylight outside the tall windows was grey. As Nellie and Janey went up the bare stairs, the clattering of their steps sounded angry. Alan Breck Stewart sitting on the tribal rug in front of the fireplace began to describe to me in greater detail the great ice ships of the Habakkuk Project, impatiently, almost accusingly, as though I had been one of the brass-hats who had frustrated him.

They were not long upstairs, five minutes at most. The telephone pinged in the sitting-room as the receiver was replaced. And we heard the long moan and the cry. Then there was silence and they came down promptly.

'Could you drive us to the hospital,' Nellie said. 'She died ten minutes ago.'

'Why wasn't I there?' Janey said.

'Because they told you to go home and see Fanny and Jack.'

'I never *thought*.'

'You couldn't know.'

Even now, so long after the event, I find it hard to put down on paper the terrible numb things that were said. What I can really remember is only how cold and bereft the room was. It seemed no more than merely a first rehearsal for the real tragedy, the session when we just ran though our lines, not yet trying to give them expression – or perhaps not so much a rehearsal as a premonition of the horrible thing that was indeed going to happen, but not yet, not here and not in this way. Undine would die young, perhaps in a road accident, and we would be all together to hear about it, and it would be real and we would believe it and mourn. We would be adequate.

As I had done before, I dreamed the old dream of a time when everything came directly to us, and people felt things directly, fully, genuinely, whether they were true or not, because they minded so little about the truth.

Out of the corner of my eye, I could see the fair-haired young man clamber down from the green mound. He continued talking vigorously, pointing at a hedge on the right of the screen.

'A virus they think, probably a type of meningitis,' Nell said.

'Oh yes, that's always dangerous, isn't it?' I said.

This last remark hung in the air, twisting in my mind to show each side of its idiocy.

Relief was at hand, of a sort. The front door crashed open as we stood in the hall plucking coats off the over-tenanted row of hooks. Rob appeared, scooping in his arm his elder daughter, a plump eleven-year-old in grey school uniform, embraced, kissed, wept, snorted, hugged, knocked a flowerpot off the table, told Janey to get in the car, Nellie to look after Fanny and Jack, me to pour Alan a drink. The little girl clung to him, crying into his woolly jersey. For his part, tears streamed down his thickened florid cheeks. The energy of his grief unlocked our laggard tears. Now that Rob was here, I felt the absence of the thin serious little girl with a long nose who did not look in the least like him, taking entirely after her mother. He knew no more than the rest of us what to say … 'this is bloody horrible, bloody hospitals, two days ago she was oh what's the bloody use of saying anything, oh come on, let's go, stay here, darling, with Nellie, oh bloody.'

We watched as he bundled Janey down the garden path, through the little wooden gate in the privet hedge out into the old blue Volvo, Fanny running after them, shooed back up the steps again. Grieving couples always looked smaller. Such a loss deflated everything that had seemed large. That too is awkwardly put, but it is right to be awkward in talking of the death of a child. The sonorous eloquence of the old preachers does not come close enough to touch us.

Some evenings Nell reads passages from the Crupper Diaries which she is editing. She settles the stained old leather-bound manuscript book in her cardiganed lap and lets her reading spectacles fall down her nose so that she looks like a quite young actress pretending to be a grandmother in one of those films that spans several generations, and then she reads in her low precise voice these outpourings of this seventeenth-century Puritan merchant, a dreary prig who seems to use his diary as much for an account book as for emotional release. 'Towards eleven of the clock, my little and my only James fell dangerously sick, stuffed with cold flegm, could not slepe, had no stomach to eat or drink. Small hope of his life was left unto us. God hath been touching us in a very tender part. Hath threatened to take from us the Delight of our Eyes, our little bird not yet fledged before struck down by this Arrow. I liked not the chairs my wife had of Mr Grimwade for 14s a pair.' We no longer had access to such language.

In the thick hedge in front of the Bunsens' house were caught a couple of rocket sticks from the fireworks the night before. Rob had taken Fanny and Jack up on the heath to see them and told us afterwards that he had prayed for Undine as the set piece depicting the borough coat of arms had fizzled to its end.

We went back into the sitting-room. Alan was sitting on the kilim rug, his bony knees now drawn up to his chin, sniffling and wiping his nose. 'I wish I'd known her,' he said.

What difference would that have made? I felt like saying, not without resentment at how easily he mourned a child he had never met.

'We lost a baby too,' he said.

We? I wondered, but then why should he not have been married,

41

several times if need be?

'That was years ago. She would be twenty-two now.'

'And your ... wife?'

'She'd be my age, still is, I suppose, wherever she is, America when last heard of. She lives in some sort of hut in Florida, in the orange groves. It was losing the baby that turned her against me. The marriage didn't last long after that. Nothing much seems to stick to me, you know.'

When written down, his words suggest self-pity. Well, so they did when he spoke them. Yet there was also something clinical about his tone. He could have been a scientist describing some material which defied adhesion.

On the television screen, some men in olive combat gear were walking through thick vegetation in what looked like a hot country. They were holding rifles and their pink faces seemed nervous.

CHAPTER 4

Far from resenting his intrusion, Janey honoured Alan for sharing her grief. She herself was contained and upright but bedraggled, a chaffinch in the rain. He seemed puzzled-miserable, like a child experiencing death for the first time, and went on talking to Janey about Undine when the rest of us shied away from the subject. He said how much he wished he had known her before she was ill. Janey was moved by Alan and drawn to him. In fact, he told me he had mentioned to her that he did not like to go on imposing on us and she had asked him to lodge with her.

I sat in our attic nursing a cup of Nescafé on a wet Saturday morning. The room was filled with piles of books, pamphlets and page after page of a manuscript in his own neat hand, often interspersed with diagrams and strings of equations. Despite his talk of renewing old friendships, he had scarcely left our house except to walk over to call on Janey Bunsen.

'She has a room free now, you see. Sadly,' he added, as he sorted through a shelf of his scribblings. He was wearing well-buffed brown corduroy trousers and a speckled oatmeal sweater with a gingery cigarette burn on the chest. He wheezed slightly as he bent and unbent in his rearranging of the papers, but he exhaled good humour.

'We would be sorry to lose you,' I said, surprised to find that I meant it. Despite my continued complaints to Nell about the signs of his presence – the somewhat military-looking underwear drying on the bathrail (he insisted on doing his own washing, using a brand of powder unknown to us), the gauloise stubs in the blue saucer, the long black plastic mac on the hall peg – I found myself seeking him out, so that he had begun to look up like a harassed executive when I put my head round the door of the little attic

43

room. Nell did not seem to mind having him about. 'Oh, he does like a chat,' she would say, but indulgently, rather in the way she reported some new caprice of Widget, our brindled cat.

'I would at least provide a little company for her. Rob is away such a lot.'

'You're going to stay on in London a bit then?'

'Yes. My work is going well. The journey would interrupt my chain of thought. London is so quiet after Rome.'

A page fluttered towards me through the air, disturbed by his ferretings. While I waited for him to stow some other papers in one of the cardboard boxes he had lined up under the table, I read it with half an eye:

'SUMMARY: Conventional thinking is non-strategic. It cannot match the linear acceleration of demo-climatic change. If we take f to be the erosion factor, s to be the population surplus, and g the trend line of green-revolution productivity, then' ... some incomprehensible algebra followed ... 'Therefore we can expect megafamine along the Equatorial belt by the mid-1980s, certainly before 1987. Only a strategy based on asymptotic planning can avert catastrophe and a starvation toll of 1.3 million–1.4 million per annum. The Breck Stewart Planning System is designed to be understood and operated by a ten-year-old schoolboy. It should therefore be within the grasp of the average politician ...'

I put it down on the pile and took up a little typewritten booklet which had *Plenty Banana* scrawled in black Pentel on its yellow jacket.

'What's this?'

'It was my first shot at a collection of Development Fables. The official literature is all such dry-as-dust stuff, so I wrote a series of little parables, one on the need for sensible irrigation practices, another on birth control, two on better hygiene, one on hygiene in the hut, the other in the village and so on. The stories could, of course, be altered in the appropriate places to suit different peoples and climates, just as the same traditional stories occur with local variations all over the world. Unfortunately, I have little gift for fiction.'

'And this?' I held up a brown booklet entitled *What Next For*

Lemka?

'An attempt to find practical uses for the lemka tree which, as you know, grows abundantly along the Selkirk Strip. Alas, its wood is brittle and not very decorative so that it is used mostly for firewood ... Now this might amuse you.'

He passed me a large chart in red and blue ink, about 36 inches by 12, mounted on stout card. Across the top, it said Strategic Civil Command after E-Day.

'What's E-Day?'

'Entropy Day. The day when the system of government in this benighted country finally seizes up. I work on the realistic assumption that none of the numbskulls will have the sense to adopt a rational systems analysis until they are forced to.'

I peered at the chart in the light of the rain-streaked dormer window. I had to bend my head under the sloping attic roof. Parts of the chart were familiar enough: Cabinet Office, Treasury and so on. But in the middle of the diagram there were two boxes, a blue one labelled CDM Body and a red one below it labelled CDM Antibody.

'Central Decision-Making Body. That is, so to speak, the command module which takes the strategic decisions which are first passed to the Cabinet for confirmation and political fine-tuning and then sent out to the Ministerial Departments for Implementation.'

'And the Antibody?'

'That's my little team. We sit next door to the Body and subject its entire output to rigorous criticism, night and day. We are a permanent opposition inside government.'

'And have you got anyone to look at it?'

'Oh, I can't spare the time for politicking. I showed it to a numbskull in the Foreign Office. He could not make head or tail of it. But they'll have to come round to it in the end.' He emitted an emphysematose chuckle at the thought of the inevitable triumph to come. The chuckle turned into the cough like a man imitating a faulty two-stroke engine.

Then at the far end of the pile, leaning against a rafter, I saw something else, a familiar sight. It was a battered, black civil servant's briefcase, the Royal crest almost buffed into oblivion, the gold-stamped initials A. B. S. scarcely legible now.

'When did you get that?'

'Oh. During the war. My Mountbatten period,' he said, with irony.

'Is it still full of secrets?' I said, reaching out my hand to grasp it.

'Would you mind awfully not ... I'm sorry. It's so silly, but it is supposed to be ... what is the ludicrous word ... classified.' I could not tell whether he was agitated or making a joke of it. I put the case down.

Great bolsters of black cloud rolled across the sky. The corners of the attic grew dark. Fumbling for the light switch behind me, he rested his other hand on my arm.

'Dear boy,' he said. 'You are kind to have put up with me. I'm getting so creaky.'

This change of manner, and the sad sour smell of his closeness unmanned me. Yet, at the same time, the abruptness of it suggested that he had not lost the power to manipulate. The will could still be put into gear when it suited.

'Poor Janey,' he said, meditatively, calmly. 'I think I ought to go there, you know.'

He used pity as a substitute for feeling, I thought. In that he was a modern. In the classics and the sagas, when a man was full of pity, he was described as racked and torn by feeling; there was nothing calm or meditative about the experience.

We started humping Alan's cardboard boxes to Janey's house the following afternoon. The distance to The Laurels seemed too short to use the car, so the children and I followed Alan in convoy round the corner, a file of native bearers behind the district commissioner. His long highstepping stride like that of a horse in the showring; Thomas and Elspeth scuffled along in his wake, peering round the boxes to see where the kerb was coming. As we climbed the steps of Janey's clean bare house, she came out, trembling with alarm at the sight of this travel-stained and heavy-laden party.

'Don't worry, they pack away quite neatly,' Alan said.

'Well, it is a small room.'

'Oh, I'm used to squirrelling myself away.'

Even on the brief journey from our house to the Bunsens, 400 yards and two streets crossed, a certain exhilaration took hold of him. 'On the road again,' he had said mock-ruefully, as I slammed our front door behind us. Yet I felt a tone of reproach somewhere twitching in him. Had we not pressed him to stay effusively enough? Had we treated him too negligently, indifferent to his age? Or had we been too respectful, failed to treat him as an equal in expectation of life? Or all, or none, of these things?

Perhaps it was nothing to do with us or our house. What we were seeing was merely the coming alive again which happened to all true travellers as the man at the gate stamped the papers and the bearers swung their packs up on to their backs – anticipation, zest and scorn for those they left behind being flecked with irritation, anxiety, even regret.

What there was no sign of was the numb gloom which travel-haters like myself felt at the slightest change of scene, the feeling that, far from being a chance to live life more fully, every journey was a rehearsal for the final journey, in itself a little death.

'What a beautiful house it is,' he said, running his hand round the curved end of the stripped-pine banister. Thomas and Elspeth looked round the hall, bewildered; to them it was just a house.

'Yes, isn't it lovely?' said Janey, herself looking round her hall as though she too had just noticed its loveliness. How clean their houses were, the Bunsens and the Littlejohns. The objects they had collected seemed to sweat on the pale wood and the white walls as if embarrassed to have intruded into such temples of austerity. Along the bookshelf in the sitting-room at The Laurels were ranged a collection of performing toy animals, many of them playing musical instruments – two bear-drummers, a monkey cymbalist, and a perky little black-and-white dog with a violin. When they were all wound up or switched on, the room was filled with whirring and little tinny clashes and thumps.

'Oh, those. No, they aren't mine. Rob collects them. I don't really like them. I think they're cruel.'

'Cruel?' Alan said, but not in a puzzled way, more appreciative, allured.

'Cruel to the animals.'

'Yes.'

'It's making fun of them.'

'And what do you think? Do you like the animals?' said Alan turning to Elspeth.

'I don't know,' said Elspeth, uncertain what she was meant to say.

'Rob always brings one back when he goes abroad. The cat came from China. Its eyes light up when it plays the trombone.'

We stood in silence, reflecting on the coarseness of it, picturing Rob, probably hung-over, outside the Forbidden City bargaining for the cat, which wore a little tartan waistcoat.

'I've always rather liked them,' I said.

'Oh, dad,' said Elspeth, now well up with what was expected.

'I haven't seen that one before,' I said, pointing to a little wooden horse or mule, much more crudely made, which had kettle drums made of skin slung either side of its saddle.

'Isn't it awful?' Janey said. 'He brought it back from the Selkirk Strip the time when he did the story about the sandstorm graves.'

'Oh yes.' That terrible incident was still fresh enough in our minds to reduce us to silence again. Again and again, the régime had denied the persistent rumours of mass executions somewhere in the scrubland between the jungle and the strip of desert which Selkirk had claimed for the British Crown. Then, in a unique combination of circumstances – a freak storm out at sea, a wind of unparalleled ferocity from off the mountains – and the narrow desert was swept by a sandstorm such as no man had seen before. Nagala the Thunderer was angry, so the British tabloid newspapers said. At any rate, the sand blew away, and there were the great shallow pits, thirty foot and more across, with the heaps of bodies lying in them. The régime tried to blame both the British and the régime before, but the bodies were too well preserved for the latter to be guilty, and since the bodies included those of several well-known pro-British public figures the British seemed to be ruled out too. And so, next time the régime engineered a motion at the UN declaring its inalienable sovereignty over the Strip, several non-aligned nations abstained. Her Majesty's Government expressed its horror at this mass slaughter, and condemned the gross intrusion into British territory involved in the disposal of the bodies. HMG raised its voice with great reluctance for, as the Foreign Office representative on COCUPA had told me, 'the low profile's our only hope'. A few wandering tribesmen; a couple of petrol dumps on the road across the Strip; the small port where the coastal traders collected the low-value lemka wood and the diminishing catches of fish; the even smaller capital in the dusty, barren foothills which made veterans of the Colonial Service dream fondly of Aden; there was not much to the Strip. Its very existence stirred the dumbest soul to ponder on the purpose of empire.

Its sheer nothingness had sent it limping into the arms of COCUPA. 'It's not just an MoD thing. The ghastly place needs a police force, and a development programme and some irrigation people. And we don't want to make a great song-and-dance about it, so why don't we just keep it as a fairly low-level contingency exercise? Who knows? If there's a bush fire, they might even need the Niffies as well as the Green Goddesses,' Puttock said, welcoming the orphan in our midst.

'I think you'll find that only tracked vehicles can get across the Strip,' said Riley-Jones.

'Just the sort of point that needs to be sorted out in advance if the Strip Club is to establish viable parameters for action,' Puttock said, unfazed and smiling in anticipation. Already we hugged the secret of our existence, gave ourselves a nickname, walked the streets with the deep satisfaction of cradling between us the shape of the future.

'I like to think,' Riley-Jones said as we settled ourselves round an umber plastic table in the Cabinet Office canteen, 'of Puttock preparing for the Second Coming.'

'Ministers have asked us to work to a tight timetable ...'

'It behoves us to consider the implications of an Armageddon scenario ...'

'No doubt our Welsh colleagues will wish to consult the Church in Wales ...'

'The Home Office might care to advise us on the status of the so-called Messiah nationalitywise ...'

Even as the Strip Club entered upon its deliberations, darker events began to cast their shadow. There were riots in Mogana City across the border calling for the return of the Mogana Desert – alias the Strip – to its rightful owners to whom the desert was a sacred place. For it was not only the martyrs of imperialism in the mass graves who were buried there. Beneath the low jagged rocks which broke the dull outline of the sandy wastes – the Place of Many Teeth – were also buried the ancestors of the Mogana people; their spirits were affronted by the usurpation of the Europeans. In the Mogana tongue 'Selkirk' – pronounced with the strange aspirated click characteristic of the region – had long meant 'bastard son of a diseased prostitute', a perhaps accidental allusion to the humble origins of the man whom we thought of as the discoverer of a desert then wholly uninhabited. The two leaders of the Mogana Liberation Party who had been kept in jail by the nervous régime were let loose upon the streets. The National Guard had been in forward patrols to the very edge of the jungle, perhaps further still into the first lemka groves of the scrubland, into British territory. In Europe, the discovery of the graves had been promoted from a trivial incident in a faraway country to a cause of international concern. This was partly due to the report that the sandy pits were disused fish hatcheries belonging to the British-owned company which enjoyed a monopoly of the export trade, such as it was. Even after this had been shown to be false – there was no water to speak of within thirty miles of the graves and never had been – the small demonstrations were still being held outside the London headquarters of the trading company. There as even an all-night vigil in which the Mogana-Liberation-Party-in-exile joined forces with the Animal-Rights campaigners who suspected the trading company of being mixed up in the whaling business.

But there was by now no doubt about it. The Selkirk Strip was unmistakably crisis-torn. Rob Bunsen was sent for.

'There's some funny buggers stirring it up down there. I don't just want a story saying the pineapple harvest will be a little late this year. I want you to trace the connections, really do some digging.'

Rob received this summons with the same serious pleasure as Puttock had initiated the Strip Club. Such missions were becoming rarer as the last vestiges of empire slipped away into the misty uninteresting realms of independence. Dependence was the story; complicity and moral responsibility, the hinges of the plot.

'He looks so happy when he goes away,' Janey said.

Now, ten days later, her sadness had sunk into her. Her pale eyes were still rimmed with red, but her grief now seemed full and deep. She spoke now of her work as other people did, without the same exuberance of self.

'I'm doing a new Grubbleys story. One of them loses his tail and it's about the adventures the others have trying to find it for him.'

She sat on a high stool at a draughtsman's table aimed to catch the north light of the fading afternoon. Neat on her perch in bleached dungarees, she was of a different species from her lodger. Alan Breck Stewart was sitting on a little folding chair in the middle of the room, surrounded by his cardboard boxes. He was making notes on a sheet of paper crinkled over his left knee while referring to a pile of pamphlets balanced on his right knee. The lack of organisation was as remarkable as the willpower which had won him the privilege of polluting the empty whiteness of the sitting-room, a privilege like a child's, hedged with conditions and rewards.

'Janey's so kind to let me work in here. I do make rather a mess,' he said.

'Oh well. Does it really matter?' Janey said in a vacant way, neither aggressive nor appeasing, so far removed from her normal self that it was hard to make out. She herself was tidy as ever.

'A cup of tea?' Alan said, as if appealing to her better nature.

'Yes *please*.' A domestic scene in a low key, in keeping with the fading of the late November day.

He got up awkwardly, limping a little as his long legs regained the swing of walking and loped off to the kitchen.

'Have you heard from Rob?' I asked.

'No, he hasn't been there long enough. He only sends postcards anyway.'

Staring out of the window down the garden, I remembered why I had come.

'I could fix the trellis now. It's still light enough.'

On my way home the night before, I had noticed the trellis lolling over the side wall in the cold night wind and I looked up and saw a single rose-branch waving from the dark lattice.

'Don't worry,' Janey said. 'Alan says he'll fix it.'

Alan looked up from his papers and nodded with an abstracted smile. I began to feel interfering and even fussy, the kind of person who asks his friends whether they have installed fire extinguishers in their kitchens yet, obsessed with the dreary hobby of prolonging his own earthly existence.

'That is not the end of it,' Nellie said when I told her that Alan had become the man about the house at the Bunsens. 'He wants to be a substitute husband too.'

'How do you know?'

'Janey says she's frightened to wear a skirt now, not that she does much anyway, his hands are so quick.'

'It's unlike her to talk about that sort of thing.'

'Liz was describing how he groped when she was serving the quiche, and Janey says even at breakfast when she reaches for the toast those boney fingers are half-way up her thigh. She says he makes her feel so guilty.'

'*Her* feel guilty?'

'He talks about his youth and how girls then were anxious to give themselves because it was the war and they never knew if it might not be the last time they met. Love was *urgent* then, he said, apparently, which made Janey feel terribly un-urgent and dried up. And then last weekend he came into her room when she was asleep, wearing only the top half of his pyjamas and saying things like I can't stay in this house unless you can be close to me.'

'She'll have to throw him out.'

'She can't. The more he goes on, the more she feels sorry for him. And, whenever she's just about to think why doesn't he go back to Rome, he says something which makes his life there sound so sad and lonely.'

CHAPTER 5

It was not often now that I made the pilgrimage. Still the old unease came upon me as I turned off Tottenham Court Road down the alley between the audio and video shops. There was a sign at head height, once neon-lit, now dusty but still stark enough in its plain red capitals: G. CLAPP and an arrow pointing slightly upwards. Clapp's was only a couple of paces down the alley: a green shop-front with some wine-making equipment on show adorned with a cluster of flyblown mauve plastic grapes behind a row of small open sacks of assorted beans, grains and dried fruit. This display was flanked by two narrow bookcases. The right-hand case was labelled 'Occult', the left, 'Politics and Erotica'. Books which were neither lined the shelves inside, interspersed with jars of herbs, spices, currants, some used as book-ends on half-filled shelves. In one corner of the room by the window there was a small case full of honest wooden children's toys, blocky simulacra of unwooden things like trains, elephants and hedgehogs.

'The arts of living, that's what we celebrate,' Clapp would say with a melon-grin on his melon-face. 'I refuse to be typecast.' He had cards printed with the Egyptian sign of life surmounting the words G. Clapp, Lifemonger, Books, Food, Toys, Talk, Love. The cards had been printed by a Chinese printer round the corner on extrabiodegradable wood-pulp, slightly cumin-flavoured and brownish in colour; a little pile of them sat on the counter looking like the accompaniment to an Indian meal. Indeed, Willie Sturgis had once circulated them at a *Frag* lunch when curry had been served, and several had been eaten without observable ill-effects.

'I know you can't stop talking, Clapp, but where's the bloody love?' Rob Bunsen said, peering at the flaky brown card.

'There's plenty of it for any nice girl who wants it,' said Clapp with a melon leer.

'When did you last see a nice girl?'

'I have had my moments,' Clapp said, reaching over to clear the plates.

In his bristly woollen jersey and gigantic spectacles, short in stature and mostly spherical, Clapp himself looked more like a toy than any of his wares, something bouncy and cuddly but also slightly repulsive. He lived partly off another shop he owned in Soho and partly off the rent paid by *Frag* magazine which tenanted the upper floors.

In earlier days, Clapp used to prowl around in his shop and buttonhole visitors to the office, ply them with a dried apricot or invite them to look at some rare work of nineteenth-century pornography or necromancy. The office lunches were then done by the secretaries on the first floor who were known collectively as The Fionas and so addressed singly too to save the trouble of remembering their names, much as male waiters in some London clubs and female cooks in private service used to have their individual identities obliterated by their employers. This practice, at first a stray whim of the editor, later came to be rigorously insisted on as a counterblast against feminism. The Fionas used to call Clapp 'the Gonk', and indeed he did look like the grotesque furry toys they kept on their beds at that period.

Moonman and Willie Sturgis, nephew of the poet, had founded the magazine in the heyday of the protest against the Vietnam war. They had taken its title from the slang word for shooting up your superior officer, usually but not always in the back. There had been a lot of it about at the time.

'You're class traitors, that's what you are,' Clapp used to say, gurgling with delight.

'Shut up, Clapp, and bring the soup.' It had eventually turned out to be cheaper for Clapp himself to do the cooking on his little stove on the half-landing. The Fionas had been inclined to go out and buy expensive delicacies from Selfridge's or Fortnum's. In any case, Clapp always insisted on joining the lunch, so that it had seemed simpler to keep him busy and prevent him from dominating the table altogether. Even so, he continued to constitute a roving nuisance, interrupting either to praise his own cooking or to put somebody right on any known topic. His range was as wide as the magazine's and his information no more accurate.

Moonman treated Clapp as his familiar, perpetually abusing him, sometimes physically assaulting him, with a kick of his long leg at Clapp's baggy bottom or a mock-throttle of Clapp's invisible neck. That violence between prince and jester which seems so senseless in old plays came to life when they were together. Willie Sturgis, by contrast, perpetual schoolboy, open-eyed, open-necked, treated Clapp as a fellow-member of the Lower Third, always game for an inky jape. This, in fact, pained Clapp far more than Moonman's brutality.

'Willie doesn't seem to understand that I am an intellectual. Deep down he is a shallow youth.' Another chuckle of self-congratulation, Clapp being convinced that he had invented every old joke.

Moonman himself (never Gerald) was a grave and stately man in his late thirties, some twenty years younger than Clapp. With his long shapeless beard, droopy limbs and general air of melancholy, he looked amazingly like the portrait of Lytton Strachey in the Tate Gallery. He was the son of the vicar of the next village of my childhood. I remembered him as a small boy standing in a lane and refusing to get on to a pony (his parents were quite rich). When the person in charge – mother or nanny, I cannot remember which – persisted, he kicked her, hard. What I remember is the calm with which he withstood the adult recriminations and eventually blows. He just stood there as his mother – it was her, I remember now – hit him about the face. She was wearing a large blue cloak, like a nun or a nurse. Even from the glimpse I had riding past on my bicycle, I could feel the pleasure he was taking. This quality had stood him in good stead.

'I sometimes think Moonman is the only saint I know.'

'Well, not a saint exactly.'

'No, but he is awfully sweet, you must admit.'

'Not to Ziegler, he wasn't.'

'Well, Ziegler was a bastard.'

And, in truth, there were times when Moonman gave off as much sweetness as the baklava which Clapp brought in a tray from the Greek delicatessen next door ('I know you public-school boys have a sweet tooth'). You would come upon Moonman in a shop selling old woodworking tools, holding a well-worn adze or awl up to the light, speculating on the honest men that had clasped these tools, summer and winter, bundled them on their backs as they trudged home disconsolate unhired from the hiring fair; simple decent things left unregarded by the back door after the funeral, and now, generations later, gathered here as 'antiques' on a stall like so much fashionable tat. Such speculations could be attributed to him from the mere pushing up of his spectacles on to his forehead to stare more closely with his milky eyes (milky like the eyes of a blind man) at the cutting edge. These mild excursions only lent extra ferocity to his attacks on the unspeakable villains who were to blame for such suffering – the speculators and cozeners and aliens and deviants.

To be with him was memorable, even mesmerising, no less when he sat in priestly silence than when he was conducting a Grand Inquisition on some villain who had fallen into his clutches. His silences were hangovers of the great Victorian silences which so marked our grandparents' lives. There was an intense absence of anything like canned music or small talk. Lunch in this draughty upper room off Tottenham Court Road had something of the uneasy quality which must have marked the Last Supper – the feeling of impending doom, the uncertainty whether your neighbour was to be relied on. Moonman was of course above politics, one might almost say beyond them. Willie Sturgis, by contrast, was supposed to be a man of the hard Left.

You would never have guessed it to see his friendly face and his jolly tomato-and-yellow jersey. Nor indeed were his political views treated at the *Frag* offices with anything other than total derision. It was hard to imagine that there were halls all over the country which had resounded to the most rabid rants from Willie. Even on the hard Left, his political views were treated with some contempt, but he was a terrific ranter. If your bill of speakers looked unlikely to draw the crowds, consisting of, say, a fraternal delegate from Chile, a theoretician from *Marxism Today* and the secretary of the local trades council, then the thing to do was to ring for Willie. I heard him once in our local town hall talking about Ireland. When he got up to speak, I scarcely recognised him. He was so pale and sombre in the dark-green jersey he had put on for the evening; he still looked in need of mothering, but more as if he had been on the run for ten days without a proper meal than as if he had just come in from rugger and was ravenous for hot buttered toast, which was how he usually looked. And, when he spoke, his rhythm was different – clumps of words gobbled out staccato with no great respect for their meaning and without that underbubbling which made his talk so pleasant to listen to round the table in Wilkes Passage: 'There's-only one-thing-left-for them-to-do: get-out-of Ulster-and leave Ireland-for-the Irish people' – with a querulous up-beat on 'people', as though to shout down those who would prefer Ireland to be left for Irish fairies or Irish rabbits.

Willie drew to him women of a gaunt and handsome type, often astringent, usually activists. Lured, I suppose, by the pale figure on the platform and won by the off-stage schoolboy, in the end they found the off-stage half too much to take; there were muddy shirts to be ironed, dubious unpolitical, uncommitted friends to be entertained – schoolmasters, potters, even chartered accountants, figures from institutional pasts, from university and National Service; his friendliness, his simplicity drove his women wild. But, curiously, one or two of them took and kept his name and others liked to talk about him so that you would often come across a fine-looking woman at a conference or reception for some good or goodish cause who would say 'I'm Tamsin Sturgis' or would drag the conversation round to Willie, perhaps not meaning to, and certainly not intending to complain about the way he had treated her, rather more in the way we talk of a film which we saw several times and which seemed to describe that part of our lives.

Moonman had no such entanglements. His life outside *Frag* was as private as that of a member of the Politburo. It was known that he had a wife and children who lived somewhere in very North London, far away from the swim. At least, he had had a family, but so little was known of them that idle tongues began to invent domestic dramas, even tragedies. Moonman, it was said, had put the house in his wife's name to avoid being bankrupted, and during a tiff she had thrown him out of it, and he now lived in a shed at the bottom of the garden, quite a comfortable shed, according to some sources, book-lined even. Others claimed that his wife had to be physically restrained at certain times of the month, or conversely that she was as sane as anything and that it was Moonman who was inclined to go berserk and attack her with some of the sharper old wood-working tools, after which he would suffer terrible fits of remorse and go into a decline or, according to one account, a nearby Catholic retreat – a great redbrick mansion in Crouch End, surrounded by dripping laurels, typical of Moonman to avoid anything at all picturesque. This seemed unlikely, given that Moonman declared himself 'an atheist with Buddhist leanings', especially fierce against Catholics; on the other hand, his ferocity was so great that there was always the chance of overnight conversion to the diametrically opposite view. Or so it was said.

For my part, and it was only a guess, I believe that, as everything about him was intensified, so he was merely an intenser case of the mystery of other people's marriages – which are unknowable not because the 'facts' cannot be observed from the public behaviour – quarrels, contradictions, echoings, putting-down, silences – but because it is the complexity, the detail, the texture, the day-to-dayness which are the reality of it, and which in the end determine the outcome if there is one to be found - whether in the last resort the arrangement is tolerable, one bed or two, one home or two. Probably Moonman spent most of his spare time quietly whittling wood in his garden shed, if there was a garden shed, while his wife was quietly baking bread in the house. She would have had to be doing something quiet. The truth is that nobody quite knew the truth of it, and this was a tribute to Moonman's willpower and the firmness with which he imprinted his personality on those around him.

'There's a silly twat up there in a bow-tie,' Clapp said, turning round balancing a steaming cauldron on the banister as he went ahead of me up the stairs. 'Never saw him before in my life.' The presence of strangers was an insult to him.

'Gus, have you met Dr John Tasman Smith? Dr Tasman Smith, Dr Aldous Cotton. Dr Cotton, Dr Tasman Smith,' said Moonman, parodying an academic introduction.

'I'm not a doctor, I'm a civil servant,' I said.

'Hi, I'm Tazzy Smith,' simultaneously said the little man in the bow-tie, neat of face and suit, with big eyes, a tiny nose and a luscious mouth, like a pinstriped marmoset.

'Dr Smith is one of Australia's leading monetarists,' said Moonman, beaming at the degree of fluster, however minuscule, which his introduction had caused. 'He is also a henchman of the wretched Ziegler.'

'Ex-henchman,' said Tasman Smith. 'I did a consultancy job on his construction operation. We blew the whistle on some of the nonsenses in the building regs. He got the contract completed in half the time and at 25 per cent lower cost.'

'Jerrybuilding,' said Moonman with glee. '*And* sweated labour.'

'I don't mind raising a bit of a sweat,' said Tasman Smith, with a pleasant smile on his cupid's lips. 'In essence, what we did was to provide Zig with a sophisticated self-employment package, the kind of deal that, I believe, used to be known over here as the Lump. We had people queueing up to sign on.'

A beatific expression spread over Moonman's priestly profile, all the more beatific since he was caught in the dying rays of the sun through the dusty window. He looked the same as he did when running his hand along the surface of the wood after trying a battered old plane, his confidence in the consistency of things confirmed. It would have distresssed him had he heard that Ziegler was a model employer, or a model husband, come to that. Indeed, he generally refused to pay attention to information which suggested mixture or confusion of motives in anyone, friend or foe, even if the information was saucy or startling. In this quality, he was precisely the opposite of my father who was a collector of mixed motives, never happier than when ferreting out uncharacteristic characteristics in the people he came across — generosity in an austere tax inspector, punctuality in a drunk, sycophancy in a war hero. In fact, with practice, one came to see that some of these characteristics were not as uncharacteristic as all that, in fact that, if they were opposites at all, they were necessary opposites created by the very force of the prevailing tendency - 'he has the virtues of his defects', to use one of my father's favourite phrases. Moonman would have none of this; the idea of tension between two opposite magnetic poles as an image of how people behaved would have seemed to him a pretentious evasion. For him, people were not only morally black or white; they were one-way forces, pushing, shoving, kicking relentlessly in pursuit of their goals. Hesitation, change of heart, velleity – all were treated by Moonman with stern suspicion as subtle moves in some unwavering strategy which had to be decoded.

'Why did you fall out with Ziegler?' I asked.

'I didn't. We just finished the job. I thought Zig was a decent bloke. You'd love him if he was sitting round this table.'

Moonman and Willie Sturgis chortled with pleasure at the thought.

'No, really, he's got charm.'

At *Frag* this was equivalent to saying someone had got leprosy and provoked more gurgles of delight.

'You're a lot of spoilt kids,' said Clapp, pausing behind my chair.

'Shut up, Clapp, and bring some more of that filthy red wine.'

'What you totally fail to understand,' said Clapp, ignoring the order, taking a chair at the end of the table which had been left fatally empty and sitting down in it, depositing the cauldron in front of him, 'is that your Mr Ziegler started from nothing, like me, and he has made something out of himself.'

'Unlike you.'

'If I had been renting office space to Mr Ziegler, he would have cut me in on some of his deals. We would have gone up in life together, instead of me being dragged down by you. No, let me speak, that Ziegler, he's got his faults, haven't we all, I mean he probably cut a few corners now and then, but you have to if you're a creative force in society. You wouldn't understand that, because you're purely destructive, you are. Watch 'em come down, that's your motto, Demolition Men to the Nobility and Gentry. I can reveal that Lady Ermintrude Molesworthy is up the spout by Lord Egbert Whatnot – that's your contribution to the sum of human knowledge, isn't it?'

'Clapp, this is a Swiftian lampoon with a genuine radical undertone. That's what it said in the *New York Times*.'

'You can keep your precious *New York Times*. I've got eyes in my head, and I can see it's a load of upper-class filth and tittle-tattle, that's what it is. I don't know why I go on giving you house-room.'

'I never realised you were quite such a petit-bourgeois fascist, Clapp.'

'Don't give him ideas above his station.'

'Just because I choose to run this place as a charity,' Clapp said rising from the chair, 'Don't think I don't understand proper business principles. Dr Smith might like to pop round and see my other shop.'

'I wouldn't bother, Tazzy. It's a crummy little tobacconist's in Soho.'

'I'd be delighted to see it,' Tazzy said, his puzzled look melting back into his habitual smile.

'I'm glad some people are interested in what's paying for their hot dinners.'

'Hot? We haven't had a hot meal in this place since Nixon resigned. What is this muck?'

'It's chile con carne à la Clapp, with special peppers from my Nicaraguan friend in Frith Street.'

'It tastes like a vulture's crutch.'

'I suppose you'd prefer fish fingers and rice pudding. Well, I'm afraid I don't serve nursery food. Have some more.' Without waiting for an answer, he deposited a menacing spoonful of the dark brown substance on my white plate which bore the crest of the Commercial Hotel, Hastings.

'Couldn't we have a simple steak-and-kidney-pie?'

'Or a decent hamburger.'

'Something from the pub.'

'A sandwich, a nice ordinary sandwich.'

'With lovely sliced white bread.'

These plaintive cries had the ring of calls from the schoolroom, seagulls mewing for scraps, Oliver Twists holding up their bowls, please, nanny, the very request a boast of security. A pleasant haze of nuances, ironies unstressed, the gentle half-light of English conversation which has no stronger designs on meaning than the chatter of Italian markets, being mere assertions of conviviality and belonging.

'In my view the fast food industry is still only in diapers here compared with the States,' said Tazzy Smith. 'Still, even that's progress. When I was last here, it was positively mediaeval.'

'*Mediaeval?*' said Moonman.

'Well, practically pre-Norman Conquest,' said Tazzy Smith, chuckling.

'And you regard that as a bad thing?' asked Moonman with the academic severity which was the sign of growing fury in him.

'Well, one has to regard the Conquest, by and large, as an influence for civilisation and modernisation.'

'Does one?' Moonman's voice slipped away into a quietness of extreme scorn. Poor Tazzy Smith could not have known that Moonman was an obsessive Anglo-Saxophile, as contemptuous of the vapourings of the Pre-Raphaelites – 'Old Morris utterly missed the point' – as of the Arthur-Bryant-Our-Island-Story whitewash of the Normans who represented everything he most detested: 'thugs, crooks, bureaucrats'. The feudal system he regarded as some gigantic mediaeval scheme of local government reorganisation thought up by the Department of the Environment and the European Commission acting in cahoots. He believed wholeheartedly that the Norman yoke had been laid upon honest, democratic Anglo-Saxon necks and that the Conqueror, in the manner of tyrants, had immediately rewritten history in the most shameless fashion, appropriating all the beautiful Anglo-Saxon achievements in art and architecture, law and politics. 'No idle Frenchwoman stitched an inch of the Bayeux tapestry,' Moonman was fond of saying. Or: 'There was no power worship in England before the Conquest, and no sex worship either. 1065 was about the last reasonably sane year in English history.'

In the summer, he visited Anglo-Saxon churches by bicycle,

pedalling on his Raleigh Tourer, a dark green and stately machine, upright in the saddle with his guidebooks in the front basket and a small squashy kitbag tied to the pillion. He made complicated cross-country journeys, from Bradford-on-Avon to Brixworth, from the Humber to the Sussex Downs, with the aid of British Rail. This brought him into conflict, as most things did, with the forces of rationalisation. The little branchline trains, no more than two coaches long, would often have no guards van and refuse to carry the Raleigh; the high-speed trains were also inclined to bar bicycles as though mere association with these antiquated contraptions would taint their image of speed. Including in Moonman's luggage was a copy of the British Rail regulations covering these points. I had seen him at Paddington once arguing with the guard while rush-hour passengers swirled round them: the guard plump as a pouter pigeon in his continental-style uniform and *képi*, Moonman tall and droopy, leaning on his bike, pointing with soft persistence at an open page in the booklet. On his return to the *Frag* office, he would compose biting letters to the General Manager of the Western Region. Replies which seemed to him more than usually pompous were stuck up round the walls and had darts thrown at them. There was also the weather to combat. He wore a long black overcoat for cycling, although it flapped against the mudguard and absorbed the rain, taking on the consistency of soaked peat. And yet when I once saw him on a wet spring day, pedalling along in the lee of the South Downs, just beyond Firle Beacon, his face shone with exultation.

Moonman would bring back from these trips tales of the terrible vicars he had met. He lingered with glee on their stupidity, vulgarity and lack of manners as well as on the frightful things they had done to their churches. 'You could hear the automatic flushing of the toilets during the Magnificat, and then he said "it's down to us to relate to God" ... he complained that the council wouldn't give him planning permission for a carpark behind the apse ...' His loathing of priests did not extend to his father whom he was fond of and used to visit in his retirement cottage in Norfolk. And yet I am sure that it was from the emotional cataracts pent up from his vicarage childhood which, as so often with children of the manse, gushed forth in these views which seemed so strangely assorted. For, if the articles of Christian faith were as repellent to him as the priests who were supposed to uphold them ('I sometimes think the Incarnation is one of the most disgusting ideas man ever had'), then why pursue with longing or even interest the vision of a true Anglo-Saxon church which, in Moonman's view, must have reached its peak towards the end of the reign of Edward the Confessor? These were deep waters, and only the bravest plunged into them when Moonman was on patrol, harpoon glinting.

But Tazzy Smith swam blithely on. 'Well, if you want to go back to the Dark Ages ...'

'As the poet said, all ages are dark to the man who keeps his eyes shut.'

'That's neat,' said Tazzy Smith, conciliating. 'Who was the poet?'

'Balsaka, the eleventh-century Poet-Physician of Seville,' said Moonman, regaining his temper.

'Balsaka,' said Tazzy, making a note of it in a slim black diary with gold edges. 'Can you get him in translation?'

'Only in Arabic, I fear. There is a nineteenth-century French version, but it is unsound.'

'Utterly unsound,' said Willie Sturgis, 'In fact Jowett claimed that it was one of the unsoundest translations he had ever had the misfortune to encounter.'

'I think it was Gilbert Murray.'

'No, it was Jowett. Murray had no Arabic.'

'On the contrary, he told Bertrand Russell that he had a considerable command of spoken Arabic, or was it Bowra?'

'Spoken Bowra is not for the novice.'

Dark, dark – the word nuzzled at my brain, already muzzied by the wine and the Nicaraguan peppers, until I hit upon the unpublished verses of T. F. Sturgis which Alan Breck Stewart had recited at the Littlejohns, heard once only, yet memorable.

'We're all of us pissing in the dark
So shake your willy as you wee

The cops are coming through the park
It's closing time for you and me.'

'Ever heard that?' I asked Willie after murmuring the quatrain to him (he was sitting next to me).

'Oh yes, one of Uncle Terry's naughties. He used to recite them to us when he'd had a few. After the first bottle, he could only talk about pricks and bums.'

'I heard it the other day from a man called Alan Breck Stewart.'

'Wasn't he one of the young comrades? I never met him. I think he had to go abroad for the usual reason – well, the usual reason then, now they seem to have to come here.'

'Willie.'

'Perhaps he's dead. No, he can't be if he's still reciting naughty rhymes. They mostly are, though. Somebody remarked at Uncle Terry's funeral what a lot of loved ones he was being reunited with. I say, it is nice to see you, Gus.'

Cheerful, unlined, with a voice altovibrant, like a boy reciting some patriotic verse, Willie always lowered my spirits after a while in his company. Like Moonman, he was the son of a clergyman, a canon of Chichester, and his eagerness was as off-putting as a curate's. In any case, there is nothing like eternal youth to get you down. Peter Pan was a depressing influence on the Darling family. Moonman, by contrast, sunk so early into nostalgia and fogeydom, was a reviving, even cheering, influence. To come upon him outside the old tools shop was an encounter which you might hope to repeat for ever, a sight little changed year by year except for the marking of the seasons by the overcoat that shrouded him in winter or the dirty beige linen jacket he wore in summer, the jacket of a schoolmaster on holiday. By contrast, seeing Willie after some interval you looked anxiously for the deepening of the wrinkles at the corners of his eyes and the thinning of the tight fair curls on his head.

'What do you think about the Selkirk thing?' Willie asked.

'What do *you* think?' I said, the old cold dread seizing me. Why had I come? This was no place for a member of Her Majesty's Civil Service. And yet how feeble it would have been to duck out, pleading another lunch or a trip to the North. To remind the Civil Service that you were a free agent by now and then acting like one was the only way of staying sane in that great kindly clink. And yet was it not equally feeble to say yes solely on the grounds that it would have been feeble to say no? Decisions were often like this, although it was not often that one was aware of it; in fact the trickiest decisions in life depended on coming to a conclusion not about what was best for humanity or even about what was best for one's own interests, but about what would seem, in the eyes of posterity, the least feeble line of action, assuming that posterity was taking a keen interest in whether or not I went to the *Frag* Thursday lunch and other such challenges to the nerve.

'Well,' said Willie, 'it's pretty marginal. I mean, nobody in this country gives a bugger about the place. So I think they'll probably slide out of the commitment if they have to.'

'Hmm,' I said.

'That was a high-flyer's mm,' Willie said. 'The mm of a first-rate mind. This man will go far.'

'It was meant to be more of a hmm,' I said.

'I'm sorry. I knew it was. It will be so recorded in the minutes. Moonman, Gus said Hmm about the Selkirk Strip.'

'On or off the record?' asked Moonman.

'Off the record,' I said. 'Deep background only.'

'Pity,' Moonman said. 'It would have made a great splash. Hold the front page. Hmm – Now Senior Whitehall Aide Says It.'

'Pound Slides,' Willie took up the litany, 'And Weathermen Say There's More to Come.'

A tall girl with bright lipstick at the far end of the table laughed.

The light in the room seemed dimmer. As I took the last forkful of the sweet sticky pastry, my insides turned to water, as though melted by some instantaneous solvent in the baklava. I rose to my feet, scraping the chair-legs on the lino. My limbs felt leaden. I mumbled to Willie that I felt a bit queasy.

'Clapp's cooking claims another victim. Now Mystery Killer Sweet Strikes Aide,' said Willie cheerfully.

The tall girl with bright lipstick looked at me with a mixture of anxiety and remorse as I flattened myself against the wall to get past her chair.

In the draughty little cell in the attic, I sat savouring the solitude. The walls of dirty-brown wood, tongued and grooved like an army hut, were covered with photographs and captions cut from newspapers: a picture of Moonman and Sturgis and a pretty blonde labelled 'the dynamic new management team at the London Rubber Company' and old snaps, curling at the corners now, of Nixon eating a plate of spaghetti, mouth slobbering round the strands, and Ford stumbling on the steps of an aircraft. On one wall was written in gold spray paint 'The Fionas love ...' Beneath, there were photographs of famous men; Steve McQueen, Samuel Beckett, John Betjeman and a fat man with a beard and crinkly eyes who looked as if he might be connected with nature conservation.

Out of the little window above my head, to my right, there was a view of roofs: slipping tiles, stained aluminium flashings bent at the edges, gutters clogged with little bundles of leaves and mud, and in the foreground a flat asphalt area with railings round it and in the middle a large puddle of water, ruffled by the cold wind. I felt a longing to haul myself up to the window ledge and slither through out onto the flat roof and scarper across the jumbled roofscape. Just as the chased villain must feel, if only for a moment, the breeze of liberty as he opens the little door out onto the roof and sees the night sky, so I felt free as Clapp's chile and the baklava from the Perikles delicatessen dropped away below me and I looked up and out at the pigeons bickering on the blackened chimney-pots.

The rattle at the door-handle cut short this breath of freedom, and the age-old cry of 'Hurry up, Gus' broke in upon my meditations. For me, no dunked madeleine could more briskly unlock memories of childhood. My metabolism, distinctly adagio, strolled in step with a daydreaming temperament. On first coming across the sonnet which begins

'When to the sessions of sweet silent thought
I summon up remembrance of things past'

it was of sessions in what Proust himself calls 'the smallest room in the house' (so much for gentility) that I immediately thought. That was, I suppose, because my mother, like women everywhere, used to harp on the theme of 'your sessions, Gus. What are you *doing* in there?' In the end, I used to take a book in with me which I could brandish on coming out to the expectant throng lining the passage as if I were emerging from an international conference or a pit disaster. I did not in fact usually read the book much, but 'reading, mum' was an answer which aroused some respect even if at the same time it provoked the retort 'Gus, you know there are plenty of other places you can sit and read'. This last redoubt of meditation was still precious to me. Baulked at home – in this respect at least I had married my mother – I sought out at the office a distant retreat between the broom cupboard and the stores, equally distant from the camaraderie of the canteen washroom and from the refinements of the facilities designated for senior staff only. In this lone lavatory, intended presumably for some store-keeper caught short or perhaps installed simply because the soil-pipe passed that way and it was a pity to waste the opportunity, I could pass a half-hour or more undisturbed. There had been a brief period of tension when a security guard of Polish descent took to using it. I glared at him as he went in or I came out. After a couple of weeks, whether because of the glaring or because he had been posted elsewhere, he switched his custom and I was undisputed sovereign again. Whenever I saw him in the street, magnanimous in victory, I gave him a broad smile; which he did not return.

'Gus,' said Willie Sturgis outside the door. 'On second thoughts I think I do remember your Alan Breck Whatever.'

'Stewart.'

'I think he was one of the chaps Uncle Terry used to take us bathing with, just after the war, in Highgate Ponds. Tall, forbidding-looking man.'

'That sounds like him.'

'God, it was embarrassing. All these grown men looking at your equipment.'

'Oh, it was nude, was it?' I said, unlocking the door.

'Yuh, oddly enough it was one of the hobbies Uncle Terry and the canon had in common, so we couldn't object, as they were all starkers too.'

Downstairs, the room looked blue and dim and smoky as rooms re-entered tend to look. Moonman was leaning back in the high-priestly chair that had been dragged from his office next door. His head bowed upon his chest, his beard outspread, his long hands pressed together, he was the image of contemplation.

'Well, essentially what Zig was doing there was to lease the holding company back to the operating company and then buy back thirty per cent of the shares with the money he had realised, which put up the value of his personal holding and enabled him to borrow enough from the Liechtenstein shell to make an offer for Ziegler Transatlantic, which you will recall was the original public company. It's a relatively simple manoeuvre,' said Tasman Smith, 'but it does of course depend on the strength of the operating company.'

'You mean it's a house of cards,' Moonman said, a perceptible ripple of pleasure animating the whole upper half of his body.

'If you like. It's not against the law. But it is a kind of super-gearing,' Tazzy Smith said. 'If it comes off . . . '

'A house of cards, a house of cards,' Moonman crooned to himself, as though reciting a mantra. And indeed there was about him some of the fatalism of Eastern religions. Although *Frag* might have destroyed ministries and ministers, stripped the ungodly naked, unmasked the guilty men, and generally gone through Sodom and Gomorrah like a clean white flame, Moonman – and Willie Sturgis too – believed that the ungodly would in the end destroy themselves; if good did not triumph, well then, they stuck to it that evil would not triumph either. In the short run, Ziegler, Nixon, Pinochet, Botha, Brezhnev might get away with it, their villainy was so crude and ludicrous and shor-sighted that in the long run they were bound to come to grief. This hidden optimism provided a kind of unseen trampoline below the level of events for *Frag*'s mocking acrobatics. Moonman and Willie sometimes seemed to dance on life's slagheap like astronauts on the surface of the moon, helmeted and insulated against hard knocks and viruses alike, untethered by the gravity of time.

CHAPTER 6

Woolly red legwarmers over grey leotards, quilted red body-warmer over grey tee-shirt, billows of hair escaping the red cotton headscarf of the sort that Russian women wear in the fields, Liz's clothes gave the impression of having been put on in the wrong order, inside out. She could never have been mistaken for a dancer. The daunting swell of muscle, the implication of physical discipline, these were comfortingly absent. Even her position for relaxing – perched on the bench with one leg tucked under the other – seemed hard-won, the tucked-under leg being at an angle which implied not so much a supple nonchalance as a fear that if it was not held down it might shoot out and fell passers-by.

The dusty hall, once a Methodist or Baptist meeting-place, was now dedicated to new gods – Tuesdays and Saturdays keep-fit and gym, Wednesdays and Fridays ballet and tap (Liz had her classes on Thursdays). The instruments of these other disciplines were tucked away in a corner of the hall: a vaulting horse and a pile of mats, medicine balls, and a couple of netball baskets on their stands. In the top lights of the high gothic windows fragments of Victorian stained glass clung to the intricate recesses of the wooden frames, shrinking from the encroaching plate glass below. Under the windows, just above the grubby hessian screens that kept out the draught, an inscription in foliate and feathery letters of sage and dried blood ran round the walls; 'Young men and maidens, old men and children, praise the Name of the Lord PS. cxxxxviii.'

In the middle of the wooden floor with the netball markings painted on it children were tumbling over each other, their squawks and giggles returning a flat echo from the pitchpine ceiling. Pss, pss, went one boy, pointing at the inscription above their heads, and then made smacking kissing noises, as he pointed at the xs.

'Duncan,' Liz called. 'Duncan, no.' Her voice took on the faintest possible hint of Joyce Grenfell. Even this warning note did not make me or the children fear that her patience might be wearing thin. On the contrary, I think, it reminded us of her almost limitless reserves of good humour which were there to be tapped.

'Bright as buttons, aren't they?' she said, as Duncan went pss, pss into the ear of the little girl next to him.

'I thought they were supposed to be ... retarded.'

'Oh, only physically, and not even that really, just a bit slow. I'd have to do a course to work with the really difficult kids. I'm only in charge because Anna's away this week. I'm not really qualified at all.'

'I think they're lucky to have you.'

'You are nice, Gus. You always cheer people up.'

These statements are quite false. I am not nice, although, like any rat who has survived the race thus far, I am capable of appearing so. Still less do I cheer people up. On the contrary, I usually drain the last drop of bonhomie out of them. It is Liz's gift, *per contra*, to draw these tepid encouragements out of me and then to cradle them to her bosom and exhibit them as evidences of my kind if somewhat damaged heart, like someone showing off a baby bird with a broken wing. This is only part of Liz's general attitude to conversation, which is that true friendship consists in a mutual exchange of compliments and character analyses. You're looking so young or so thin, or you've got such a turn of phrase or it's amazing there's not a bit of grey in your hair or you're really much more affectionate than you pretend. And she says these things, not after a searching gaze or brooding on what, if anything, you have said but as a kind of teasing greeting to which you are drawn to reply, however lamely, that she is looking pretty well herself or that her new hair is a success. These gambits are not, as they might sound, simply fishing expeditions for compliments. It is more that she seems to have a constant fear that other people are falling away from her, receding into a misty middle distance at which they will perceive her less and less clearly and her own perception of them, however sharp and warm it used to be, will become an unsupported memory. Liz sees, more clearly I suppose than the rest of us, how easy it is to sink into a sort of emotional death-in-life, a region of dim indifference to other people. She teaches a kind of remedial dance for palsied emotions, exercises which may be danced solo, or as a couple or in a set, so that she will break off in the middle of an intense discussion of her own feelings or our friendship to bring in some absent person or persons who might otherwise be left out.

'I'm worried about the Bunsens,' she announced after she had handed round orange juice in white plastic cups and there was a marvellous quiet in the hall.

I smiled at the soap-opera sentence.

'Why do you smile, Gus?' she said in that puzzled way which was as near as she usually came to being cross with me. 'Janey has had a horrible time. And Rob has been so marvellous with her, but I think the strain's too much for him.'

'Mm.'

'I know you all think he's just an alcoholic old journalist, but there really is another side to him. He's awfully thoughtful in lots of ways. There's such a lot of love in him.'

'You're right there, I suppose.'

'What *do* you mean, Gus?'

'The secretary. What's she called? In fact, I don't think I know her name. The one from New Zealand.'

Liz was uncoiling herself from the half-lotus position to begin the class again, and she froze as though her limbs had locked. Then she looked at me with a long blushing stare. When she looked me straight in the eye, I knew of old that it was a sign of embarrassment; the straighter she looked the greater her embarrassment.

'Gus,' she said, rising to her feet and pushing her hair back under the ends of her red headscarf. 'I didn't know you had become a *gossip*. I won't say I'd expected better of you. But I do think that sort of talk is basically unkind, however you try to justify it by saying I thought you ought to know or something, because there's really no ought about it, is there? I mean it wouldn't matter if nobody else ever knew, would it, even if it is true which it may well not be because that's the sort of thing people always say

72

about a one-to-one office relationship and most of the time there's really absolutely nothing in it. Duncan, put that shoe back, please. He's probably just taken her out to dinner a couple of times and kissed her goodnight. There is something rather narrow and, well, puritanical about you these days, Gus, no, that's unkind, I didn't mean that and it probably isn't true really but you have to understand how easy it is to hurt people. Duncan, put that shoe back now, please. Right, children, now into one long line, because we are all going to be mice, and we are all going on a long trip.'

'To Disneyland, Miss?'

'No, not to Disneyland, Debbie. We are going to look for the cheese. And we have to crawl through a very long, very thin hole to get there. And we have to crawl in time to the music, otherwise we shall all fall on top of each other. So if you will all get down on all fours and get into a long snakey line and start wiggling. No, I said a line, not a heap, Duncan. I want a nice long wiggly line. Duncan, get *off* Lindy. That's better. Stretch, and wiggle and stretch. That's right. Listen to the music, Duncan. Now you're coming through the hole and you're going to make a huge great jump because there's a horrible mouse-trap just where you come out of the hole. Stretch and wiggle and *jump*.'

It was only when the children began to dance that I really took them in. Or was it because the midday sun outside had at that moment broken through the grey sky and down through the long windows, pouring light, dusty pale gold, upon the upturned faces of the jumping children? When they had been tumbling over one another, they had been as indistinguishable as puppies. Now as they leaped over the invisible mouse trap and shuffled into a chorus line in front of Liz, there seemed fewer of them and they stood out from one another: the wide face and the black eyes of Duncan, the slow plump limbs of Lindy, the surprised look of another little girl in a pink tracksuit at the end of the line, and towering above them in her inside-out red-and-grey dance gear, rosy and strong in the cold hall, Liz, goddess of health, Atalanta and Athene in one. She told me she often cried when she got home after her class. Her tears redeemed her good works. In any case, what other moral vision was left to us? Since health was the only thing we still knew how to worship, how could we show ourselves more devout than by handing out that last great good thing like the soup that was once distributed to the poor?

'There now, you've come out of that nasty dark hole and you've jumped over that horrible trap, so now you can show how happy you are. So we'll just jump about and throw up our hands as high as we can and do a happiness dance.'

'Better get shifting now, Mrs Littlejohn. Kungfu blokes will be here in a minute.' The caretaker, solid, unfit guardian of the shrine, pottered in, cigarette drooping from the corner of his mouth.

'Oh, Don, just a couple more minutes. We started late.'

'Well, that's not down to me, is it?' The caretaker said, ashing out in the fire-bucket by the door.

'All right then. Now then, throw your hands up high, and dance with your feet, and now link hands and swing them backwards and forwards and now up on your tippy-toes and now back down on your heels and whirl round and clap your hands, hard as you can, harder, harder.' The instructions came faster and faster now. The children whirled and stumbled and flung out their hands as if they were trying to keep their balance on a floor which was itself moving even faster beneath their feet. Liz seemed to be driving them and herself to a point at which they would have to cry Stop it. And indeed, laughing hysterically, pink-cheeked, beside themselves, the children did collapse onto the floor as the gallop from *William Tell* rose to its thunderous, heart-hammering finish.

The caretaker lit another cigarette. Two men in white robes came in and stood beside him, passing the time of day. The sun fled from the high windows and the crackle of the finished tape filled the sad and darkened hall. Liz chivvied the children on to their feet and led them off to a cloakroom.

'She seemed so upset,' I said.

'Wouldn't you be?' Nell said. 'I mean. She and Janey — they are best friends.' Some fleck of irony, the merest ion of jealousy there? But not to be spoken of.

'Yes, but — I would have expected oh no, how awful for poor Janey and so on. But she was so sharp and disapproving. After all, best friends' husbands are committing adultery all over North

London and one says, even the most saintly of us says oh no, meaning how fascinating, tell me more.'

'She has got a disapproving side,' Nell said.

'She is awfully good, really, I suppose. I can never quite get over that.'

'Being good is not at all the same thing.'

'I meant good in inverted commas.'

'Inverted commas don't make as much difference as you think,' Nell said. 'Good is good, and I'm not sure Liz is.'

'Well, anyway Rob certainly isn't. Just when you're beginning to think he's not such a bad old thing, he behaves like a very bad old thing indeed.'

CHAPTER 7

'It's yucky, her food,' Elspeth said.

'It's not yucky,' Thomas said, in his more reflective pedantic way, his father's image. 'It's just dried up and skinny. Like she is.'

'Oh, poor Janey,' said Nell, perhaps a little mechanically.

'It's very nice of her to have us.'

'It's not nice to make us eat her horrible lunch.'

'It's not horrible. It's just grown-up sort of food.'

'Grown-up food is horrible. I'm not going, anyway, I'm staying here.'

'You can't. There's nothing to eat here.'

'Yes, there is. There's frosties. And peanut butter.'

'You can't have frosties for lunch.'

'Yes, I can. Frosties are my best food.'

'Well, you're coming anyway.'

'No, I'm not.'

'And I'm not if he's not.'

'Get into the car before I lose my temper.'

'You have lost your temper.'

Their talk battered at my head like a man beating out a car panel, flat hard hammering around the same spot. Subject-verb-object, subject-verb-object; no adverbs, adjectives only as predicate; no doubts, no hesitations; simple, clear, packed with will and power, the way it takes years to learn how to write. The learning of language is a curious round trip. You learn to modify and qualify, to catch the nuance, to inflect to the will and match the mood of other people, and then you are told you must become as a child again if you are to be great. Be plain and brutal and repeat yourself and you will be a true poet or a politician. Was it always like this? Or does civilisation often go through these periods of artificial infancy — times when the surface noise is so distracting that only the simplest, flattest message can get a hearing? How odd it is in the morning to go from Thomas and Elspeth to a meeting of ministers and see the same recipe for success followed: the flat assertion, the scorn for subtlety, the indifference to evidence. And yet even politicians would not think of teaching their children to behave like they do; only the most libertine of parents actually encourage their children to be wilful.

'Put that leg in or I'll shut the door on it.'

'I'm not going.'

'Yes, you are.'

'Well, I'm walking then. Go without me. And I'll walk.'

'No, you won't. You'll just stay here and make a mess.'

'I won't, I promise.'

'Get. In.'

Janey's food was daunting, not in the way that Liz's food was daunting — adhesive and mountainous — but rather minimal, effortful and lowering to the spirits. One could not help thinking of how much time she had taken over these scanty salads. They lay in rows of oval dishes like boats at anchor in a deserted harbour.

'You must have taken ages,' Nell said.

'I skinned the broad beans last night, when I was hearing Fanny's arpeggios.'

'They look lovely.'

'You are lucky having Gus around. Rob never helps even when he's here. I hope you'll like the lentils. It's mostly pulses today.'

Thomas and Elspeth glared at the flat pink roundels of mortadella which lay in chaste solitude on their plates. They did not eat pulses.

But the wine flowed at The Laurels. Rob over-compensated for the food. He ambled round the room in a huge floppy pistachio-and-cherry cardigan, grey curls flopping over his bulging forehead as he bent to pour red wine from a big beaker into big glasses, no longer a golden Bacchus but a dishevelled North London Silenus, purple and swollen.

'Never knowingly spilled a drop,' he said, refilling my glass with the exaggerated precision of a barman pretending not to be drunk. 'First thing my grandfather ever taught me, how to pour a tot in a force ten gale. In fact, it was the only bloody thing he ever taught me. He was a Danish sea-captain, in Hull. Lovely man if you kept on the right side of him.'

'Your mother said he worked for a shipping company,' Janey said.

'Well, she wanted to make him sound more genteel.'

'No, she was quite precise. She said he was a clerk in the offices of the Danish shipping company, whatever it was called.'

'I dare say he did work there for a bit, after he'd retired.'

'No, she said he worked there for thirty years and saved quite a tidy sum. I can see her saying it.'

'My mother was a snob. Anyway, you have to retire young from the fishing game. Even bloody Conrad never went to sea after he was thirty. I suppose you're going to say Conrad who?'

'I know perfectly well who Conrad is. Don't try to put me down.' Her voice sounded like she looked, small and pale and determined.

'Well, who started it? Your grandfather was a clerk, in Hull. How frightfully amusing.'

'You always squash me in front of people.'

'Come on, children, eat up your beans. We all love beans, don't we? Beans means Janey. I expect you've been looking forward to your beans all morning. Please, mummy, can we go to the Bunsens now? We can't wait for those scrumptious bloody beans.'

'Oh, do leave off, Rob,' Liz said.

'The beans are lovely,' Nell said in her vague way, as though taking part in a gentle culinary discussion. She had a knack of failing to tune her responses to the prevailing tone. Her ears screened out any rough noises that did not take her fancy – anger, ferocity and the cruder kind of sarcasm. At first, I took this for a symptom of the self confidence of the old upper-middle class, but I have come across it elsewhere, in people who combine self-confidence with a sleepy gentleness. Indeed, a sleepy manner often indicates an inner sureness, one which lies not too deep to irritate people who are already on edge, as it did on this occasion.

'So I'm up against the monstrous regiment of bean-fanciers, am I? I'm not back five minutes from a tough overseas assignment and

I can't even mention my grandfather without being contradicted. Well, all I can say is fuck your bloody beans and fuck you.'

Janey rose from the little folding chair she was sitting in, and went upstairs, face twisted with tears, followed by her daughter.

Rob went to the foot of the stairs and called up to her, his great woolly arm wrapped round the banister like a bear on a branch. 'Janey, come on down, I'm sorry. Come on down, Janey Juggins. I didn't mean it. Jugs, please.'

Silence came from above. Rob shrugged at it and came back down into the well of the room with a rueful smile which incautiously suggested not so much repentance as that this sort of unfortunate incident tended to stick like burrs to a happy-go-lucky fellow who meant nobody any harm.

'Rob, I really think –' Liz began.

'No, hold it there, Elizabeth. I don't want to know what you really think. In fact, I know what you really bloody think. You think I'm a shit.'

'I just don't think it matters that much who or what your grandfather was.'

'Oh come on, Liz. If I can't have a row with my wife, who can I have a row with?'

'I don't think you know how unhappy you make Janey. I mean you're all used to shouting at each other –'

'Because we are great big coarse men and you are sensitive and wonderful women' - but he was smiling now, and, although she wasn't, it was impossible not to see how his rapid changes of mood took her fancy, gave her steady, serious manner something to aim at, so that he was for her both an entertainment and a case to work on. You could lie there all afternoon, on your back or not, and watch the clouds scud across the face of the sun and listen to the wind get up and die down. Rob's own face changed marvellously according to the conditions; a skinful acted literally upon it, crowning empurpled cheeks with constellations of erysipelas; yet I had seen him on that awful morning looking pale and almost noble in the mild light.

Even now, when Janey came down again with Fanny behind her like a lady-in-waiting, he took on another guise, the tender,

79

thoughtful swain, putting his arm round her and bending over to murmur something into her ear, re-establishing a separate intimacy, leaving the rest of us feeling inadequate and static.

'Would you like to hear the band play?' he said, turning to the children.

'What band?' Elspeth asked.

'Robbie's Ravers.' He gestured at the animal musicians ranged along the shelves.

'Oh. Yes.'

'Right. Let's move it then.' He began winding up the toys with brisk twists of the wrists, looking round at the rest of us with a beam on his face as each furry virtuoso went into its stiff little routine. Soon the whole cool white room was buzzing, ringing, tinkling and poop-pooping.

'He always sets them off when he comes back from a trip. It seems part of coming home,' said Janey. Yet the noise was not homely. In fact, its queer, clanging buzz was distinctly alien, like the feeling that comes upon you when you have wandered far from the hotel in the mid-day heat and the glade is filled with cicada noises and the harsh cries of unknown birds. My nerves, still ruffled by the sea-captain row, twitched to the changes in rhythm as the clockwork ran down, or the battery began to fail. Our voices rising above the noise seemed to sound not only louder but shriller.

'This is the only one that doesn't play,' Rob said, picking up the little mule with the kettledrums. 'It comes from the Selkirk Strip, well, from Mogana City in fact, typical of that bloody place. Nothing works there at all. But I always like to bring something home and this was all I could find. Bloody awful place really, and awful people too. They think they know all the answers. This last time I met the Minister of Something-or-Other, Commerce I think, and I said are you worried about the situation in the Strip, sorry the Mogana Desert? He said Oh no, Mr Bungson, we know everything your government do before you know yourself. What do you mean, I said? We know all your top secret plans. Really, I said, have you got a bloody mole? And he did a lot of winking and ah-ha-ing I-say-no-more, Mr Bungson.'

'Well, they might have a mole. Everyone else seems to have one.'

'In Mogana, sweetie, they can't even get through to the next town on the telephone. I hardly think they're up to bugging the British Embassy. The only reason they're so cocky is they are so incredibly bloody stupid.'

'What did *you* tell him, Rob?'

'Well, he was so cocky he didn't actually ask me anything, so I had to carry on both sides of the bloody conversation myself. While he just went on grinning. I expect you're wondering, I said, how the British government would react if your troops moved into the Strip. Grin. Well, I said, I think they probably have not yet decided how to react, we're great ones for not taking our fences before we come to them. Grin. But if you ask me − grin − I think they'd probably take a dim view. Would it come to military force? Well, I said, there's the bloody 64,000 dollar question. The Strip is a hell of a long way away, but there is the refuelling base at Victoria. Grin, grin. So after a bit I gave up and asked for a fishing permit instead.'

I realised that Rob's bloodshot eyes were fixed on me, trying, while pretending not to be trying, to gauge my reactions to this intelligence from the front. Yet, if my face was blank, it was not because I was being discreet. I was imagining the scene in the air-conditioned office with venetian blinds turned down against the mid-day glare and the grinning official leaning back in his chair, his belly spilling over his knife-edge creases, his moustaches twitching with glee and guile as Rob, puce and sweaty, floundered on answering his own questions − and then Rob's rage as he came out into the dusty, tenth-rate main street and looked back at the ugly little white government building with its ludicrous pretensions to power and wondered what he was doing in this godforsaken place. Yet, at the same time, I could see that this interview in retrospect − unsatisfactory as he said it was − held for him a certain glamour, not, of course, because he had been talking strategy with (or, more precisely, at) a government minister − Robbie had fried far bigger fish than that in his time − but just because of the godforsakenness of it all, the flies, the old men sitting on petrol tins, the dung in the gutters, the broken-downness of Grimmonds

Hotel with its great fly-spotted fan creaking all through the airless afternoon.

'Marco's going out there, you know. Instead of Java. Of course, he'll be staying up in the hills as usual with some bloody tribe. You wouldn't catch him down in Grimmonds with the ex-pats. I don't know what he does there all day. There's nothing to see in those hills.'

And yet the lure was the same. It was distance that still lent enchantment. There were more people within a mile of this lunch-table who held in their heads a map of the Selkirk Strip than could find the way to some nearby London suburb.

The red wine began to buzz in my head. The torpor of Sunday afternoon invaded me, as suffocating as the English Sundays our grandfathers had known or had fled from, as Marco had fled. And with the torpor and the talk of schools and wine merchants came stealing in the longing for elsewhere, the conviction, lurking in the most settled among us, that there was somewhere else where we were meant to be, a land of instinct and authenticity where we could find ourselves and be ourselves, and this belief never quite defined, concealing within it a still less defined feeling that the voyage was the thing, that nothing worthwhile was to be achieved without a journey, that even if at the end of the tramping – though this far we did not pursue the argument, even to ourselves – there turned out to be no such place, the journey would have justified itself and those who had made it were entitled to a spiritual title of some kind, like Moslems who had made the pilgrimage to Mecca.

Even in Thérèse, sitting curled like a leaf beside the fire, I could see the belief in the journey shimmering. The theatre was her project, the platform with the aid of which her proud shy person was to be launched upon a proper life. To talk of acting or indeed of any way of life as a mere matter of technique and practice was to play it false, to reduce it to the humdrum and the bogus. It was a journey, a becoming.

How these ingrained assumptions of our time left us vulnerable to the call of action. Where the action was repugnant to our principles, we hurriedly called upon all our reserves of fastidiousness to resist it. Yet still the call came. I was conscious all the time of this tug, this call that could not be denied, calling to attention, to alarm, to action – a slow throbbing, irresistible beat – a siren call which said this is real life, this is your destiny, your purpose, forget the soft erosions of hearth and home, this is what you have blood in your veins for, come away, come on, play up. The match is not over yet, the clock was misread in the half-light, stumps have not yet been drawn. Even down in the airless calm of Conference Room K4 you could feel it, hear it, thrill to it, through all the suffocating mediations of our profession.

Riley-Jones looked bad. He had been working eighteen hours a day for the past week, he told me. And he had still failed to convince his minister about the logistics of the operation.

'The operation?' I said, nodding at a dried-up little dark man opposite who appeared to be deputising for the usual man from the Welsh Office.

'The options for response, I meant,' he said.

'There is a difference between an operation and options for response.'

'Like the difference between war and peace.'

'Quite possibly.'

'Well, shall we start, gentlemen,' said Puttock with a kind of good-humoured briskness which suggested that we had kept him waiting long enough but he didn't mind because he knew we only did it to irritate him. 'Since our last meeting our remit has been somewhat clarified. We are to consider the civilian implications of a fast response scenario. In fact, for those of you who have not already been briefed, I should perhaps say that troops were sighted crossing the border into the Strip at 0300 hours GMT this morning.' There was a barely repressed whistle of excitement on the T of GMT.

'Do we know that they are Moggies?'

'We have as yet no positive identification. We know they are not ours. I have taken the liberty of asking Air-Marshal Gallowglass from Transport Command to join us.' The dried-up little dark man opposite me nodded. He might have been a jockey or one of the six richest men in the world.

CHAPTER 8

'I'm looking for some trousers,' Hector said, his slow mournful gaze travelling along the unpromising shopfronts as though hoping to see the pair he wanted flapping from some shop-sign or belisha beacon.

'I'll come with you,' I said, always happy to be a companion. To my surprise we turned in to Wheelies, the cycle shop, ducking under the children's chopperbikes suspended from the ceiling.

'What I want, I think, are the Facchetti Hi-Rides, in black.' An unfamiliar precision seized him.

'Size?'

'Medium, I imagine, but I'd better try them on.'

'You can't try them on here,' the assistant said. 'We haven't got the facilities. You can take them home and bring them back if they don't fit.'

'I'd prefer to try them on here. I could go behind there.' He pointed to a dark corner behind some cycling capes dangling from a rusty gibbet.

'That's not a changing room.'

'I can see it's not a changing room. But nobody can see me behind there.'

'We haven't got the facilities.'

'My friend here will keep a look-out,' At Hec's beckoning I shuffled forward. 'Hang on, Gus, hold this for a minute.' He passed me his executive wallet, a slimline thing in the limpest morocco.

'Oh well, perhaps that's all right then,' the man said staring at me thoughtfully, granting me conditional approval as a guardian of public morals.

I stood with my back to the dangling capes, gazing at the rows of bicycles on their metal stands, silvery tangle of spokes and tyres, while Hec bumped and grunted in the confined space behind me. At the end of the battered hardboard counter in front of me there was a mug of tea half-drunk, a little blue transistor radio playing 'Swedish Rhapsody' in Radio Two bouncy tempo, and beyond it, coming to the front of the lunch-hour queue which had already built up and which lasted deep into the afternoon, sometimes winding half-way down the street − women in anoraks with children on their backs and tall, awkward men in trouser-clips leaning on their bicycles with an air of almost sepia antiquity, recalling central European refugees fleeing in World War Two from the advancing enemy − was the drooping bearded figure of Moonman, in his long black winter overcoat. He held in his hand an inner tube, held it with the stillness of a man of God bearing a consecrated Element.

'The puncture repair kit you sold me does not contain a patch large enough to cover this hole,' he said gravely, pointing to the spot.

'The assistant took it and held it up to the light to inspect the damage.

'Oh, that's a slash.'

'Call it what you like. There isn't a patch in the tin big enough to cover it.'

'No, no, your tube's gone. You'll have to get a new one.'

'Surely you must have somewhere a piece of rubber roughly two inches long.'

'A new tube will only cost you £1.28.'

'This tube is less than two months old. I don't want a new one.'

Hector emerged from his hide-out sporting the close-fitting cycling trousers, sheeny and skinny below the jacket of his city suit: a figure miming Big Business in a modern ballet. He made out a cheque for £39.99. Moonman continued to argue in that quiet, unyielding way, inquiring at one point about the possibility of a second-hand inner tube.

It was a sweetly lassitudinous place, grubby and simple and gentle. By different routes, Hector and Moonman were in pursuit of the same idyll, chasing an age, imagined or remembered, of innocent machines: for Moonman, Victorian cycling clubs pedalling down country lanes bushy with wild flowers, the world of Cummings and Pooter and the *Bicycle News*; for Hector, the Tour de France of the 1950s, old men looking up from the *boule* under the plane trees as the pack of brown-kneed sinewy cyclists flashed past the fading red and blue ads for Ricard and St Raphaël on the gable ends, a sight first seen on a summer morning years ago and forever associated with French bread and apricot jam and *café au lait* with the white bits floating in it. Together, their fingers scrabbled to find a grip on a congenial ledge of time, a temporary refuge from the abyss.

But Hector had moved on a little. A month or so earlier, he had cornered me one evening and said, 'I'm going in for agonistic cycling now.'

'For what?'

'It's a whole new scientific approach to competitive cycling. The Italians started it.'

'What does it involve?'

'Well, you have to measure everything — the glycemia rate, lipidic attitude, proteic profile, you don't want to overdo the proteins, surprisingly enough. Essentially, you have to treat the body as respectfully as you would if it was a machine which has to be oiled and cleaned and have its tyres pumped up.'

'I see.'

'You start with general aerobic work, and then work up to maximum speed legs, just like running in a car. You have to watch out for the haemochromes.'

'I bet you do.'

'Too much haemoglobin means there's something wonky with your liver or you're short of vitamin B12.'

'And do you feel terrific?'

'Not yet. In fact, I feel pretty bushed usually. But it's great to know that you're taking your body to its natural limit.'

'It must be.'

'And of course it's a marvellous age retardant. You can go on competing into your sixties and seventies, and winning. Remember Reg Harris. *Ciclismo elisir di lunga vita* it says on my cycling vitamin pack.'

'Swedish Rhapsody' stopped abruptly, and an announcer's voice broke in with that menacing grown-up tone which reminds the listener that all the rest of it – the records, the interviews and the disc-jockeys – is contemptible wallpaper and must be torn away in the interests of real life and the bare wall revealed, stained and crumbling.

'This is a newsflash,' the voice said. 'Unconfirmed reports in Washington are claiming that British forces in the Selkirk mandated territory have been overwhelmed by invading forces from the Mogana Republic. So far the British government has refused to confirm these reports or the further report that the officer commanding the British garrison has surrendered.'

'Hullo, Gus,' said Moonman, 'somebody will have to resign after this, won't they?'

'I expect so,' I said, 'if it's true.'

'The Minister of Defence,' he went on, brushing aside my qualification, 'or the Foreign Secretary, or both. It's a glorious cock-up.' His face shone with happiness. 'They haven't a hope of getting away with it.'

'This is terrible,' said Hector. He diffused misery. Even his new cycling trousers seemed to have gone baggy at the knees. 'What will they do to them, do you think?'

'This is Hector Littlejohn,' I said to Moonman, but the introduction dribbled into the sand, for Moonman had gone into trance, a holy smile suffusing his features, both innocent and gloating – or perhaps there is no contradiction, for gloating requires a kind of innocence.

'What will the government do, Gus?' said Hector, standing there, dripping melancholy over the dark tyre-tracked lino. With his head on one side and his rumpled mien, he now reminded me of a more traditional part of the mime's art, which comes at the end of the sequence in which he daringly, ever so hesitantly, woos an unseen lover, plucks a flower with a little seizing gesture, offers it to her with both hands cupped around the calyx, these are moments of ardour, hope, one giddy instant of believing that she loves him back, and then the cold shoulder, the farewell, the being left alone, all alone, the crumple, the heavy floppy dragging limbs, and behind all this the bitter, impotent, sentimental rage and self-pity.

'What they ought to do is send a couple of fucking Vulcans down there and take out the Moggies just like that,' said the assistant, making a low, scything, chopping motion with Moonman's inner tube which he was still holding.

'What do you mean, take out?' said Hector.

'Bomb the shit out of them.'

'I know that. But do you mean military targets or what?'

'Go for their main barracks and the airport. There's no point frigging about in the bush, bombing a whole lot of banana trees.' The assistant was a blond sturdy youth, with a fine delicate face, and a faint lisp which a white fleck across his upper lip suggested might be due to having had a very slight hare lip. Hector looked at him.

'We couldn't get away with it. There'd be the UN and the Americans.'

'Who cares about the UN? Lot of fucking coons. And don't tell the Yanks. Just do it. And tell the Moggies there'll be another dose where that came from unless they get their lads out sharpish.'

'You'd steer clear of civilian targets?' said Hector, leaning forward intently.

'Well, you can't always guarantee to hit the target spot on, can you? I mean, they started it. They got to take the consequences. You got a cheque card?'

But Hector, in that sticky, lingering way of his, would not let the conversation go. Heartened by the thought of reprisal, indeed positively glowing at the prospect of action, he persisted.

'But would the Vulcans have the range?'

'Of course they got the range. They could fly twice round the frigging little country and still have enough gas left to get back to Victoria. I mean, that's what they're designed for, isn't it? If we don't have the bottle to let them have a go, we might just as well flog them for scrap.'

'But couldn't the other side retaliate?'

'With their peashooters? Do me a favour, squire.'

Moonman took no interest in this conversation. He had a gift for making his indifference felt, and for distinguishing it from his disapproval – another formidable weapon in his arsenal. He stood looking down at a selection of bike locks festooned along the front of the counter, cradling the chains in his hand, as though testing some arcane quality in the metal, its ductility or specific gravity.

'Do you think, Gus, that the Moggies had some kind of advance warning?'

'About what?'

'About where our troops were. I mean, they seem to have overwhelmed them rather speedily.'

'Come off it, Moonman. You don't have to know much to find out where the garrison is in a tinpot little place like the Strip.'

'But shouldn't they have dispersed into the hills, or something?'

'There are no hills near the town. Anyway, what would be the point if they were outnumbered?'

'I expect you're right, Gus,' Moonman gave me a warm old-friends smile, different from the gloating one.

All the same, the whole business did seem to have been a bit quick. Even Puttock, reconvening our little group, seemed irked at the enemy's lack of consideration.

'We shall, I fear, have to move onto a different time track. I trust that we shall be kept properly informed of developments, whether diplomatic or military, insofar as they affect our deliberations. Now to the question of the police contingent. We are, I think, agreed that if it is to be the purpose of a task force to reinforce the civil arm, there should first be a civil arm to reinforce. A dozen part-time officers, or, as we would call them, special constables, are scarcely likely to impress world opinion, particularly if two of them keep the local liquor stores and several of the others double up as local magistrates. Our American friends will, I fancy, be keen to see some separation of powers, particularly since HMG in its wisdom seems to have omitted to provide anything in the nature of a democratically elected council. Are we then agreed on the numbers: a dozen police officers, two sergeants and an inspector? And three stipendiary magistrates? Insofar as possible, all these officers should be drawn from outside the Metropolitan Police area, since provincial officers are more likely to adapt to conditions in the territory.'

'I don't think we want to overdo it,' Riley-Jones said. 'Otherwise it'll look as if we'd completely forgotten about the place until the invasion.'

'Well, we have,' I said.

'I'd prefer it if that remark was not minuted,' Puttock said. 'Now, the question of medical personnel.'

As he gradually assembled – at least in his mind's eye – this army of civilian helpers and their equipment, they seemed to dwindle in my hazy afternoon brain until they were like the toys of peace in Saki's story, little tin soldier substitutes to be boxed up in Hercules transports and scattered as moral largesse all over this desolate terrain, like the huge bundles of flour they dropped on areas of famine which bounded away, leaking on impact pale trails of nutriment over the barren ground as the aircraft soared up away back to the comforts of base.

'. . . and then agronomists. Or is the committee of a mind to postpone that issue to a later stage?'

'I think it's a bit early for agronomists,' Riley-Jones said. He spoke mildly enough, but his old blandness was running ragged. His eyes were baggy, and his hands were twitchy until he pressed them together. Only the voice kept most of its old velvety quality, trained by long years of suppressing his own feelings and calming those of others, a voice training as exacting in its way as any opera singer's and surviving the rudest shocks to personal self-confidence and hope. I remembered from my first days in the service a meeting at which Roddy Bowle, my immediate boss and a legend in his day, had delivered the most graceful, lucid, and even amusing summary of a very rough cabinet committee on the graduated pension scheme and had died, of cirrhosis as it turned out, five minutes later in the permanent secretary's toilet in the permanent secretary's arms.

Even at this remove, in this secure bunker, the prospect of action played upon our nerves, brought out into crude relief the lines of character which normally remained muzzy and indistinct in the comforting smog of routine: Puttock brisk and large, more bull-like, the Harvard-Business-School-geniality fallen away; Riley-Jones a sad sight shorn of his silky vinyl finish; myself a sadder sight still – I felt a curious urge to giggle, mostly at things that were not particularly funny, punctuated by periods of boredom and an indifference so extreme that I seemed to float away from the meeting altogether, like a man going mad in the snow. History of a sort was being made, vestigial no doubt, a footnote to empire at best, yet history none the less. But, on picking up my part, a few lines only, I felt little urge to play it, still less any desire to ask for a larger one.

The evening was cold. The sore patches on my skin rubbed against my thin cotton shirt as I hugged my overcoat to me. Home-going north through the dim streets – the street-lamps' glare seemed diffused by the snow-promising light – the whole enterprise was dismal and remote to me. The British garrison – a company of infantry with a handful of technicians – was now known to be imprisoned in the town lock-up, and long columns of troops were marching in along the dusty road which led down from the hills through the lemka forests and on through the narrowest part of the desert where the track was marked by oil-drums. All this we had confirmed from Washington. Our own links with the Strip had been cut by the invaders. Our impotence was magnificently complete. As a compromise, we had asked the Agricultural Research Council to nominate a team of tropical agronomists who might be willing to serve on a mission to the Strip 'in due course' – a form of words which had required a little drafting since we did not wish to encourage false hopes of an immediate return to normality. On the other hand, there was the question of morale.

The pale faces scurrying past me to Euston and Kings Cross cheered me up; their bustling purposeful steady aiming for Much Hadham and Princes Risborough restored a sense of home waters and anchors which never dragged. It was in such eddying crowds, anonymous yet compatriot, that I had always felt most at ease. As a child, in a small village of the kind unhappy people dream of retiring to, I had experienced, perversely according to conventional ideas, an invasive insecurity; this stillness, this prettiness could not last.

Under my arm, I felt the limp morocco executive wallet which Hector had forgotten to ask for back as he pedalled off to the City. His forgetfulness, mine too I supposed, rather pleased me, if anything; I like running little errands, dropping in on people, picking something up or putting in a word for someone, that kind of thing. These minuscule services are so finite, and so much to be preferred to the vast responsibility of having a good time. I have the good humour of the low-key busybody who is only at ease when he has something to do and who stands shifting his feet, awkward and brusque, at functions dedicated solely to pleasure.

There was no answer when I first rang the Littlejohns' bell. A longer peal did no better. The third blast produced footsteps scurrying and the door half-opened by Hector in a scarlet towelling dressing-gown.

'I'm sorry. I was in the bath. Oh, thank you.'

'There's nothing like the teatime bath,' I said in a friendly relaxed waiting-to-be-asked-in way.

'Well, thanks for dropping it in anyway.'

'Well, it's not really out of the way, is it?'

'No, not really.'

His panic was manifest. Each fresh move in the stilted conversation sent a jab of desperation across his face, which was, unlike his usual moony pallor, flushed and rumpled. And then over his shoulder, crossing the half-landing, I saw a pair of long brown hairy legs, walking with stiff springy gait to the bathroom. At mid-thigh, there was a gingerish tweed jacket being used as a wrap-around skirt held in place by a bony forearm. The ceiling cut off my view at the waist.

'Well, see you at the weekend probably, Hec.'

'Yes, absolutely. Thanks again, Gus.'

As the door closed behind me, there came a rasping cough from the landing, a man imitating a two-stroke engine failing to start.

CHAPTER 9

Nobody quite knew where it started and, as with things of this sort, nobody seemed to care much. The life of a rumour is too brief to need a history. For my own part, I first came across the story in Robbie's piece after the invasion. By his normal flamboyant standards, the reference was guarded: 'The public will want to know who left our troops to be picked off like ducks sitting on a pond. And they will wonder just how the enemy knew exactly where to find them. Did someone tip them off? Would *you* have gone straight to a meat cannery expecting to find Her Britannic Majesty's Resident Commissioner cowering amid the rotting carcases?' Such was indeed the place where the officer commanding the British garrison had escorted Sir Terence Wheelock for his own safety, in the belief that the slight hill on which the cannery stood would provide a first-rate field of fire, as it would have if only the invaders had not arrived through the dispatch yard at the back. The rotting carcases were a poetic touch, for the cannery had been out of use since the meat trade in the territory had collapsed some years earlier.

'Smug young men in the Foreign Office,' Robbie continued, 'may mock the intelligence-gathering capacities of our opponents. But I, for one, would never underestimate the shrewdness of the dreaded Fosec – the Foreign Security Branch of their Military Department. On my last visit, one highly placed official boasted to me that they had access to all our top-security information, down to the vital statistics of the Commissioner's wife.' This final flourish, inserted for euphony no doubt, slightly damaged the alarming build-up. I had noticed before that Robbie was unsuited for panic-spreading effusions of this sort, since he could never refrain from throwing in a flippant postscript. This worked well enough when a touch of humour in the midst of disaster was what was ordered. But, when stately gloom was required, his copy needed editing.

Whether or not Robbie was the originator, within twenty-four hours the security issue was undoubtedly major. Who blundered? How did They know? The enemy's timing was described as brilliant – even fiendishly cunning. Only two weeks later, and a British destroyer would have been lying out in the Bay of Mogana on a goodwill mission. A week earlier, and the Marines would have still been on station, not as it happened a great number of Marines, thirty-six to be precise, but still. British correspondents in Washington, having little else to report, reported that American intelligence sources were furious at the security lapse and were threatening to withdraw co-operation in the region. And then the Bristow story broke.

I say Bristow, although the word was spelled in several different ways – Bristo, Bristol (in Mogana they do not pronounce the final 'l'), even Brisco. But the origin of the story was agreed. A group of Western reporters had been lushing up a Mogana diplomat in New York the night before he was called home (whether in disgrace or genuinely for consultations was not clear) and virtually the last thing he had said to them before they shovelled him into the back seat of his Skoda, the only car available to the official classes in the unhappy country, was 'Naturally we owe it all to Bristow/Bristol/Brisco', and he made a funny face.

From there on, it was anybody's guess. The British reporter in the group suggested that they might have an agent who was the image of Bristow, the *Evening Standard* cartoon character, a fat, bald, moustached clerk, since the diplomat had worked at the country's press bureau in London and would know about such things. Other suggestions were that there was a mole in a Hotel Bristol somewhere, perhaps Athens, since there was an obscure but long-standing connection between the whole Mogana region and Greece, which had sent many of her less successful sons there (hence the old saying: 'for the lucky, Manhattan, for the unlucky, Mogana'); or that there was a key listening post at Brisco, a dismal fishing village further along the coast. Anyway, the government was by no means anxious to discourage any of this speculation, since the more fiendishly brilliant the enemy and the worse the treachery by person or persons unknown, the less the government was to be blamed for failing to deter or to foresee the invasion. Ministers accordingly told Parliament gravely that these were serious accusations which deserved to be treated with the utmost seriousness and would certainly be given the most rigorous investigation.

'But surely Selkirk's quite a small place?' Nell asked, as I watched her cutting back the buddleia with slow, languorous snips.

'Quite small.'

'And it wouldn't be hard to find the British soldiers wherever they hid.'

'Not hard at all.'

'Well then, why all this fuss ...?' She trailed away, as she bent to prune the new wood near the base.

I remembered from previous spy scandals how hard she found it to understand such things. Her assumed dumbness is provoking. Why does it matter whether he's one of ours, or one of theirs, or one of ours pretending to be one of theirs, she asked once in the middle of a spy film, what's he *doing*? The 'doing' spat with something so nearly approaching ferocity, for her anyway, that I could only shush her and explain afterwards that it wasn't what they actually did that mattered. Well then, it's all just a silly game, she said. They know *that*, I said. But, she said, I mean a really silly game of the sort children play, not amusing at all. Well, it's a question of taste, I said, to placate and end it.

'Have you felt Elspeth's forehead today? It's awfully hot,' she said.

'It's not awfully hot. It's no hotter than my own was.'

'I shouldn't have let her go to school. She's got that myxy look like Undine had.'

'She has not got a myxy look. She's perfectly all right. You promised you wouldn't go on comparing the children to Undine every time they get a cold.'

Every morning now we had the feeling of the foreheads – a rite of greeting. I placed my hand on Thomas's and Elspeth's clear pale brows, then on my own corrugated and eczematose strip. Once I rashly said that in the old days when everyone was ill all the time I bet they did not spend their whole time feeling each other's brows.

'Oh, they did, I promise you,' Nell said. 'Even more than they do now. Their diaries were full of symptoms, their own, their wives', their children's, and other people's if they were interesting enough – old Amos Crupper has a bunion in his ear. They were obsessed by illness. They just didn't put it in books, because they didn't think that writing about diarrhoea or pre-menstrual tension was literature.'

'Perhaps they were right.'

'Not if not writing about it gives us such a peculiar picture of what they were like.'

'Does it matter what they leave out?' I said.

'Yes, because if you think that people only care about spies and kings and economics and so on, then you can do anything to them, take their children away, or rape their wives or anything, and say, you know the sort of thing historians say: although his radical policies met with some opposition, on the whole Henry VIII's reign was one of progress and consolidation.'

Nellie spoke with a cheerful fire, removing the outer husks of the brussels sprouts with rather the same sleepy discarding motion as she sent the buddleia branches toppling onto the frosty ground. Standing at her side, I felt my own heart slow. Her presence seemed to stretch out the passing moment so that, as my attention wandered, I fancied myself once again able to acquire all the experience and skills which I knew I had missed for good and all – sailing in a caique along heat-hazed shores, drawing a pert, dark-haired life model in a north-lit attic, polishing the work of immense scholarship on the Cathar heresy for which I had once made notes and which would involve climbing Pyrenean crags for a year or two. Assistant secretaries often have such dreams, but it is only those with pushy, harrying wives who dream them bitterly. It is one of the satisfactions of vegetable love such as ours to be able to gaze on hopes abandoned with only a saccharine regret. But these are insufferable reflections at a time of national peril.

For the great adventure was under way; well, it seemed to most of us rather more than a medium-sized undertaking, although by the standards of past rescue missions it was modest enough. Around me, colleagues were quietly putting up barricades; I felt like a Parisian householder going out for his morning walk to find that all the pavements have been ripped up overnight and great ramparts of rubble erected at the end of each boulevard. The Home Office reported that regional police forces could not spare any men who would be capable of making decent colonial policemen; the Foreign Office was warning of international repercussions, and whuffling about international law; the Ministry of Defence stressed the logistical difficulties, the length of the supply lines, the danger of being lured into a protracted and perhaps ultimately doomed guerrilla conflict in the lemka forests. And we at COCUPA supplied our masters with carefully illuminated options in which we nuanced the milder possibilities – do nothing much, appeal to the UN – in the most delicate shade of rose, while the more robust alternatives were subtly blackened as much as we dared. Even amongst ourselves, we dared not quite admit that we were involved in a conspiracy to avoid bloodshed, still less did we state openly how ludicrous, how bathetic, how atavistic it seemed to us to contemplate the loss of life in such a cause. But we knew what we were up to, and we were, I think, secretly proud of ourselves, still are if we bother to think about it. In that vast scrubland of government life, what exactly we were supposed to be doing was not clear even to us; none of us had ever thought of defining precisely the boundaries of our little domain; we lived the unreflective life of nomadic tribes, grazing on traditional pastures, and then, by some unspoken agreement, striking our tents one night and silently moving on to fresh fields.

But stronger, swifter, far more terrible and powerful than our little raids and traps – at best, a few sticks and grass concealing only shallow pitfalls – came the tidal wave of public opinion. The politicians, poor lambs, who normally liked to think of themselves as doing things like providing strong leadership, were knocked off balance by the ferocity of it, swept along, mere straws, their faint babbling quite inaudible in the roar of the waters.

'I don't care for the way matters are shaping up.' Puttock said as we stood side by side in the urinal. He always knew what to say in such circumstances.

'Look here,' said Riley-Jones at the next meeting hurriedly summoned later that evening, 'we're backing too many losers. When I showed my minister our last draft, he said, don't give me all this crap, options one to six are so wet you could shoot snipe off them, it's a waste of time even putting them up to ministers. We've got to smarten up the two task force options and circulate them by midnight.'

The Air Marshal came in and nodded to Puttock. He was wearing uniform. He looked even smaller in the blue with the ropes of gold braid on his shoulder.

'Surely,' said Puttock miffily, 'the task force options are strictly an MoD concern. We included them in our own paper only in outline and for the sake of completeness. Surely the essence of our brief is the non-military response.'

'No, because ministers are still anxious to keep the whole operation within a civilian framework. The military presence is simply to back up the reinforcement of the civilian arm.'

'I scarcely think,' said Puttock, miffier still, 'that this posture is likely to carry much weight with world opinion. A handful of country policemen "backed" by six warships and two commando battalions and almost a brigade of infantry as adumbrated in Option A, scarcely sounds like a civilian mission.'

'I don't think our masters are much concerned with world opinion at the moment,' Riley-Jones said.

'In my view, the Home Secretary and the Attorney, who is unfortunately not represented tonight, would be reluctant to have their officials agree to a report which did not fully explore the possibilities of first carrying the matter to the bar of world opinion.'

'There's no bloody time for that,' Riley-Jones said, departing from the decorum which we are taught to maintain on these occasions, 'they're digging in and laying mines round the town already.'

'I feel bound to insist on retaining the original shape of the paper.'

'Insist away,' Riley-Jones said. 'They won't read it if you do, and this committee will have lost its opportunity to influence events in a rational direction.' This code phrase for avoiding violence struck home to the rest of us who wanted to get on with plotting how to make military retaliation seem relatively unappetising. Quite hopeless. You had only to read *Hansard* or the tabloids to feel the irresistible tug of events. But Puttock, burly, bullying, bullshitting Puttock, wanted to go on defending his vision, an ideal, almost platonic vision of rational non-violent government. Puttock, who not only played hockey for the Home Office with terrible fierceness but was ready to elbow aside the halt and the lame in the race for preferment, had once confided to me that the moment he had finally decided to join the public service was after first contemplating Ambrogio Lorenzetti's fresco of the Allegory of the Good Government of Siena in the Palazzo Pubblico – which before he had actually seen it was to have been the subject of his thesis had he chosen an academic career. Here in this benighted underground conference chamber was to be found the final resistance of the peace party.

'We are all aware of the political constraints,' Puttock said. 'But it would be a radical departure if, in default of explicit instructions, we were to depart from our original brief which colleagues will recall was to prepare a comprehensive list of options for response ...'

As he emptied himself of the last polysyllables in his bandolier, my mind strayed to the young Puttock – or Hilary, as I now thought of him – bending low, no doubt in khaki shorts, to inspect, perhaps even to sketch, some faded detail of the fresco, then hurrying, muscular-thighed, back to his *pensione* by the cathedral, to collate his notes then to be worked up and dreamed over in the library all winter long: *Rhetoric and Harmony in Lorenzetti – the iconography of Renaissance Political Theory* by H.R. Puttock. And then the call to active life, to realise the allegory.

'If I might say a word,' said the Air Marshal, 'may I apologise for parading in this get-up? I have to be at Lyneham at first light. I do think it would be valuable if the paper were to concentrate on the task force options. The civil and diplomatic implications could perhaps be studied in an appendix.'

'I am most grateful,' Puttock said. 'I entirely understand the anxiety of the chiefs for early guidance on those matters which fall within their bailiwick. But the Committee's remit goes somewhat wider, and I think we would be failing in our duty if we did not provide the comprehensive review for which we were asked.'

But he was beaten, slowly and not without a struggle, beaten nonetheless. We knew what our masters wanted to be told. And we gave it to them. As we tottered back along the passage into the night air, the clock struck three, and ministers had been told how to launch a counter-invasion.

'It will be a damned close-run thing,' Puttock said as we stood side by side in the urinal again, 'but I'd back our side to pull through. The government's authority will be enormously enhanced if it comes off.' The moon gleamed on his spectacles. He was gung-ho again, four square behind the policy, a biff-em-all-the-way man.

'Well, they were going to fight anyway, whatever we told them,' I said.

'Yes, yes,' he said, appearing not to listen.

We walked together up the vastness of Parliament Street, the wide-cambered road black and shining from the rain, statues of soldier-statesmen strutting against the sky, transmuted into legends by the mist of the Whitehall night, part of that frozen niagara of bronze and stone, which swept and leaped and reared through the middle of the city. Caught as they fell in their moments of glory, lamented by angels and erected by public subscription, Ponsonby with his broken sword, Wolseley all Sir Garnet on his horse, and Bobs from private soldier to Field-Marshal on his and Florence Nightingale with her lamp and Sidney Herbert with the testing of the first Armstrong gun, and David leaning on Goliath's sword in memory of the Machine Gun Corps, and the gigantic umpteen-pounder to remind us of the Royal Artillery, and Captain Scott with his ski-ing stick and Nelson with his telescope and Sir Colin Campbell with his telescope and Captain Cook with *his* telescope; guns and telescopes, telescopes and guns; nothing and nobody and nowhere out of range. Even for Lemprière and Kay, commemorated only by a brass in the Great Lecture Room of the Royal Botanical Institution, nothing was out of range – the Caucasian highlands from which they brought back those eggy little crocuses and that delectable pigeon's-eye iris, the Tung-su mountains with their camellias and the rainforests of South America and central Africa from which Mr Kay, such a stubby unassuming little man with a pointed beard, but so dauntless, brought back those positively vulgar things which now decorate every south-facing herbaceous border (not to speak of the appallingly sturdy lemka tree which will fill an awkward gap, or make a windbreak or hedging plant, whichever you need). Everything known, marked and classified by his fierce beady eye, so that to this day Kew is still trying to undo some of his more impetuous classifications of sub-species.

And the unknown world shrinks and imitates and surrenders; even its unknownness is tracked down and catalogued and celebrated, by Marco Bunsen and his friends. For Marco has to live; he must write travel books, make films, lead treks. He must return, a little shamefaced, to his old kraal with camera crew in tow and introduce his blood brothers to the world he himself has been fleeing. Since he last came, they have built a road to the village; there is a mobile clinic, a resident government official; necessary things, part of a process which he too is part of, more telescopes, more lamps, more guns. At the corner of Trafalgar Square, the lights of a café still flickered on a candyfloss machine, turning the pink, still revolving floss red, blue and yellow. I had a sudden painful longing to see a statue to the man who invented candyfloss.

'Integrity, Gus,' Puttock said suddenly, 'in a world like ours, integrity's the only thing that really counts.' He hailed a cab and heaved his muscular fawn-mackintoshed bulk into it.

'We seem to be going to war,' I said as I climbed into bed.

'Oh, do be serious,' Nellie mumbled from her doze.

CHAPTER 10

'It's a bloody disaster, and we should just accept it. What's the point of men getting killed for that? Have you *seen* the place? It's the arsehole of the universe.'

'Well, it's ours,' Hector said, 'we built the country, what there is of it. And anyway, they voted to stay British.'

'Only because they didn't want to pay any bloody taxes.'

'Rob, you know you're trying to get out of it.' Janey's voice had that firm littleness. 'They've simply walked in and they've invaded, and it's wrong.'

'Walking in *is* invading. And of course it's bloody wrong. You don't drop a bloody atom bomb on everyone who does something wrong, do you.'

'We're not dropping an atom bomb. We're just sending a task force.'

'It's no good saying task force in that prissy way as if it was like sending a bad school report. If you send a force, you have to be prepared to use it, and that means people get killed.'

'I do *know* that,' Janey said.

'I know you were brought up in a barracks, bloody Judy O'Grady, but you could rise above it, you know.'

And at that moment Janey did for the first time remind me of the army wives from the nearby camp whom I had met as a child, with their steel voices and their suspicion of any flippant or blurred or ambiguous thought. Mumbling was for them, I think, a sure sign of defeatism; and paradox or any other such trickery they thought of as a kind of smokescreen for avoiding straightforward decisions – which perhaps it is. But then who wanted to live in a world swept so clean by lucidity? For me, blurring and obliquity are the breath of life.

'I don't think it's rising above it to pretend that we don't have to do anything about it.'

'It *is* a moral issue,' said Hec parodying a *Times*-leader voice.

'It is,' Janey said.

'It would be like Munich if we hadn't sent the task force.'

'Oh, come off it,' Robbie said. 'People are massacred in thousands, millions, all over the world every day. The Moggies haven't killed a single person, as far as we know, and suddenly they're the worst thing since Hitler. Don't be such a prickface.'

'Don't use that horrible language.'

'You mind more about rude words than you do about your beloved Selkirkers. What about Marco? He's smack in the middle of it, you know. I suppose you don't care what happens to him. You probably want the extra bedroom so that the weirdo can move up from the basement.'

'Oh, *please* don't talk like that. Alan's perfectly happy in the basement. and I am extremely worried about Marco although I must say I don't see why he had to go there now.'

'I wouldn't call him a weirdo exactly,' said Hector.

'Why not?'

'Well, I rather like him.'

'He's a weirdo.'

'I think he's intriguing.' Liz was always supportive when anyone was being defended.

'And he really understood about Undine,' Janey said. There was no answer to this, or none which could be given out loud. Janey herself had been so brave, so touching, no, there is no room here for condescending, so *nice* – the only word in our shrivelled vocabulary which confers equality on its subject. And Janey in her grief had been nice, in the way she talked about Undine, with a warmth and dignity which was almost poetic in its way and was certainly shaming, because it made one see that what was jarring about her the rest of the time was really only a way of keeping up with people who frightened her a little and who, if they stopped to think, knew they frightened her.

All the same, Alan Breck Stewart did not seem to me to understand about bereavement, or other people's bereavements at any rate, for he made them his own in a way which I thought rapacious. Throughout the terrible days which had followed Undine's death, there he had been in the front row of the group, tears treacling down his Easter-Island cheeks, blowing his nose noiselessly and putting his arm very gently round everyone, including me, which, if he had one-tenth of the sensitivity attributed to his kind, he ought to know is the cardinal sin. I found Robbie's bawling and blustering grief a truer comfort, but then Undine had not been my child, and it was not for me to judge, certainly not for me to say.

'Oh, Alan's been so wonderful,' Liz said. 'Not thoughtful exactly, because that sounds a bit as if he's putting it on, but really sharing. When there's somebody who isn't part of your family but who genuinely shares in your troubles and knows how you feel, it's the best thing, isn't it? Because I suppose it makes you feel the world understands and you're not just isolated in your nuclear family situation having to keep up a front. I expect it's partly because he's older. I'd like to know more old people, wouldn't you, Gus? We get so cut off from different generations, don't we? In other cultures, some of one's best friends would be older women, grannies and so on but not just one's own grandmother. We'd all be part of a richer kin network. But it's not really possible now that we all live in these little boxes and don't even know our next-door neighbours although actually we do because the woman went on a course with me once and Hector knows the man vaguely, to do with work. Hec would be rather good at living in one of those Borneo longhouses, because he likes to have a lot of people about, although you wouldn't think so because of him being rather shy, especially about things like undressing. Isn't it odd how opposite one can be, because I don't mind taking off all my clothes anywhere, well not quite anywhere, Gus, but I'm basically a loner, I like to be on my own. Alan's like that too, you know. Solitary.'

'Where is Alan?'

'Oh, he's taken Thérèse and the children to the Zoo.'

They must make an odd group walking the damp tarmac between the cages, among the access fathers and the shrieking South Americans in their tactless furs: Thérèse with her straggling dark hair and her liquid eyes, Alan, a tall and withered stick of celery, and Fanny and Jack, a study, bumptious, curly-headed duo. They brought back those pictures of wandering acrobats or pierrots which Picasso used to do in one or other of his saccharine melancholy periods.

'They're a long time.'

'The Zoo always takes ages. Just as you think you're over the worst, one of them will catch sight of a sign saying To The Giraffes.'

'But Jack hates giraffes,' Janey said. No, not a stick of celery, I thought, a giraffe: long, yellow and blotched, proportioned to browse off the highest foliage only, useless for the common pastures.

And when he came in, as he did a few minutes later, with Jack in his arms, he seemed ill adapted for carrying a child. He carried him so awkwardly, much like one child carries another who is almost as heavy as he is. Jack's head was covered with blood. A handkerchief tied across his forehead was soaked rust-red.

'He fell off the swing in the playground. I don't think it's very deep,' Alan said, as Janey examined the cut.

'It wasn't anybody's fault,' said Fanny, in the way of children who know the importance of getting in quickly to ward off blame which may spread like a forest fire to consume the most innocent bystander.

'Oh, poor Jack. Poor Jack.' Again, she shed all the cooing when genuinely occupied by a mother's anxiety. Grief is nobler than we have come to think, and so is anxiety. I suppose they are devalued by the ego's parodies of them, which we meet more often in the shape of self-pity and funk.

Thérèse stood, useless and brimming-eyed, one hand playing with her straggling hair, beside the group examining Jack.

'You *know*, Thérèse,' Janey said, squeezing the wet towel she was going to wash the wound with, 'he's so awful in the playground. You have to watch him the whole time.'

'I know, I was. But he's so quick.'

'You have to watch him. Do you think he's got concussion?' Janey said.

'I'll run him up to the Royal Free.'

'There's no point, Rob. You just have to keep him under observation. You must remember from when Undine fell off the slide. Can't you remember anything?'

'Sorry, sorry.'

'Alan, did you really carry him the whole way back? You are good. You must be exhausted.'

'Oh, he's not so heavy, are you, Jacko?'

'I'm nearly six stone, Uncle Alan.' Who, I wondered, had instigated the uncling? It was the kind of usage which people like us shied away from, too cosy and greasy and old-fashioned. Applied to genuine uncles, it licensed the stifling intimacy which we had had enough of in blood relations, and to uncle elderly friends of the family was, I must confess, rather too working-class for us. Curious, when one thinks about class – and in North London there are people who think of little else – how few working-class mannerisms the pseudo-prole bourgeois really will adopt and how many they fiercely revolt against – the sweet tea you can stand your spoon up in, the dazzling clean front doorstep, the tidy suit on Sundays. Yet all these things have something to do with the warmth we are supposed to be longing for.

A day or so later, when we knew that Jack had nothing worse than a deep cut, Alan said to me:

'He's a dear little chap, isn't he? I asked him to call me Uncle. You don't think Rob and Janey will think it too cheeky?'

'I'm sure they don't.'

'I think it makes all the difference if children have a decent time with adults, don't you? That's what we missed so dreadfully in my generation. Of course not everyone was put through it quite like I was.'

'How were you ... '

'Well, my father had left when I was very small, I'm still not quite sure when, but he used to write from Germany telling my mother not to let me grow up into a milksop. There was little chance of that.' He gave that dry, rasping laugh which I had now heard so often. 'So I was packed off to the training ship HMS *Horncastle*. An aunt who lived in the neighbouring seaside resort

106

had recommended it, said it was character-building and that sort of rot. What it was was cheap, particularly since I stayed the holidays with my aunt to save the fare back to Scotland. It was a dreadful old hulk moored off the marshes, cold as sin, the heads smelled like death, we lived on suet, margarine, and cocoa. I suppose the Bollock – Captain P.F. Gurney-Pollock R. N. – wasn't so bad by the standards of his day. Most of the beatings I got were from the other cadets, especially when I was a new shit. I couldn't sing for toffee and we had this barbaric ritual in the hold called new shits singing, when they made you stand on a stool and sing something. I sang "Poor Old Joe," and by the time I got to "Gone are my friends from the cotton fields away" they had me off the stool and were hitting me with these knotted ropes. You can't imagine how it hurt, like bare knuckles punching you all over your body' – he patted himself all over, with quick tense dabs of his bony hands – 'and then they made me go on till I got to the chorus, you know, "I'm coming, I'm coming, for my head is bending low" and, of course, I didn't know then what coming meant, and so they had me off the stool again and toggled me all over again, for singing such a disgusting song, they said.'

'Horrible.'

'The worst times of all were the parades on deck, especially the church parades in that terrible damp air with the Bollock booming, almost invisible from the bridge, about God and the Royal Navy which God seemed to be part of, though not a very high-up part, somewhere around a rear-admiral, I think. It must have been worse during the Great War. I was told by one of the younger officers who was himself an Old Horny that you should have heard the Bollock reading out the death roll of old boys followed by "For Those in Peril" rolling out through the Thames fog, really made him blub.'

'Why wasn't the Bollock at sea himself?'

'Something wrong with his leg. He had a limp. Of course, we all thought he was putting it on. But he wasn't entirely bad. He was very keen on nature and on cooking, at least for himself. In the summer we used to go for rambles on the marshes to collect samphire which he made into salad and I held hands with my jam when the Bollock wasn't looking. When we were allowed ashore on half leave, we went a bit further than that.'

'Your jam?'

'My best friend, a pretty little boy called Wykes. Don't know what became of him. Every senior had a jam. Somebody told me it comes from the French *jamoir*. I don't know about that. I wonder whether the Bollock ever noticed. Whenever a boy had to lean over a bank to get a clump of samphire, he would boom out "half way down

Hangs one that gathers samphire, dreadful trade!

Methinks he seems no bigger than his head."

No, he was a ghastly man. But the Bitch was worse, his wife, she lived on board. I think she had the money. He was certainly scared to death of her. She'd have us in for cocoa and read the most peculiar things aloud to us, sea stories but with stirring moral lessons attached. So you see, boys, she'd say slamming the book, you need a rudder in life. Frightful woman, frustrated, I suppose. But I'm afraid my generation still believed, you know, in rudders. Not in the old Victorian ones of course, we prided ourselves on that. But we did think we had to look for new ones. You all seem to be blessedly free from that compulsion.'

'Are we?'

'Take Freud, for example. Now in our day, ah well ...' He paused, staring into his drink, seeming to have lost interest in what he was saying. Then he said, 'May I confide in you, Gus?'

'Please,' I said, expecting some further light on life aboard the training ship.

'When Jack fell off the swing –'

'Yes.'

'Well, I suppose it was really my fault. They didn't want to go to the swings at all, but I challenged him to see how high he could go standing up.'

'I see.'

'It was a silly thing to do.'

'But they all insisted on not telling, Thérèse and Fanny too.'

'Did they?'

'It was awfully good of them. Fanny said her mother would be so cross. And I do depend on Janey so much. I would be desolate if anything were to upset our friendship. It means a lot to me. Well, friendship always means a lot to lonely people, and I've always been a lonely person, or rather an alone person. I plough my own furrow. This is clearly connected with my sexual orientation and my inability to form lasting relationships. Yes thank you, another small pink gin, a peculiar relic of my naval past. Have you had any adult homosexual relationships, Gus?'

'I don't think so.'

'I stress adult because it's an entirely different matter from the kind of romantic friendships one has in adolescence. The awakening consciousness scarcely knows what it is doing. One is simply gathering samphire, so to speak, living in a glorious daze. But, later on, the matter is not quite so simple. One gets this thing about vaginas. The literature is lamentably vague and flowery about these matters. There's nothing hidden about it. It's not a dream, you know. It's an appalling reality every time you have a woman.' He was speaking louder now, slapping his long bony hand on the bar as he spoke. 'The trouble is that most homosexuals are dishonest people. Never trust a homosexual, Gus. They're always after something.'

'So are most people.'

'I think it is important to be honest. Everyone says that, don't they? But not many people mean it. I think honesty is the most important thing there is. I can't stand people who won't face the truth. It's not an easy way to live, you can probably see that. I haven't given myself an easy life, not an easy life at all. That's because I'm an idealist. You can be a dishonest idealist and tell yourself lovely stories, or you can be a more or less honest cynic like most of these people' – he condemned the saloon bar with a bony sweep of his hand. 'You probably never were an idealist, Gus, probably never went through that stage.'

'I did. In my teens, I had an elaborate scheme for world government, like the United Nations only with teeth. It involved a kind of super supremo who, oddly enough, turned out to be me.'

'I never thought much of the UN,' Alan resumed, gliding elegantly over my intervention. 'I could see from the start that it was doomed to dribble into the sand. I'm afraid experience has taught me that most of these international bureaucracies are run by frustrated old women. You very rarely find a man of any quality in a position to really influence events. Just one more gin, thank you. I don't often find the time for pub-crawling these days.' From the faintly foreign stress which returned now and then to his voice, the heavy-labialled 'b', the softened 'i', the twanged 'g', one might have thought we were half-way through some epic bender, involving the grossest excess in a variety of licensed premises.

The gin was hard-won, the noonday topers pressed in upon the Australian barmaid, a big-rumped, gingham-girt girl rather like Liz and with her sweetness. There you go, she said, with a flash of strong white teeth. I held the glass out over two burly men standing shoulder to shoulder behind me. Alan started forward, in that jerky way he undertook motion from a position of rest, as though he had been trying to move for ages and the sudden eventual success had taken him by surprise.

Then, abruptly, he disappeared. A loud crash and the two burly men turned round. Between them I saw Alan flat out on the ground stiff as a board, heels to the ceiling. One of his blue training shoes had been twisted half off in the fall, and the heel of his thick grey sock was to be seen, worn brown with a small hole in it. He did not move. I waited for someone to say I think he's gone, or some such lapidary comment, but no one said a thing. His stillness was awe-inspiring. I have not seen a deader man.

His scuffed, lived-in aspect only emphasised how dead he was; the worn soles of his trainers, the thin grey flannel bags with the network of wrinkles at the back of the knees, the flat old man's bottom disclosed by the thrown-up flap of his tweed jacket, the wrinkles at the back of his brown neck, the iron-grey gorse of his hair.

'Christ,' said one of the burly men. He instantly relieved the tension. The corpse gave a small groan, almost a whimper. Several of us knelt down and began to pull him up. He was still stiff and inert. It was like levering upright a large component in a civil engineering project, some rib or girder which could be restored to the horizontal only by a painstaking arrangement of chocks and pulleys. Just before he was finally on his feet, there was a moment of uncertainty when he threatened to crash back to the floor. Once up, he swayed only slightly and began to dust his jacket down with slow careful movements. Then he flattened his hair with his hand hurriedly, like a schoolboy late for assembly.

'Oh dear. What an exhibition.' A melting Easter-Island smile.

The word 'exhibition', pronounced with that rasping italianate precision, further relaxed the crowd. They were dealing with an educated man. In England at least this meant there was nothing to be frightened of; there would be no difficulties with the police; the man would have a home to go to; and he would be unlikely to turn nasty.

'Perhaps I've had too much to drink.' Alarm melted into smiles. A recognisable type, the absent-minded professor who had unwisely accepted another gin. It was at precisely this kind of moment that Alan resisted inclusion. Where a genuine example of the type would have gone and sat down quietly, he stood there swaying and continuing: 'While it is true that I do not drink a great deal these days, in the 1940s I certainly did my share and was reckoned to have a tolerable head for it, although, of course, my height-weight ratio is far from ideal for the pastime. As a boy, I often fainted on church parade. One used to be taken below and be given tea and biscuits by the orderly, who was, I regret to say, an uncontrollable pederast. I expect you all thought I was dead.' He turned from me to speak, rather sharply, to the rest of the people at the bar whose attention had been waning. They shifted in some discomfort at this accusation. It is, after all, the ultimate accusation, more damning in its finality than if we had thought him anything else – mad or drunk or a raving fascist.

'I think we ought to push off,' I said. 'You could probably do with a rest.'

'Rest, yes.' He gave his rasping two-stroke cough. Rest, he implied, true rest, was not for him. He would go through the motions of repose to please those timid souls around him who pretended to take an interest in his welfare, but he had not been placed on this earth to relax, his mind was too alert, his purposes too high to slack off.

111

We stood outside a golf shop waiting for a taxi. The shafts of gleaming steel in the window, the scarlet and blue and yellow golf bags, the background of emerald green baize — everything was bright and shop-fresh. Alan inspected the merchandise. His hair stuck out at the back in dry grey spikes. There was blood inside his ear from a nick on the rim.

'I used to play a bit,' he said, 'as a schoolboy before the war. In fact, I was a good player. That was how I got mixed up in the Pyke survey.'

'The what?'

'Geoffrey Pyke was a brilliant man, a genius in his way. He could see that the German people didn't really want war. He was convinced that Hitler was hopelessly out of touch with public opinion. Well, the only rational answer was to get some opinion research carried out to persuade Hitler of the true state of affairs, but time was short — this was in 1939 — and he knew the Gestapo would not take kindly to a team of British researchers charging all over the place and asking questions. So he had this first-rate idea — which, like all first-rate ideas, is quite simple when you think about it — of disguising some of his researchers as a team of visiting golfers. Perfect cover. Nobody would suspect them. And of course they could fall into conversation with pretty well anyone. The trouble was that most of the chaps he had signed up couldn't play golf, so he had to go out into the highways and byways at the last minute to pick up a few who could.'

'Here's a taxi. But didn't the Germans think you were a bit odd?'

'Nobody suspected a thing. It was a glorious summer. I was playing down to four that year. I went round Frankfurt in three under par. After playing, we stuffed ourselves with huge cream teas and then went back to the hotel to write up our reports. Later on, some of us would go out again to dance with the girls we had met on the course. The only trouble we ever had was from ordinary Germans who feared we might be Gestapo spies. But, as soon as we showed our British passports, we were fêted royally.'

'And what did your researches show?'

'The results were staggering. Only 35 per cent of our sample supported the persecution of the Jews — I remember that finding very well – and 60 per cent, I think it was, didn't want war at any price. The tragedy was that the British authorities were not in the least interested. I don't think the War Office even bothered to reply. Blind, blind as bats, the whole lot of them.'

'Only 35 per cent.'

'Extraordinary, isn't it? And yet there was the Führer marching into Poland not a fortnight after I had returned to England. Not a fortnight. It makes you think.' He lit a gauloise and stared at the ceiling, doing some thinking. 'Forty million dead, and it could all have been stopped,' he resumed.

'Would you mind not smoking,' said the taxi-driver. 'There's a notice.'

'I worked with Pyke later on in the war, of course. That was how I first came into contact with him, you know.' This information was bedecked with generosity. It was an act of enlightenment, a favour conferred on me, as one among a host of scholars dedicated to filling in the missing link in his life. 'A remarkable man, but too abrasive for the Whitehall world. He had no time for Mr Facing Both Ways.'

'I said no smoking.'

'Take those ice ships. Could have saved hundreds of lives on the Atlantic convoys. Perfect example of what they now call lateral thinking. Mountbatten saw it, Churchill saw it. But the brasshats couldn't begin to get the point. They were bound and gagged by conventional thinking. Tragic, utterly tragic.'

The cab stopped. And the driver turned round.

'Look, I'm warning you.'

'What did you say?' Alan said, dropping his elegiac tone and leaning forward to press his mouth and nose through the glass very close to the white face of the driver.

'I said no smoking.'

'That's what I thought you said. And by what right do you say it?'

'It's my cab.'

'So it is, and we shall leave it to you.' With surprising agility he flicked open the door and hopped out.

'Go fuck yourself,' said the driver.

I crawled out more clumsily and stood beside Alan on the deserted pavement as the taxi sped away.

'Typical petty bourgeois fascist,' Alan said shouting to make himself heard above the grinding of the North-bound lorries changing gear as they came up the hill. 'Obsession with hygiene combined with foul language. Shall we sit down for a minute?' He pointed to a bench by the low parapet, behind which you could hear trains snuffling. The weathered wooden slats of the bench were broken or missing. Only the concrete supports were intact. The wind whistled dust and sweet papers around our ankles, the cold street dust of a cold spring.

'Of course, my finest hour with the Pyke outfit was the broomstick.'

'The broomstick?'

'I must have told you about Breck's broomsticks. They were the talk of Whitehall – for about three months, ha.'

'No, I don't think you have. Was that what was in the HMG briefcase?'

Alan looked at me vacantly.

'The briefcase?' I wondered if he was going to pass out again, then I realised that his mind had discarded our wet morning in the attic as it discarded all personal trivia. 'Yes, I do keep the papers in that briefcase as it happens. They're classified, you know, but it's high time the whole scandal was exposed.'

'I'm sure,' I said.

'Once again it was a perfectly simple idea. They came to us, after Dieppe it was, and said, look, our chaps are sitting ducks on these raids because of all the equipment they have to carry. By the time they're half-way up the cliff, every German within miles has them in his sights. It's like a tortoise-shoot. And, even if they get over the top, they can't make ground inland quick enough to carry out their mission. Well, I said, what you need is a broomstick and I roughed it out on a blotter there and then. It started as a skeleton trolley, self-propelled, aluminium.' He began to draw with his finger in the dust in front of the bench. 'Its wheels fitted onto a railway track, continental gauge naturally, and you could wind yourself along by means of a handle and a rope which shuttled to

114

and fro like a typewriter ribbon. All amazingly light, fifteen pounds approximately, and pretty nippy, I got up to 20 mph on the prototype at the Bedford test track. But the really ingenious thing about the Broomstick was the way you could collapse it like a baby buggy. In fact, I suspect the man who invented the baby buggy had access to the Broomsticks file. And it turned into a light cradle attached to a winch mounted on a tripod. First man up the cliff could set it up in thirty seconds and have the next man abseiling up to him on the cradle in no time. Advance party sets off down the line to blow up the points or the marshalling yards or whatever before they all abseil back down again.'

'What happened?'

'Beaverbrook wouldn't let us have the aluminium. And the Prof poisoned Churchill's ear against us. It was a tragedy. Could have saved thousands of lives, perhaps shortened the war.'

How long we sat there I do not know. Behind and below us, the trains clanged and snuffled. In front, the lorries chugged, sighed and chugged again as they bounced over the canal bridge. Few people passed along this desolate pavement and those that did were not glancers but heads-down, muffled-up, and one or two talking to themselves. And, as we sat, I began to gather something of the atmosphere in which Alan lived his life, for moments even to fancy myself inhabiting the same air: the urgency, the feeling of time running out, time for him and time for the world being wasted by irrepressible human folly − if only they could see, the answer was so simple − and yet at the same time, because somehow all time *was* the same although there was this shortage of it, the sense of liberation from the usual constraints − breadwinning, home, family, civic duties, petty allegiances − so that he was free to waste time − at least as the world saw it, for it was not really wasting at all. In his own eyes he was using time as an artist uses it, seeming to fling it away with a princely disregard for consequences, yet in reality husbanding every drop, digesting, turning to good use every scrap of experience.

It was tempting to imagine him putting 'lateral thinker' on his passport, but he clearly scorned the commercial popularising of the phrase, its degeneration into a mere box of tricks. For Alan, intelligence meant something grander, gustier than a smart short cut round the side of a problem; it was the way one set one's sails and headed for the darkest of the stormclouds, clad only in a pair of old khaki shorts, indifferent to discomfort mental and physical alike. He was a wandering Jacobite, true to the old faith. Well, one said old faith, but what was it? I suppose, simply the faith that there was a faith worth having, despite all evidence to the contrary, somewhere a king who deserved to come into his own again.

The king himself was not to be dumbly worshipped. In fact, a true Jacobite frankly admitted his sovereign's faults and foibles. What mattered was the enchanted realm the sovereign brought with him, that kingdom of secrets and magical knowledge, for adepts only, with broomsticks reserved for alpha minds. How glorious to be able to lift oneself up by one's own intelligence, unaided. How intoxicating to be able to transform a cradle into a broomstick, as though one of the balls on Hector's toy had been able to shed the iron weight of Newton's laws and take off into space. Why should action and reaction always be equal and opposite?

I had read, of course, the stories of the great betrayals — the romances of well-brought-up young men who had done such peculiar things in the name of faith. But then what was really more peculiar was that they had done them also in the name of intelligence: 'every rational man now recognises, any thinking person today must ...'; that was how the Thirties Communists started off their screeds. At the very moment they were checking in their intelligences at the door like so many overcoats, they were claiming to be super-rational. Or was it more like checking in your gun at a Western saloon, intending to pick the hardware up again from the barkeeper and blaze away when you had had enough? How strangely aggressive was this idea of intelligence, or not so strange. We all spoke of grasping things, of penetrating gazes, of getting to grips with the problem. That softer, negative, absorbing kind of understanding, well, that was something different.

'Why was fascism so attractive to homosexuals?' Alan was saying. 'There is a mystery which nobody much cares to go into. I wrote a paper once which — '

'I think it is time to go home now,' I said.

'It was a terrible country, you know, Gus. England in the Thirties. Terrible, like being suffocated.'

'Yes, I know. I think perhaps –'

'It still is terrible. But none of you seems to care any more. Terrible in a different way. I suppose the difference is that you don't care. We did care, you know. We did. We knew we had to get out and start again. You remember the Sturgis poem?'

'You mean – the cops will be coming –'

'No, no, not that one. A real poem. Dead Ground, There's no breathing done in England now ... You must remember ... They've all flown to Moscow, fled to Rome, swapped dreary spire for sunkissed dome ... somewhere south and warm's the place to be.'

'Oh yes. History bereaves the rotten bough.'

'Well, it does.'

.

CHAPTER 11

Woken from brief conjunction, the sweet declivities of sleep still running with the dew of love, already half-forgotten – all of which was rare enough these days, what with one thing and another – I stretched across sleeping Nell and grasped the telephone which began to squawk authority.

'Ah, Gus. This is Hilary.'

And although it could not have been anyone else, at that bleak hour, the name seemed worse chosen than ever. It was an hour for stern names, unambiguously masculine, names like Robert.

'Yes, Hilary,' I said.

'Hilary who? We don't know any Hilaries,' said Nell, not asleep, her mind running on Hilaries full-breasted, creamy-thighed, on bicycles, she said later.

'Could you report to Bluefield by 0700 hours?'

'What is it now – quarter to five – yes, I expect so. But what for?'

'I'm going in to open the batting.'

'What?'

'You remember the original plan was that I should go in first wicket down, but the skipper thinks I ought to be out in the middle right from the start.'

'Skipper?'

'God, man. This is an open line.'

'Oh, I see. Yes. Open the batting. Well, jolly good. They'll need you out there – in the middle.'

'Thank you, Gus,' Hilary said, after that tiny pause for registering appreciation which people who know how to receive compliments know how to allow.

'But,' I said, a terrible thought striking me, 'does that mean that you expect me to open the batting with you? I thought of myself more as, well, more like the scorer in this match, you know, the fat boy with thick spectacles who comes along with his pocket computer and eats a huge tea.'

'No, no, Gus, you misunderstand me. I simply thought we should have a pre-match pow-wow with our friends in blue before our ways part.'

'What, the police?'

'No, not that sort of blue. *Sky* blue.'

'Oh, I see. All right, I'll be there, at what did you say seven o'clock?'

'0700 on the button, please. ETD is 0745.'

'Ah,' I said. 'Yes,' though what the little Air Marshal would gain from my presence I could not guess. On the other hand, it was easy to see that Hilary himself would be glad of a supporter or two to bolster the civilian arm in the face of overwhelming military force.

The sky was the pale blue of an Air Force shirt by the time I drove out of the Hampshire heathland and on to the chalk down along empty arrowing roads, those old open roads which woke up in me that mixture of hope and fear, familiar from childhood: the hope of release from duty and constraint, the fear of the future. I suppose hope and fear of the same thing: liberty, the prospect of free play for the peronality, like. being suddenly turned into an American. Why was it that I alone dreaded the holidays more than the term?

The military policeman at the white guard house saluted with gusto as he saw my pass. For him I was perhaps a fabulous creature, one of the spiders at the heart of the web who knew what it was all about, my briefcase bulging with secrets – or perhaps he was merely a keep-fit enthusiast who just liked saluting smartly. A man in a jeep swung out from behind the guard house and beckoned me to follow. He went at high speed round a couple of right-angle bends between the nissen huts and the low flat RAF buildings. Creaking along at a more tepid pace in the Escort, I lost him and overshot into a cul-de-sac ending in a high wire-and-concrete fence. As I backed up into the main roadway, a black limousine blazoned with three silver stars on a blue ground came charging forward, horn blowing, and screeched to a halt a yard or so from my back bumper before jinking on past with an Air Force driver shouting, red in the face. In the back, I saw the little Air Marshal, smiling.

I regained contact with my guide who led me to a small white hut in the shadow of some fir trees with two military policemen standing outside. The Air Marshal was already trotting through the door.

'Ah, Gus,' said Puttock. He was standing by the table looking at a half-unrolled map with some men in uniform. I noticed with a stab of horror and envy that he was wearing a flak jacket. Oblivious to my stare, he introduced me.

'Air Marshal, you know Gus already. This is Mr Cotton, gentlemen, my colleague from COCUPA. I thought it might be useful if he sat in on this briefing.'

There was a burble of very-usefuls which, if anything, tended to suggest the opposite. There was a time for penpushers, one gathered, and it was past; real men were in the driving-seat now and any information they wished to impart to civilians would be imparted as and when they felt like it. One very good reason for getting airborne as soon as possible was not to have to listen to such persons.

But Puttock was already different. I knew for a fact, for all facts about him were memorable, that he had not done National Service because of weak stomach muscles; possibly he drilled somewhere in the evening or went to Territorial camp in the summer; possibly it was simply his ability to soak up atmosphere and blend into backgrounds, a gift for camouflage far more impressive than any flak jackets. This was not just a readiness to adopt military slang or jargon, although he was quick enough on to that. His whole manner was now that of a serving officer, brisk but only pleasantly brisk with the mixture of strongmindedness and sycophancy delicately adjusted to make the maximum impression on his superiors. As only a motor mechanic can tell from the noise of a particular engine whether it is rightly tuned, so only a bureaucrat like myself could really appreciate that his present performance, though superficially not so very different, would not quite have done back in his own office, a little too full-throated, a few too many revs perhaps.

'Gus, I wonder if you could stow your briefcase somewhere,' Puttock said, unrolling the rest of the map in my direction.

As I put my briefcase under the trestle table, memories of the July plot on Hitler's life began to stir. A meeting much like this, I suppose it must have been, in just such an austere settting: the bare cream walls, the trestle table which creaked slightly when you leant on it, the brown lino on the floor, the drab greens and browns of the combat uniform; the only specks of colour here were the ribbons on the chest of the Air Marshal and the General who was not accompanying the mission. Such a cold, plain gathering – perhaps that was half the point; there was nothing there to remember, except the excitement, the sheer thrilling nakedness of the choices that were to be made. People sought out settings like this in private life too – bare, quiet rooms to come to a decision in or to think things out. Strip away the noise and smell and interruption of daily life, and you will see things more clearly, face reality more bravely. Mmm, well, up to a point. For what are you stripping away? – crying children and herbaceous borders and tumbledown chapels. If you have to guess how people will react, which way they will jump, what they will fight for and what they won't, you might be wiser to do your thinking in Sainsbury's or hold a Cabinet in a saloon bar. But that would undermine the aesthetic of domination. Ever since Philip II in his bare little cell in the Escorial, power had excused itself on the grounds of the suffering and solitude inflicted on those who – enjoyed it was not the word – shouldered the burden. Being in charge was a sort of deprivation; one was not as other men, the lucky multitudes. What a curious charade, what comforts had to be squirrelled away to keep up the myth, what sumptuousness hidden behind the smoked glass. While we were standing in the cold air – faintly pine-laden – there were grosser souls in England now abed, half of them watching breakfast television.

'Sorry about the kit,' Puttock said to me as we walked back through the camp to the aircraft hangars, huge and black against the pale spring sky. I caught a scent of melancholy, as faint as the pines, beneath his gung-ho mien. The night we had peed side by side in the Cabinet Office urinal and he had said, 'I don't care for the way matters are shaping up' – that night was buried as such things have to be. But even now the distaste for the whole enterprise was not quite rinsed out of him.

'It rather suits you,' I said.

'They said it was a standing ground-rule on active service. Makes everyone feel part of the team.'

'You could hardly wear striped trousers and a bowler hat.'

'Well, Gus, that's not exactly my scene, as you know.'

'I was thinking of a civil servant in a Giles cartoon.'

'Right,' Puttock said in a vaguely disapproving manner which put it on record that he had of course instantaneously grasped the allusion but ventured to question whether it was an allusion worth making at this or indeed any other time.

As we approached the little knot of officers standing by the transport planes, Puttock stopped and turned his back on them. He put down the black briefcase which he was, rather incongruously, carrying, and took out a small phial of pills. His big fingers had some trouble in extracting the plug of cotton wool.

'I'm afraid I still have this hang-up with the Hercules,' he said.

'Ah yes.'

'Concorde or Jumbo, no problem. But these old transports can be a bit hairy.'

'Indeed. How long is the flight?' I added cruelly.

'Eight hours' flying time.' He braced himself and turned to greet his comrades in arms.

The officers stood at ease in the air, which was fresh and bright now as the sun climbed high over the distant downs; they stamped their feet or rocked to and fro on their heels, hands in pockets, one or two junior officers with hands more respectfully clasped behind their backs, cheeks pink and fresh shaven; laughter broke out, briefly ringing round the group, then dying in the morning freshness, and finally being drowned by the roar of revving aero engines.

Across the grass from behind the hangar two columns of soldiers in combat gear began to embark. They moved at a slow, dragging pace, weighed down by their equipment. They seemed passive, like sheep being dipped, beside the little knot of buzzing, excited officers. I could not see where the columns finished at the assembly points behind the hangars. They might have wound away to the far horizon for all I knew. The airfield seemed as vast as a Russian steppe; it surrounded the men tramping on to the two Hercules transports with ample dignity. By the standards of our times, it was a tiny operation – a couple of battalions at most from this airfield. Yet the sight of a marching column moves us with a violence our grandparents could only have guessed at. There is no demilitarised zone in our imaginations. Hour after hour, the D-Day troops marched through our village. There was no end to them, or to the white caterpillar trails left by the tanks rumbling across the downs where the chalk lay only a few inches below the grass.

I had turned to go back to my car, our business done; my visit had been a formality, to make contact. But the sight of the troops embarking held me. And I stood a little apart from the rest of them, watching them go up the steps into the aircraft. There was the odd shout of Good Luck Charlie and Didn't think they'd get you up in time. But most of it was drowned by the crescendo of the engines. The last man to go in, a short, fat fellow with a bald patch, gave us a thumbs up. And then the officers followed him up the steps. As Puttock stooped to enter (he must have been 6 feet 5 inches at least), his great bottom stuck out at me in that familiar way. The size of it in unaccustomed khaki denim seemed poignant. And then the first Hercules was off down the runway and up, banking round the corner of the wood at the end of the runway and away soaring high over the edge of the plain. As the second one followed it, there was a cheer of sorts from the groundstaff and a few canteen girls in front of the main building, a hovering, uncertain cheer.

'You know the story about the tall Englishman?' Moonman said over the telephone that evening.

'No,' I said.

'You must know. The story about the tall Englishman who gave the Moggies all the details of the British positions.'

'Haven't heard it.'

'Ah, Gus, come off it. Anyway, I think it's untrue. I think the government's just putting it out to cover up their own massive incompetence.'

'Well, where does the story come from?'

'From an AP correspondent in Mogana City, but they could easily have been fed it by a British agent.'

'Why are you so keen to tell me all this?'

'I just thought you might have an idea about it.'

'Well, I don't. It sounds to me like the sort of story you always hear when there's a phoney war on.'

'Is this a phoney war, Gus?' Moonman said with a wheedling, chortling tremolo in his voice.

'You know perfectly well what I mean.'

'I only wish I did.'

By now I had come to recognise that tremolo, and not in Moonman alone. I had heard it in the office, in the white hut under the pine trees, in Robbie Bunsen discussing his travel plans, and in Hector crouched in front of the television as the wide-eyed announcer began to read the six o'clock news. It was unmistakable, this trembling note of exhilaration suppressed, this underground hymn to adventure, this exulting in the derailment of routine. Nobody dared say so, but it was like the thrill of art, only far more potent.

'They'll be there by midnight,' Hector said.

'It would be great if there was live coverage of them landing,' said scramble-brained Pete Bunsen. Hector and Pete often sat together in the early evening, the best time for both of them. Pete went to bed very early, then wandered about his room in the small hours – Janey said the sound of his feet overhead drove her mad – and went back to sleep on into the late morning. Hector too went to bed quite early, after News at Ten, but also had to rise early to go to the City. He would often have a bath after work if he and Liz were not going out and then sit about in his heavy woollen dressing-gown. Pete liked to come round and fix him a drink. Padding about in his long floppy jersey and chunky baseball boots,

Pete also had a convalescent air. The two of them together behaved as if they were in the dayroom of some institution where the patients were intended to regain their responsibility by helping each other.

'What do you think, Gus? Will there be live coverage?' Pete turned to me, beseeching, his pale mad eyes full of hope.

'No,' I said, 'there won't. But they'll probably film it for later.'

'It might make the early evening news tomorrow then?'

'No, much later. After it's all over.'

'Oh,' he said. 'It won't be the same then.'

'It was terrific watching them come across the tarmac this morning.'

'Yes, it was,' I said and could not help adding, 'I was there.'

'Gus.'

'I thought,' I said, regaining my spoilsport persona, 'that you were against war and all that.'

'But this is *action*,' Pete said. 'And it's all right, isn't it? I mean, we're right, aren't we?'

'Of course we're right,' Hector said in a strange growling voice, crouched there with his arms clasping the leather arms of the chair, Churchill in a woolly dressing-gown.

'My dad thinks it's a lot of fuss about nothing,' Pete said. 'But I think we've got to stand up for ourselves.'

'I'm worried about the Harriers,' Hector said, almost musingly. 'Have they got the range?'

'Well, according to the specs ...' Pete consulted a chunky blue book at his side, putting on some rimless glasses.

'That's all theoretical,' Hector said, 'the kind of range you'd get flying in a straight line from Farnborough on a clear day with no extra equipment.'

Pete had had his breakdown when he was working on a pop magazine years earlier. I suppose it must have been at about the time that Rob had left his first wife. Pete and Marco had continued to live with their mother, in Kent somewhere, until she had died, young, in unclear circumstances. Then they had come to live with Rob and Janey and their three babies: Marco migrant, only an occasional visitor, Pete a resident except for periods of stress when he would go into hospital, not for very long, a couple of weeks at most. These downs came at longer intervals now. He was, as they say, better.

In all sorts of ways, he was well, terribly well. He was master of a variety of martial arts, or so we were told, for he was too mild to demonstrate in company. In the summer, he wore tank tops which revealed wonderful biceps, the kind which have veins riding precariously on top as though the sheer mass of muscle had left no room for them inside. And he had a mathematical bent. He would no longer play the piano because, he said, he was not good enough; but he played chess with Hector, slow games drenched in theory. Sometimes he brought round a kitbag full of books on chess, and they would analyse openings and endings together. He shared Hector's taste for tricks and knacks: mazes, prime numbers, ley lines, constellations – more interested in these things for their ingenuity than for their mystical significance (he liked reciting the books of the Bible in order, or backwards, although hostile to Christianity). When Pete was talking about such topics, his eye would be bright, his tone lively; on other subjects – how he spent his day, his health, his family – he would sink into a listless monotone.

'How's Alan?' I asked. 'I'm still rather worried about him, after his fall.'

'Oh, all right. I think he's borrowing money from Dad,' Pete said in just such a monotone, erasing from his voice all the light and shade of cause, effect and connection.

'I didn't realise he was short. He could have come to me,' Hector said. 'What does he need the money for?'

'I don't know,' Pete said.

'Well, he probably hasn't got much,' I said. 'I suppose he gets a pension, but it would only be a small one.'

'He could have come to me,' Hector said.

'It was quite a lot of bread. Hundreds of pounds,' Pete said.

'Did Rob cough up?'

'No, he was angry. Janey said he didn't have any compassion. Then he was very angry.'

'But he paid?'

'I think so. I don't know, really.' Pete's voice trailed away into total lack of interest.

Rob attracted such responsibilities despite himself, or so it seemed. While he rumbled on complaining about them, disclaiming them even, (bloody man, parks himself in my house and then starts bankrupting me), they homed in on him, attached themselves to him like limpet mines – wives, children, houses, pets. A colleague of his left a basset hound at The Laurels for the duration of a posting to Lima from which he never returned since he married a Peruvian and settled there. Rob disliked dogs, never ceased to dislike the basset hound which lived out its days by his fireside, growing older and smellier without ever succeeding in endearing itself. He was not one of those characters who occasionally reveal a glint of gold beneath a gruff exterior; still less did he present himself as a dependable character who could be relied on when fairweather friends might fail. And yet it was clear there was no accident about the cluttering up of his life, for there is no person with a more dazzling turn of speed than the man who wishes to escape responsibility. Rob allowed himself to be trapped, and there was about him too some sensitive receptive quality which would once have been identified as 'feminine', a quality not so much hidden beneath the rough exterior of the hard-hitting columnist as perching on his shoulder and indicating by the odd cluck or ironic trill that none of it was to be taken too seriously – and perhaps, if only by implication, also suggesting that there was something in life which *was* to be taken seriously and which – and here I really am guessing – could be identified as one's responsibilities, although if you looked at the way Robbie actually behaved, to his wives, for example, the identification was sketchy, to say the least.

No, that last is too simple a jibe. That is not quite how responsibility works; to be reliable is not enough, is not even necessary sometimes; it is some subtler quality which encourages the distressed to deposit their luggage with people like Robbie, something half-moral, half-aesthetic, a substantiality, a being-thereness as German philosophers might say. Whatever it was, I was conscious, intensely so, that Hector lacked it. As he sat in his woolly dressing gown watching the newscaster bat her eyelids at him, you would not have confided in him so much as your telephone number. Pete had lost interest in the television and had begun playing with the Newton's cradle which had acquired a period charm in the twenty years since it first crept onto coffee tables. Well, to say Pete had lost interest is a sentimental way of putting it, like attributing irony or compassion to a spaniel, for he had that flatness of affect which the sane find so unnerving in the deranged; there were none of those undulations of feeling which nudge the rest of us through the day with the soft persistence of the large intestine at work; first he did one thing, then he did another, that was all.

The profoundest melancholy lapped me round as the clicking of the metal balls on the Newton's cradle accompanied the newscaster teleprompter-reading; one non-rhythm working against another. The uselessness of my companions, far from making me feel confident of my own sterling worth, eroded my sense of self, encouraged the onset of the same helplessness as when the patient surrenders his clothes to the nurse and puts on those humiliating garments which tie at the back and leave his orifices exposed.

Liz entered and I rose like a trout to the fly in a cold spring. The briskness, violence even, with which she plumped her shopping bag down on the table; her high colour – she was a little out of breath from bicycling, she said – her response, so quick and bright to each of us, even her gabbiness, restored me although it seemed to cast Hector into a deeper melancholy; Pete did not look in her direction when she came in; but, a minute or so later, he stopped playing with the metal balls and went across and looked in her shopping basket where he found an apple.

'What are you all doing? Watching the news, isn't it terrible? I suppose you haven't heard from your brother, Pete? There was this woman in Tesco's who's got a son in the Commandos. She was crying and kept dropping her change. I think it's terrible. Gus, doesn't everyone think it's terrible?'

'Some do, some don't.'

'Nobody with any sense can support it. It's mediaeval.'

'In mediaeval times,' said Pete, 'they settled arguments by single combat. Two knights jousted and the knight who knocked the other off his horse won the war.'

'It would be fun if that happened now,' I said.

'I don't believe it was ever really like that. I think all that's just a myth,' Hector said.

'No, it's true,' Pete said. 'It's historical.' He ate the apple with neat, careful bites as if avoiding some dangerous or infected part of it.

How the middle ages still kept their emotional charge, perhaps even boosted it as time went on. The very mist and dark surrounding them allowed each of us to keep his own middle ages intact: for Moonman, an era of common sense, earthy democracy and unaffected craftsmanship; for Liz, a time of cruelty and barbarism from which we had escaped into the brighter world of clinics and advice bureaux; for Pete, a land of colourful simplicities, as satisfyingly flat and bright as a heraldic blazon. For all of us, there had to be an olden time to give us purchase on the present. Once the notion had crept in that it was up to us to make some kind of sense of history, it would not go away.

It was a month or so since I had noticed the Littlejohns together. To be honest, I had not taken much notice of them as a couple for a long time, perhaps for years. After people have become friends, individuals to be sized up and noticed, after those first moments of intimacy and attention, they tend, if coupled, to subside into an unexamined duo – 'the Littlejohns'. Only when something happens to them is the eye drawn back as to a patch of listless grass ruffled by a wind getting up. How marked now was the width of the berth she gave Hector. After she had hugged me, perching one knee on the chair in order to put her arms round me, she went over to Pete and slipped her arm though his, squeezing his elbow now and then as she talked about him: 'Isn't it lovely to see Pete looking so *well* – and so terrifyingly fit – I've been feeding him up on pasta. He was an absolute skeleton when he came back from St Bott's.' The mention of St Botolph's, the hospital which Pete had last been in, seemed to make Pete the hero of a parable, a sadder, less hopeful version of the Prodigal Son. Pete smiled in an unconnected way.

Liz herself was the first to say, 'I'm a terrible toucher, I'm afraid.'

She seemed to have invented new forms of pawing – some semi-erotic, others more like a physiotherapist's rubs and pummels (a strange little kneading of the small of one's back being the most unnerving), all calculated to make the Anglo-Saxon male shudder, and not only the Anglo-Saxon male. I had seen her once with a Spanish student who was lodging with them; his dark eyes filled with terror and his Castilian buck teeth flashed like a horse's as she began to stroke the top of his hip. What strange demands were to be made of him, would he have to seek fresh lodgings, what would his mother think when the story reached her? How hard, perhaps impossible, it would have been to explain that the pawings were signs not of uncontrollable desire but of friendly indifference, or rather of a wish to generate an utterly platonic affection which did not yet exist, like a boy scout trying to make fire by rubbing two sticks together. When serious feeling was involved, she did not touch.

But her agitation charged the air, and so did Hector's. They could not look at one another; yet neither could keep still. The room was filled with a flickering, darting restlessness – the terminal signs of breaking up, a station far down the via dolorosa of marriage from the sly dig, the public put-down and the stand-up row. Marriages going wrong seemed to progress from melodrama to minimal drama, ending like Beckett playlets in a few sighs and twitches. It was a condition beyond speech; almost any remark would indeed have been an opportunity for a quarrel, an opportunity which would have been seized earlier on when rage and bitterness were in their fullest flush; but now the exhaustion and the fear of exhaustion were too great to risk it. Hector and Liz had reached that stage of misery which is a sub-department of hypochondria, where most of the time is spent thinking about how unhappy one has been made and how one's health has been broken by it – the sleepless night, the excesses, the pain in the chest, the ache in the head.

'Well, I'm glad someone's feeling all right.'

'Oh, Hec,' she said.

'Nobody understands about back pain, until they've had it. I mean really understands.'

'Nothing more boring, love, than other people's backs, except other people's sinus.'

'They may not have to operate after all. The doctor says I've got what's called a clever vertebra which teaches itself to adjust and relieve pressure,' Hector said.

'Perhaps Liz could massage it?' I hazarded.

'I'm not letting her near me. She's got hands like a bloody docker's.'

'Some people think I'm rather good at massage. Pete likes my hands, don't you, Pete?' She burrowed under Pete's long woolly jersey and began to rub up and down his backbone with small, fierce, scrubbing movements. Pete smiled and said, 'That's great,' holding on to the bookcase.

'Sometimes, at work, I have to lie down and stay completely motionless for a couple of hours,' Hector continued, 'my boss is American and understands about back pain.'

'Where do you think Marco is, Gus? Could you find out where he is? It's terrible not to know,' Liz said.

'Well, we think he's up in the hills with the mountain people,' I said. 'He should be out of harm's way there. It's miles from the fighting, if there is any serious fighting.'

She went on rubbing Pete's back. The ripples up and down his woolly jersey made me think of the humpings of some dim brown mammal.

'You must be building up a lot of static electricity in there,' I said.

'Whee, my head's lighting up,' said Pete. He stuck his arms out sideways, fingers outspread, and gave a mad wide grin. With his hair sticking up, he did look like the way cartoonists draw a light bulb smiling.

'Marco really helps the mountain people, you know, Gus. He teaches them how to look after themselves, elementary hygiene and keeping wounds clean and so on. There's not a Mogana doctor for hundreds of miles.'

'Marco's not a real doctor,' Pete said with a sharpness I had not heard from him.

'Well, he may not have quite finished his exams, love, but he

131

knows an awful lot. And I expect he knows lots about tropical medicine that he wouldn't have learnt if he had done the last year at St Thomas's.'

'He's not a real doctor,' Pete said.

'You remember, Gus, it was just after Olivia had died, and it was an especially difficult time for Marco.'

I did remember. It had been a time that was not easy to forget. It was also a time that I thought ill recalled with Pete in the room. Perhaps it would have been wrong elaborately to avoid mentioning his mother's suicide if it was suicide; to turn any subject into a great unmentionable produces perverse effects. But Liz went to the other extreme. She believed in mentioning other people's tragedies in their presence like schoolmasters once believed in cold baths for their pupils; it braced them up, brought them face to face with reality and had other such therapeutic advantages. Like old-fashioned schoolmasters too, she did not spare herself the same treatment. She would often say, 'It was about the time my father left my mother,' to date an event, rather than saying, 'It happened just after I left school,' or 'at about the time of the Profumo affair.'

'I wonder what it's like up there, in the mountains. Marco must feel so free, don't you think?'

'Mm,' I said, not wanting to wonder. But it was hard not to conjure up the slim fair figure, in his Sketchley-fresh denim, kneeling beside some ailing mountain person, cleaning the wound with brisk dabs of cotton wool, moistened with Dettol from his first-aid kit (a chunky fibreglass box – I had seen girls down the King's Road shopping with them). And then as the sun fell behind the mountains Marco sitting amongst the elders of the tribe neat as a lotus with folded petals, listening to their grave courtesies and stately reminiscences, then some ritual of brotherhood, and a dreamless sleep beneath the velvet sky. Simplicity and purity itself, and yet all the time, one was drawn to suspect, there must lie beneath it an image of the tensions he had left behind. He could not help hugging to his chaste chest some faint consciousness of the spiritual desolation he had escaped; indeed, just as old planters used to talk about Surrey cricket matches in their youth while they watched the sun go down over the Bay of Bengal, so the modern traveller, solitary, unsettling and unsettled, might reflect on the divorces and breakdowns that had dominated his childhood and adolescence, and think that he was well out of all that.

Perhaps he could envision Hector as I saw him now: too fat to wear a dressing gown by daylight, dark round eyes slipping into darker pouches, jumpy and fractious, drinking too much, seeing not enough people and saying less to those he did see; his half-mock melancholy thickening into true gloom.

'I've been thinking,' Hector said, producing, as though from the sleeve of his dressing gown, a can of lager.

'Oh, love,' Liz said.

'I've been thinking about giving up my job. I mean, what's the point of it all?'

'Money,' I said.

'But what's money for? All this money, what's it all for?' He gave a great sweeping gesture, as if he were standing in a bank vault. 'We haven't got any children. You know Liz can't have any children. Her tubes are like that, like a bloody cat's cradle. So all this money —'

'All what money?' Liz said. Her hands had stopped massaging, but they were still under Pete's jersey. Pete began playing with the Newton's cradle very quietly, as if there was nobody else in the room.

'All this money will go to my nephew Angus. To my horrible nephew Angus. Every time I get up in the morning and go to Leadenhall Street, all morning, I am working my arse off for my nephew Angus, and after lunch I am working for the Chancellor of the Exchequer. No, don't interrupt, I've done it on the computer. It's only the last two-and-a-half hours of the day I'm working for me. The rest of my life I am working for people I don't like and, in the case of the Chancellor of the Exchequer, people I don't even know, although he would probably be just as horrible as my nephew Angus if I did know him. But my point is, that's not living. Marco is living, he's up in the mountains putting elastoplast on a lot of piccaninnies —'

'Hector,' Liz said.

'Lovely, black, *grateful* piccaninnies. Marco is alive. And there's

Gus, starting wars and bidding godspeed to his comrades-in-arms. I have no-one to bid godspeed to. If I died this minute, nobody at Berle, Hoyte and Engstrom would play the Last Post for me; they'd just cable the headhunters for another oil analyst. I'm not alive, Gus. I'm just going through the motions.'

'As far as I can see, love, you don't seem to have even gone through the motions today.'

'You don't know about pain. That's the trouble about big fat *stupid* women, Gus, they are insensitive to pain. If you knew how I longed to get out of this house —'

The new Hector, crouched in the chair gripping its arms like Churchill in Sutherland's portrait, was an inflated, unreal character. His mock despair was too theatrical, at odds with that sidelong melancholy which was what we thought of as his real personality. Yet, because it was theatrical, it was sad too, for the soft blurrings of his old way of talking had been a comfort to us. Hector, we had thought, was all right; his gloom was put on, but it was only put on because he was at ease with himself. Hector would not change. But here he was, up from 10 stone 4 pounds to $12^1/_2$ stone, those panda pouches disappearing under a fat man's cheeks, and self-dramatising like someone having a breakdown in a soap opera. But then what other language is there for having a breakdown in? Deep down, though we would not admit it, we do expect people to go mad in a distinguished way. How irritating it is to have to listen to the thin whine of paranoia, the gross blubbery moan of the depressive. And how unsettling that all they can talk about is themselves. No, worse than unsettling. It is that which is the awful vision of solitude. Left to ourselves, in the abandonment of madness, all we ever wish to talk about is ourselves. Hector's taste for gossip had quite gone. Perhaps therapists were all wrong; instead of encouraging their patients to talk about themselves and how they related to this or that — encouragement all too rarely needed — they should teach patients to gossip, to busy themselves with rumour and anecdote about the doings of other people.

As Hector described his last agonising bout of back pain, which had seized him during a strategy meeting at Berle, Hoyte and Engstrom, my gaze wandered to the window. Across the road, a tree surgeon was cutting down a tree. The main branch had fallen on a lilac bush. The bush was just coming into flower. Heavy swags of pale mauve blossom shuddered under the impact, shaking off the raindrops from the showers earlier in the day. The burly young surgeon must be drenched in rain and scent. I had heard he had a reputation for laying his female clients as fast as he lopped their trees. Only a few months ago, that was a piece of information which Hector would have swallowed with delight. But now when I tried it on him, he said only that he suspected, although his doctor would not confirm this, that the vibrations from the noise of the chain-saw made his back worse.

'I do wish you'd let me find someone who knows about backs,' Liz said. 'There's this lovely man I heard about at the centre today. He seems to do a mixture of osteopathy and acupuncture.'

'Oh, fuck off, I don't want to be crippled for life by one of your fucking quacks.' Even the swearing sounded false, for Hector's old style, oblique and nuanced, was also curiously pure.

Pete stopped playing with the Newton's cradle and with great care, using the palms of both hands as though the toy were much heavier, pushed it along the top of the bookshelf until it fell off the end onto the floor. The balls clicked as it fell. The fall broke two of the glass pillars off from the base and tangled the strings and balls together.

'Oh, you stupid bugger, you've broken it,' Hector said. 'It's the only possession in the world that I really like.'

'Well, you can always get another one,' Liz said.

'I don't want another one.'

'Pete, I think you ought to apologise for being so clumsy.'

'He doesn't need an old slag like you to tell him to apologise. Anyway, he did it on purpose.'

'I'm sure he didn't.'

'Of course he did it on purpose. He did it to make you shut the fuck up. I could have told him he was wasting his time.'

'There's no need to turn on me just because your silly little toy's broken.'

Pete began to cry, and I said I had to get home and suggested he walk with me, which was escape masquerading as charity. Pete

135

cried most of the way home. Even to leave the house was not to break free of the quarrel which still seemed to ring in my ears as I said goodbye to him and I watched him climb the steps to the stucco portico of the Bunsens' house. He looked all the wearier because his body was so karate-fit.

CHAPTER 12

'You will find us Cubitarians quite a mixed bunch,' said Tazzy Smith, tweaking his bow-tie straight as we climbed the steps to the white stucco house in St John Terrace, a grander version of the Bunsen house.

'Cubitarians?'

'From *cubitus* – elbow in Latin. Admirers of the late George Elbow of Chicago and the LSE, *né* Georg von Ellbogen of Vienna, free market economist, lover of beautiful women and champion shot.'

'Oh, I thought he was just an economist.'

'The old boy was getting on a bit when I was doing my doctorate at the LSE, but he was still smart as paint. At dinner one night, he had us rolling in the aisles with his Erich von Stroheim act – monocle, white tie made out of a paper napkin – the whole bit. Then he'd go straight into a hot streak on supply side theory. A great guy. They don't make them like Elbow any more in the groves of academe. There are usually a few interesting people here,' he said, as be embraced a couple of short men in spectacles in the half-lit hall. To my surprise, one of them was Clapp. He was wearing the sort of jacket worn by the late Pandit Nehru. In one hand, he was carrying a steaming plate of courgettes.

'I'm afraid the paper tonight will be pitifully superficial,' Clapp said to me.

'I didn't know you were an expert on supply side theory.'

'There's a lot of things you don't know, cocky,' he said as he took the vegetables over to a side table where several of his familiar cauldrons were already bubbling.

'We used to just have a cold buffet,' Tazzy said, 'but I thought it would be more Cubitarian to try Clapp's cuisine.'

'Living dangerously, you mean?'

We came out of the gloom of the hall, dodging a monstrous mahogany sideboard, to be welcomed by a dapper elderly man with surprisingly black hair, as slick as an airport runway.

'Gus, dear boy.'

'Minister.'

'Boy to you, Gus' – turning to Tazzy – 'Used to know his father in the bad old days when we backed the wrong horses and the wrong women. Then the poor chap had the misfortune to work for me. Neither of us ever got over the shock. Welcome back to my pad.'

Boy Kingsmill had not been a minister for ten years, but the aroma clung to him as tenaciously as the honey-and-flowers from Trumper's on his hair. At the age of seventy-five he seemed to be still gliding effortlessly along in pursuit of the main chance, ever on the look-out for a fresh patron to woo, a fresh fad to be up with. There was something restful for spectators of this endless pursuit, and when he used to say to me, 'Never give a damn, dear boy, that's the secret,' he was speaking a kind of truth about himself, although in the same breath he would be saying, 'You might just give the Secretary of State's office a tinkle and uncross the wires for me, would you?' And, when he called me in to tell me he had been dismissed, there was an endearing mixture of pique and serenity in the way he said, 'I have just received the most noble order of the boot, Gus – no, no, dry your eyes, there are always plenty of billets for a willing soldier.'

His good humour – inexhaustible, imperturbable – was not to be confused with goodwill. He discarded wives and allies as lightly as he took them up, retaining only the vaguest memory of the precise circumstances in which they parted company. He assumed that the way matters had turned out for them would fit as simply into the snipelike life-routes which they too must be pursuing as it had into his own plans. When confronted by an indignant ex-lover he would mutter afterwards: 'Can't quite fathom what she's up to' – in this respect being rather like Moonman faced with a victim threatening legal action, and also like Moonman, happy to confess his puzzlement to relative strangers such as a junior civil servant.

'Very clever some of these chaps,' he said with a wave at the twenty or thirty middle-aged characters now crowding round Clapp's cauldrons. 'Don't follow every word of it myself, but they're clearly onto something. This fellow here is quite bright for an Aussie,' he added patting Dr Tasman Smith on the bottom. 'He's a mon-et-arist, you know.' He pronounced the word as if it was foreign, not with irony or distaste, more as though he wished to be understood by someone only just in earshot.

'Well, they can't jail you for it yet,' Tazzy said.

'Have you *read* Sulzbach, Tazzy?' Another short man in spectacles, perhaps the one I had already bumped into, not Clapp whom I could see smirking at the far end of the room as he watched the Cubitarians having to stretch over the serving-table to ladle some green liquid out of a cauldron they could barely reach.

'The thing on private motoring courts? Fantastic. Gus, listen to this. The government puts motoring offences out to tender. Bidder sets his own scale of penalties for parking, speeding and so forth, employs his own traffic cops and collects the fines, keeps a percentage on a sliding scale according to whether road deaths go up or down, average speed of traffic over the period, etcetera. If he performs badly, he loses the franchise. That way, every guy in the company gets to be enforcement-hungry. They're trying it out in a couple of counties in Arizona.'

Eyes gleaming, bow-tie erect, Tazzy was bathed in an innocent joy. No, bathing is not the word, water was too heavy an element. He was footing it lightly through the desert air, an Arizona Ariel, inviting the heavier-laden to shed their burdens, their clogging attachments – guilt, reverence, loyalty, awe – and caper along with him in a world of perfect competition, perfect in an almost theological sense, like the freedom to be enjoyed in the service of the divine.

'Sulzbach was Elbow's favourite pupil. Sometimes he was too much even for Elbow.' The short man laughed with pleasure at the recollection. 'Of course, we thought they were all crazy then, and in any case we Reds got the best girls.'

'Frank was a horny young Trotskyite in those days,' Tazzy laughed back.

'I was assistant organiser for the South Side, June through December 1941, I split over the Pact. History hit us with a freight train as Whit Chambers used to say. My God, we took ourselves seriously. We were going to save the world from 437 Lincoln Avenue. Ho hum.' He gave a tinkling chuckle and took off his glasses and rubbed them.

Yet this transformation from Chicago ideologue to New York-erish sophisticate was not entirely convincing. You could indeed feel that a great weight had been lifted from Frank's shoulders when he joined the Tazzy camp; the idea of the free market seemed at once to dissolve all the dark sludge of centuries, untie the tightest knots of thought, simplify life without bruising it. But long imprisonment in the ideological dungeons had left its mark. He hobbled and dragged himself about ponderously where Tazzy skipped. Was Sulzbach's thesis watertight? Suppose motorists refused to pay their fines? Would they be jailed by the State? If so, these courts could not be genuinely described as private.

'Oh, they'd have their own coolers,' Tazzy chuckled, 'with the governors on a percentage, so there wouldn't be too many frills. I reckon most motorists would be pretty keen to stay out of that type of establishment.'

'This private justice all sounds a bit mediaeval to me,' I said.

'Tooshay, Gus,' Dr Tasman Smith said. 'The feudal system had its plus side, I guess. In fact, they had a much healthier attitude towards property than they let on. If you wanted to shift someone from a territory, you could always buy him out. They didn't take all that roots stuff too seriously. In the middle ages they'd have sorted out this Selkirk Strip crap, no problem at all. We'd have sold the old Strip to the Moggies and paid off the settlers with the proceeds, settlers would have gone to the States or somewhere, everyone would have been happy. Instead ...' He gave a little twirl of the hand — a wry dismissal of all the anger and violence and destruction that were to be expected of irrational attachments to blood and soil.

'They're sending half the Royal Navy, it's just incredible.'

'I must say, I do think they're overclubbing a bit,' Boy Kingsmill said, sipping a spoonful of Clapp's green soup from a bowl he had scarcely moistened – I remembered his abstemiousness from of old, he fed on sex and gossip. 'But the horses have bolted and there's no point in hanging around the stable.' His demeanour was grave. As always at moments he considered to be of significance, he spoke in a flurry of idioms garnered from all periods and spheres of life, so that at one moment you might have thought him an RAF hero of the 1940s (his war service was in fact hard to track down, 'intelligence of the military variety' he told me once but with a don't-believe-me twinkle); at another, he seemed more like a rather elderly pop promoter of the 1960s. Despite this gravity, signalled also by a slow rubbing of his jaw with his left hand, from ear-lobe to dimpled chin, first on one side, then on the other, his spare old body was clearly rejuvenated by the thought of action, throbbing with the beat of it, in fact, behind his senatorial mien. It was more even than the raw thrill of the thought. Action, of whatever sort, was a thing to be respected. I noticed how, on hearing that a colleague had taken some dramatic step, Boy would instantly think more highly of him, even if the step might well be ill-advised: 'Hmm, interesting, I wouldn't have expected him to go the whole hog on that one.' Indeed, while remarkably free from the sorts of snobbery usually to be found in someone like him, he was an action snob: 'Chap broke his first wife's arm with a croquet mallet', 'he hitchhiked the whole way back to Delhi from the Burma Road in '44', 'you wouldn't believe it, but he rogered the mother and both her daughters', these were the kind of achievements he really seemed to respect rather than undistinguished wealth or passive occupation of high office. This childlike delight in action suddenly irritated me.

'What do you mean, the horses have bolted?'

Boy looked at me, pained. Such idioms were the precious warp and woof of speech. They were not to be roughly unravelled in this fashion.

'Well, Gus, the countdown has begun. We had to ante up.'

The nauseating frivolity of action, the puerile dressing up in the language of morality, the whole dishonest reluctance to admit that boredom was the only real enemy, above all the refusal to confess to having fun, stung me into a departure.

'I must admit I don't see the point of the fucking game.'

As soon as I had said it, I realised, not the indiscretion (I wanted to be indiscreet to relieve my anger) but that, for the first time in our association, I had not only shocked Boy, I had won his respect.

'Well, Gus,' he said, putting his head on one side as though to admire a work of art from a fresh angle, 'It certainly looks like a zero sum game to me, but then when the regiment's being run by the sergeants' mess funny things happen.'

'You've got to stand up to these tinpot régimes,' Frank said, 'if the British lion allows its tail to be twisted, the medium-term geo-political consequences for the West will be disturbing, extremely disturbing.'

'Quite right, Frank, quite right,' said Boy.

'That man,' said Clapp, spooning me out a helping of curried chicken, 'is probably one of the KGB's half-dozen leading agents in London.'

'Which man?'

'Linz. Over there,' he pointed with the spoon at the short, sturdy figure who was spelling out geo-political consequences to Boy Kingsmill with large round potter's gestures.

'Oh, the one called Frank?'

'Frank, that's ripe. He's about as frank as a rattlesnake.'

'He seemed rather right-wing to me.'

'Grow up, Gus. They sent him over here in '44 to penetrate the British Establishment.'

'Oh, for Christ's sake, Clapp, grow up yourself. Isn't it about time we stopped all this spy rubbish? Everyone knows we haven't got any secrets left worth stealing.'

'You try and persuade Mr Linz's friends of that. You think the world is a nice safe place, don't you? All you have to worry about is who's winning the Test Match. Well, some people are playing real matches, you listen to old Clapp, there's a lot of dirty tricks they don't teach you in public school.' He was agitated, almost shouting.

'Clapp, there's hundreds of people waiting for your curried

chicken.' Hungry Cubitarians had pinned me against the serving-table, their voices rising as hunger sharpened:

'But, in a proper market, you could *buy* a Get Out of Jail Free card.'

'Or a free parking card.'

'I tell you, once an underachiever, always an underachiever.'

'But Chambers never trusted Nixon.'

Clapp, impervious to the clamour, seignorial with his ladle, leant forward and said to me in a fierce whisper:

'Listen, cocky, don't you patronise me. I know things you never dreamed of.'

'Like what?'

'I know who Bristow is.'

'Bristow?'

'The Moggie spy. I can finger him, just like that, any time.'

'I'd like some curried chicken.'

'Can we help ourselves, please?'

'Nixon admired Chambers, but Chambers never trusted him.'

'Help yourselves, it's got extra coriander in it,' Clapp said with the grand indifference of an artist laying his work before a public incapable of appreciating it properly. He led me off to a little side-hall. It had a round mahogany table in the middle with an overlarge Chinese bowl on it, half-full of dusty pot-pourri. Against the wall there were two George VI Coronation chairs, rather grubby. The walls were hung with political cartoons. If you looked closely, at the back of the gang of better-known faces, climbing onto a wagon or crouching in a trench or acting out any of the other metaphors of political struggle, could be discerned Boy, less recognisably portrayed than the rest – all they got right about him was his smooth black hair. It was an uncomfortable cheerless coign, with that air of neglect common in politicians' houses. Boy's house seemed to be full of such corners for waiting in. Clapp clasped my forearm and spoke to me in a conspiratorial yet rather loud voice, like some bit player in a Jacobean melodrama who has to come on during a noisy scene change and shout his sinister news to make himself heard.

'Those boys at *Frag* have got the whole story. Willie Sturgis cracked it.'

'Well, what is the story?'

'Just say Bristow to yourself, slowly.'

'Bris ... stow. Bris ... stow. So what?'

'You don't see it? You of all people?'

'What do you mean, you of all people?'

Clapp raised his eyebrows, pantomiming amazement at my stupidity or perhaps at what he took to be my sly dissembling.

The double doors behind me opened, and Kingsmill appeared, looking shrunk and for once rather old in the light of the chandelier above his head. The chandelier, a dusty octopus of red and yellow glass, might have been bought from a Murano workshop on some romantic trip to Venice – 'Delia insisted,' I could hear him say, he would have thought it unbecoming to confess to any preference of his own in such matters, an unmanly diversion from action.

'Just rounding up the stragglers. Frank wants to say a few words about our hero before the paper.'

Frank Linz stood with his large hands fiercely clutching either side of the lectern as though he intended to dazzle us with his physical strength by crushing it. Although superficially like Clapp – short, square, bespectacled – he was not so ugly or so bald. Little tussocks of sandy hair grew round his ears, and when he smiled there was a sweetness in the air, but a discomfiting sweetness since the smile came at unpredictable moments, not necessarily humorous ones, rather as though it was a barely uncontrollable physical thing like a yawn not indicating boredom at that particular instant.

'Fellow Cubitarians, subversives, and friends, I come to praise George Elbow, not to raise him. And not before time, I can hear his unquiet shade muttering as he ignites yet another Turkish cigarette, for in whatever libertarian valhalla he is presently practising the art of afterliving I am confident that there will be no restrictions on smoking there. Lay it on with a trowel, Frank, I can't stand lukewarm flattery, I remember him saying to me once during one of those Alcibiadean nights at Chestnut Acres with the incomparable Dorothy and a quart or two of potable Bourbon. How we outlasted the upstate moon and between us restored the disciplines of classical market theory before dawn laid her rosy fingers on the Catskills is a tale I have told elsewhere. But, for those who have not sojourned in my pages, let me say simply that Georgie Elbow was the Mencken of macro-economics. His breezy blasts of commonsense dispelled the stale clichés of contemporary discussion. And his subtle Viennese charm lured mugwumps and milquetoasts alike into the perilous realms of microeconomic analysis. When he envisioned a new conceptual formulation, he ran with it like an All-American quarterback. As Oliver Wendell Holmes once said of Dr Kingman Hay, 'He lectured like a man at a picnic on the Fourth of July." '

As these fine-wrought sentences succeeded one another, Clapp sitting at my side became increasingly restless. His Nehru jacket rustled as he shifted in his seat and, when Frank referred to Elbow's 'penchant for the never too blushful Hippocrene', Clapp muttered fiercely: 'Elbow choked on his own vomit.'

'What?'

'Choked on his own vomit. A week after they told him he'd got lung cancer. The man was a total alcoholic.'

'Oh,' I said.

'And so,' Frank Linz finished, 'without further extremities of ado, I shall leave George Elbow to pass the time of eternal day and share a glass or twain with his good friends David Ricardo and Davey Hume. I now pass you over to Dr John Tasman Smith who will address you on The Supply Side Revolution – Could It Happen Here?'

Through the hearty crackle of Cubitarian applause, a commotion of a different sort upped and imposed itself. The door into the hall had opened, and half-a-dozen Cubitarians had congregated around the doorway chattering like starlings. Then Boy Kingsmill detached himself from the huddle and made one of his glides across the room to the lectern where he raised his hand for silence, with the authority of an old bandleader still calling the boys together after nearly half a century in the business, having adapted himself effortlessly to every new beat and step, playing now for the children and grandchildren of his first fans who murmur 'can it still be the same man?' and take comfort from his survival, finding it easier now to imagine that they too are well-preserved and that desire has not yet failed.

'Ladies and gentlemen,' Boy said, 'I would like to thank Dr Linz most warmly for that graceful tribute to the inspirer of these little gatherings. Before I introduce Dr Tasman Smith, I have an item of news which may be of some interest. It has just been announced from the Ministry of Defence that, shortly before eight o'clock this evening, Selkirk town was relieved by men of the 4th Worcesters. The British prisoners have been released and are said to be safe and well. An armistice is expected to be signed shortly.'

The applause was tumultuous. The Cubitarians cheered and stamped their feet. Short men in spectacles embraced even shorter men with beards. Frank Linz gave an earsplitting war-whoop which he afterwards described as 'the college yell of my alma mater'. Boy Kingsmill shook hands with everyone in the front row of the audience. Faces shone with sweat and martial joy.

'Well, as Tiny Tim said, God bless us every one,' Clapp said.

'Tiny Tim has nothing to do with it.'

'I can tell you, I'm not going to wet my knickers just because they've rescued some prat in a plumed hat.'

'It's a victory for democracy, Clapp.'

'Democracy, my aunt fanny. I suppose they'll clean forget about the guilty men now. It'll be roses all the way and we happy band of brothers and jolly good show, Claude.'

'Oh you mean the mysterious Bristow.'

'Not so bloody mysterious,' Clapp said. 'Say it slowly, and use your loaf. Briss . . . stow. Briss . . . stow.' He hissed the two syllables with furious venom.

'Well?'

'Briss . . . stow. Breck Stewart, Moronic Moggies couldn't say it properly, let alone spell it. Can't fight either, it seems.'

'What do you mean? What's Alan got to do with it? Do you mean Alan?'

'Of course, I mean your bloody highbrow high-and-mighty Alan.'

'What do you know about him?'

'Of course I couldn't know anything about him, could I? Old

146

Clapp wouldn't come into contact with one of your upper-class intellectual type of traitor. You have to be a public-school man to mingle with the creamy de la cream. Poor Guy, dear old Kim, poor old Alan.'

'What do you mean? What's Alan got to do with them?'

'Nothing that I know of, yet. But we've got him by the short and curlies on this one. Young Sturgis it was — he's not quite as stupid as he looks — had this idea of checking with the Foreign Office on British visitors who'd been to both the Strip and Mogana in the last couple of years. Said he was worried about relatives of his. They sent him to the agencies that had had people there, and he suddenly saw the name of Mr A. Breck Stewart of the FAO and it clicked because of you reminding him about the nude swimming in Hampstead with Uncle Terry.'

'But that's mad. It doesn't prove anything at all. Hundreds of British people must have passed through that part of the world in the last year or so.'

'Not so many as you might think, cocky. But Little Willie didn't stop there. He got a pal of his in Reuters to check at the Mogana end with a description of the man. And the Moggies all said, "Si, si, Bristow, Bristow, he tell them all about British soldiers and guns."'

'That's still mad. In the first place, Alan wouldn't know anything about soldiers and guns. And, in any case, why would he tell a military dictatorship?'

'Search me, cocky. Ours not to reason why, ours but to do the dirty, that's the motto. If you go around poking your nose into other people's business, you've got to expect a little unpleasantness sometimes.' Clapp's humour was quite restored, indeed appearing to improve still further at the thought that there might be some miscarriage of justice.

'He was probably just chatting away in a café, explaining how hopelessly out-of-date and unscientific British military tactics were.'

'Very likely. I'll believe it, Gus, even though I have not had the pleasure of meeting the gentleman in question, but I don't know who else will. Remember what happened to Lord Haw Haw.'

'That wasn't the same thing at all. I'll get on to Moonman immediately.'

'Too late, *Frag*'s gone to bed. It'll be on the streets tomorrow. Anyway, it was you who gave us the lead, cocky. Moonman will probably think you're ringing up to ask for your fee.' Clapp's spasm of chuckles left him nigh breathless with delight,

A betrayal then? Easy enough to persuade myself that what I said to Willie Sturgis had been only a fragment of idle chat that turned out to be a piece of someone else's jigsaw. Yet even to think of myself as having supplied a connection quite unwittingly was to acknowledge a slightly grubby thumbprint on the business. To mention Alan's name to Sturgis or Moonman, even quite without motive, was to set him adrift in perilous waters. He was a fragile barque not to be allowed out in a high wind. Who could possibly imagine what he might have been up to in thirty-odd years of knocking around places where things were going wrong? Or rather it was all too easy to imagine.

I could feel excuses sidling up to me like so many consoling private secretaries: not your fault, how were you to know, Willie Sturgis would have found out anyway, how much ultimately – 'ultimately' is a crafty solace – does it all matter? Yet I found myself hanging on to my guilt for much the same reasons as one's tongue returns to a tooth that is aching, so long as it is aching within reason – the pain is less wearing than trying not to notice the pain.

'Don't you worry, cocky,' Clapp resumed above a hubbub in the room which was increasing for some reason I could not see. 'You've got your credit. "On returning to London, Superspy Stewart first took refuge with stuffy civil servant Aldous 'Gus' Cotton in his dreary North London hideaway. Upwardly mobile Cotton, worried about fading career prospects, managed to palm off his embarrassing guest on near neighbour the equally fading columnist and megadrunk Robbie Bunsen, who is too far gone to notice." Or words to that effect,' Clapp said.

'Oh God, you –' I said. My little trembling guilt vanished in a flash and gave way to fear, thus showing a proper sense of precedence in the hierarchy of the emotions.

'Ssh,' Clapp said, 'There's another announcement.'

'I understand,' Boy said, 'that there is to be live coverage from the Selkirk Strip in two minutes' time. The programme is expected to last for an hour or so. I therefore venture to suggest that we might reluctantly postpone Dr Tasman Smith's keenly awaited talk to a quieter night. Does that meet with your agreement?'

'No, no,' came a babble of Cubitarian cries, anguished and menacing. 'I've come down from Sheffield specially . . . for Chrissake . . . we want Tazzy.' These indignant voices soared above the better-bred murmuration of hear hears.

'Really, ladies and gentlemen, I think on this night we might find it difficult to concentrate . . . '

'Oh shove it, we want Tazzy. Go Tazzy go.'

And there indeed stood Dr Tasman Smith, slight and smiling, eyes aglow, his delicate hands palming his claque into quietness.

'I bow to your verdict, ladies and gentlemen,' said Boy Kingsmill, ruffled and himself not a little indignant, 'if that is your preference – ' he made a gesture which Pontius Pilate might have envied and stepped down from the platform adding, 'Those who are otherwise inclined will find a television set in my study. We may need a few more chairs.'

Those who had opted for television rose and picked up their chairs – little gold hired ones – and hoisted them above their heads. Already, it seemed on average, taller than the Tazzy enthusiasts, with the addition of these wavering gilded head-dresses, they now towered above the squatter Cubitarians who, being mostly seated to the right of the room, barred the way to the study. As the chair-carriers bumped and sidestepped their way through, the air trembled with ill-suppressed hostility; it was the joining of battle between two of those tribes which are eternally in a state of war, the tall, warlike tribe somehow never quite managing to exterminate their elusive, shorter opponents – or is it that the conflict hovers between the real and the ritual in some mysterious self-regulating way incomprehensible to outsiders so that the number of casualties never threatens the survival of the tribe or the continuance of the conflict? Battlecries of 'Oh, I *am* sorry' – said with that malevolence peculiar to the English upper orders – and 'mind your backs' – the less refined, equally offensive equivalent – provoked protests of 'hey, take it easy there'. One little gilt chair knocked against the chandelier, this one an equally elaborate brass confection of vaguely rabbinical aspect, so that the lights swayed and flickered over the scene.

The study was packed. I managed to find a corner of Boy's desk and hitched a buttock next to a silver-framed Lenare photograph of Princess Marina. Boy had kept from pre-war days one or two tenuous links with the Royal Family — 'danced with her when I was a young subaltern in Malta,' he would claim. These links were part of his curriculum vitae; he did not actively seek to keep them in good order; that was not his way of being snobbish; indeed, I suspect he thought of the Royal Family and the upper classes as a whole as being rather dull and inert; they were unmistakably not where the action was, a phrase which might have been invented for him. He liked to think of himself as beyond class — 'we common chaps' I had heard him say — but he would not have thought of concealing these trophies of his past.

The old cigar-sweat of the room was yielding to the throb of aftershave and the clean, flowery scent which Cubitarian women seemed to go in for — three of them crushed on the sofa, handsome, thickly-made up women in their forties with page-boy mops of an earlier date. Boy perched on an arm of the sofa holding the remote control panel of the television. His erect bearing and smart turn-out suggested that he was in command of the whole operation and could at the press of a button bring to a halt the column of troops to be seen jogging up a dusty main street past a blighted palm tree.

The camera paused and settled on a truck lying in the ditch with its wheels in the air. The truck looked sad and exposed like an upturned beetle. Behind the truck there was a crumbly white ruin of a building which might have been a warehouse or barracks. 'This is the industrial zone which was continuously strafed by the Vulcans before the landings,' said the voice-over of the commentator, who now came into view. He was a thin man with untidy fair hair. He was wearing battle fatigues and standing in front of another ruined white-ish building. Several small boys were playing in the dust behind him. The camera switched back to the jogging troops.

'Those aren't the Worcesters,' Boy said as the camera closed up on the face of one of the soldiers, now crouching in the doorways along the street, 'they're Dandelions, my old lot. Look at the cap badge.'

'You must feel very proud,' one of the women said.

'Well, it's not quite a clear round, I'm afraid. We've lost twenty-two men and there's another fifteen unaccounted for.'

'Still, you won, goddammit, you won,' the woman's voice startled me, more sharply American now as it rose and vibrated through the little hot, crowded room.

'We pulled through, my dear, we pulled through.'

There is a temptation to leave those words there to ring in one's ears, to let their false modesty speak for itself, and not to dwell on the ugliness of the scenes now flashing in hurried, awkward sequence across Boy's television screen. He had not adjusted the colour control properly. The men's faces were bloated and bloodshot; the green of the vegetation behind the low tin-roofed houses was a hot viridian. As the troops climbed further up the hill, the damage done by the bombing was worse. In the distance, guns could be heard booming – at what? What was there to boom at in that desolate, dusty place? The crackle of small arms fire confirmed the taming voice-over of the commentator that 'snipers are still being flushed out, there is plenty of mopping up still to be done'. Night after night, so many such scenes, resistance being mopped up all over the world, only this was our personal mopping up operation. It was a matter of national honour and the pride of old England that not a single sniper should go unmopped.

I had not suspected such feelings in me. It was a surprise to discover so much distaste for the dirty work involved in keeping up appearances. At my age, all that should surely have been outgrown. A sudden and, I must confess, shaming kinship with the lifelong infantilism of Alan Breck Stewart seemed to be budding. Talking of whom, where was he? He should be prepared for the storm that was about to break over him. I got up, accidentally knocking Princess Marina's photograph so that she turned her face to the wall, and made my excuses to Kingsmill.

'Do stay, dear boy. Just going to break open some champagne.'

151

CHAPTER 13

'Oh Gus, I've been trying to get hold of you.'

'I'm sorry. It's rather late to ring.'

'I never go to bed until much later than this.' Even without that oblique reproach, Janey always sounded erect and queenly on the telephone as if talking on it was the kind of public appearance like being involved in a traffic accident which demanded meticulous grooming. Even had I rung at 3 am rather than 11.30, I would not have found her muzzy or déshabillée. This, I should hazard, to be fair (her own fairness provoked, even demanded, a constant renewal of fairness in others) was not a consequence of her own troubles, still less a complaint about them, for she did not complain. It expressed a stoic view of life which must have been with her since her wintry and solitary childhood, for I remembered her as just the same when first I met her as Liz's friend, well before she had married Robbie.

'I wanted to talk to you and Nell about Thérèse, or rather Thérèse wanted me to talk to you,' she went on.

'Thérèse?' I said.

'Yes, Thérèse. We're very worried about her. And she's very worried too. And since she's Nell's cousin and you introduced her to us —'

'Oh, I hope she hasn't been —'

'No, no she's marvellous,' Janey said. 'She was so good when Undine died. And she has been amazing, the way she's cheered up Fanny and Jack.' Even at that late hour, one could not help noticing Janey's knack of slipping in the precisely wrong phrase to undermine the sense of what she was saying and stir up unease in the person she was talking to. Whatever Thérèse's other gifts, like me, cheering up is not what she is good at.

'Does she help with the washing-up and so on?'

'Gus,' Janey said patiently, 'in my house everyone helps. No, she's ideal, only the thing is she's pregnant.'

'Ah,' I said.

'She's very distressed and won't tell us who the father is, though I'm absolutely convinced it's Pete, because she never goes out and he's about the only person she sees. Well, of course, that doesn't make it easier, because he's not exactly responsible, is he?'

'No.'

'I've told her that she's not to worry and millions of people are nowadays and we're all delighted. But she's desperately worried about her parents. I mean, they're Catholics aren't they and terribly stuffy, Nell said.'

'So I believe.'

'I wanted to talk to Nell, but your phone just keeps on giving the engaged tone.'

'She's got an abscess in her tooth and a nasty temperature and she's taken it off the hook. I'm not there at the moment.'

'Oh,' said Janey, implying that I ought to be. 'Well anyway, what she really wants is Nell to go down with her and talk to her parents, but I'm sure you would do just as well. I know it sounds peculiar because you'd think it would be something you'd want to deal with on your own, but she says she wants an ally and she can't face doing it by herself.'

'Well, to be honest, I don't really know the Dudgeon-Stewart parents. In fact, I've only met them a couple of times. Perhaps we should wait until Nell is better.'

'Thérèse is very anxious to get it over with as quickly as possible. I mean, I don't want to exaggerate, but she is very nearly suicidal, and I think it is vital to get things straight with her parents absolutely now.'

'Mm yes, I see that.'

'I think you really ought to go tomorrow, because presumably you'll have to work on Monday.'

'Yes, I suppose so. Oh, all right then. I could pick her up in the morning. Does Thérèse know it might be me taking her down? I mean I don't know *her* that well either.'

'Yes, she does. In fact, she specially hoped that you'd be able to go down with her because she thinks you're very kind and very good at dealing with things.'

'Does she?' However, there was no standing up against this sort of flattery, even if Janey had invented it on the spur of the moment.

'Well, that is nice of you, Gus. I'm sure it will help enormously.'

'I'll pop round at nine. It's quite a long drive. By the way, is Alan there by any chance?'

'No, he isn't. Is that what you rang about? He's gone away for a few days, but I'm not quite sure where. Oh, I suppose it might be something to do with his memoirs.'

'His memoirs?'

'Yes. It was really my idea. He's been so mopey recently, wandering about the house not knowing what to do, that I suggested he's had such an interesting life and met all sorts of people he ought to write his memoirs. I mean I don't actually know if he will or not, but he seemed quite interested in the idea. I thought it would be sort of like a holiday task, you know.'

'You must remember my parents are *Catholics*,' Thérèse said as we reached the motorway.

'How could I forget it? Aren't you, any more?'

'No, no.' Beyond the distress, there was some impatience in her voice, perhaps at the suggestion that anyone her age could have clung to such a faith, or perhaps simply at my failure to have noticed. She was so bedraggled and starveling in her flappy slate-grey raincoat with wet hair straggling down her back. Even on the steamy June morning, she seemed to be shivering. Yet, on a hot afternoon the summer before, I had seen her sloping across the Bunsens' lawn in a swimsuit showing off her broad shoulders and strong brown legs like a Californian. Her mood always seemed to irradiate her so that, although shy and, in theory, inconspicuous, one was always conscious of a concentration of misery or contemplative contentment in the corner of the room where she sat with knees up to her chin.

The house was at the end of a high-hedged lane. The rain came down the sides of the valley running in errant streams across the

154

sedgy fields and through the brambles to wander red and muddy across the black tarmac. The air was heavy. I gasped for breath as we climbed the little steps up from the road to the gate in the hedge. My feet slipped on the glabrous flagstones that led between borders of old-fashioned roses to the front door which seemed to be bowed down with the weight of wrought-iron decorating it. The damp in the hall rose to greet us.

It was dark inside. My eyes, tired from lack of sleep and the long journey to Devon, took time to adjust. Substantial oak furniture loomed, perhaps panelling too. There was a fearful chill.

'Mama,' Thérèse called, half-plaintive, half-peremptory.

Mrs Dudgeon-Stewart was a tall, deep-bosomed woman with Thérèse's mane of dark hair, now greying, coiled round her fine head. I had not met her since we had shaken hands at our wedding.

'Ah,' she said. 'Here you are. It was kind of you to bring Thérèse. She could have come by train.' There was no suggestion of an embrace. The welcome was not cold exactly, more how I imagine members of some royal house might greet one another in the presence of strangers.

'Will you take Cousin Gus into the snug? I will see to the bedroom.' It sounded like an undertaking of some audacity.

Thérèse took me down a passage with uneven stone flags, partly covered by a long rug with holes in it, and into a little room at the end. The room was lined with books and contained a couple of old armchairs with faded chintz covers pulled over them anyhow. On a low firestool there was a heap of dog-eared magazines. They smelled of damp and had names like the *Catholic Quarterly of Literature* and the *Blackfriars Review*. Most of them were four or five years old.

'Jesus, it's cold.'

'I know it's silly, but I wouldn't swear when she's about. She'll say something embarrassing like "Monsignor Knox said that profanity was the mark of an incurious mind".'

'Will she now?'

There was a cough at the door, or rather a series of coughs and a roly-poly bright-eyed little man with hair sticking up on top of his ears and a bald dome came in. 'Tizzy-wizzy, ducky-wucky,' he exclaimed, enfolding Thérèse in his short arms.

'You remember Gus?'

'I say, yes indeedy. How are you, Aldous-known-as-Gus, and how is that irresistible Eleanor?'

'Nell's fine.'

'She *is* fine, isn't she? One of the finest.' Mr Dudgeon-Stewart hopped from one foot to the other as he spoke, perhaps to keep the circulation going.

As he went on saying how fond he was of Nell and what he remembered of her as a child, his wife appeared at the door of the snug and stood there, quite still, with her arms at her sides.

'The room is prepared,' she said, 'You would like to see it.'

'I'll show them the way,' Mr Dudgeon-Stewart said. He led us up the stairs, wheezing agonisingly without slowing from his cheery trot.

'There,' he said as he flung open the door to a little bedroom the same size as the room on the floor below. The brass bed was broad and high. It nearly filled the room, a mountainous mattress carrying the sleeping level uncomfortably near the ceiling. The bed was covered with a faded Indian counterpane with scorchmarks on one side. About nine inches away crouched a single-barred electric fire which Mr Dudgeon-Stewart switched on with a magician's flourish.

'Mind how you wake in the morning or you'll crack your nut,' he said. As he spoke, he crossed himself before the ivory crucifix hanging above the bed-head.

'Ah, you're not a Catholic of course,' he said. 'Mark you, not all Catholics are quite such bowers and scrapers as me. Even Athene says I go over the top.'

At lunch, it was he who held the conversation.

'I have come across a delightful episode in the Linnell papers, Tizzy. The youngest Miss L you will recall was rather sweet on one of the Graveses. Unfortunately for her, this young man turned out to be somewhat peculiar and became not only a priest but confessor and chaperone on the Grand Tour to the young Lord Nantwich, the one who later became known as the Pious Duke and who added the ghastly new wing at Bilby, but he was quite a rakehell in his youth, and little Father Graves had quite a struggle to keep him in order. He writes home to poor Miss Linnell of the most trying nights with the ladies of the opera in Parma.'

'Do you find this ancient tittle-tattle of interest?' Mrs Dudgeon-Stewart scarcely turned her gaze in my direction, continuing to raise mouthfuls of Irish stew to her mouth at a steady pace. She had a good appetite.

'Fascinating,' I said. The adjective vibrated in the icy silence.

'And how was the hay, Papa?'

'Not bad, not bad,' Mr Dudgeon-Stewart said. 'Of course the acreage is nothing like as big as it used to be in my father-in-law's time, not since we sold Bottom Field and Chaplains, but we got a decent price for the hay in the circs.'

'The farm is not what it was,' Mrs Dudgeon-Stewart said.

'My father-in-law was a marvellous man, you know, Gus. He had enormous talent as a writer and a painter too although he would never exhibit. He was a friend of Chesterton and Belloc and all that lot and then at the same time he was a jolly good farmer and knew how to look after his people, and of course the Church too. I don't know how he managed to fit it all in.'

'He is much missed,' Mrs Dudgeon-Stewart said. She seemed to finish off a topic.

'This apple pie, mother, superb as ever,' Thérèse said.

'I have decided against sultanas, in favour of cloves,' Mrs Dudgeon-Stewart said.

'In theory, I deplore the choice, belonging as I do to the sultana camp, but I can only applaud the result,' her husband said, raising a spoonful in tribute.

'Then you ought to leave the sultana camp.'

'I swore on my mother's grave to keep faith with sultanas. She was a devil for them.'

'Your mother,' Mrs Dudgeon-Stewart said, 'was not much of a cook.'

'Oh come, Athene, her pastry wasn't bad at all.'

'At best it was passable. It was not often at its best.'

'I thought the Grampus had a cook,' Thérèse said.

'On and off,' her father said. 'But there were interregna when she wielded the skillet herself.'

'She was not gifted as an employer,' said Mrs Dudgeon-Stewart.

'You may feel, Gus, that we bang on about food too much in this house.'

'Not at all,' I said.

'Was food a topic of conversation in your parents' house?' Mrs Dudgeon-Stewart asked.

'No, we didn't think it worth talking about.'

'Do you mean that the food was not of sufficient quality to be worth talking about or that you considered food in general to be an unworthy subject of conversation?'

'Our food wasn't much good.'

'Your father is happily with us, your mother, alas, not.'

'No, they're both dead.'

'What a pity. They should have come here.'

'And how are the rogues and vagabonds?' Mr Dudgeon-Stewart threw into the long silence that followed.

'Oh, you mean the players' workshop,' Thérèse said. 'Quite well really. Basil has lent us his old van.'

'Ah, the beneficent Basilio,' murmured Mr Dudgeon-Stewart.

'These entertainments are to be in the nature of masques, are they?' His wife enquired.

'Sort of.'

'Is the public eager for such spectacles?'

'Well, we don't know yet.'

'Your purpose is to instruct the audience?'

'Well, it's supposed to be quite political.'

'That would not necessarily be instructive,' said Mrs Dudgeon-Smith. She rose to collect the plates and pass them through the hatch.

'Mother, the reason I came down here is I'm pregnant.'

Mrs Dudgeon-Stewart continued out of the room into the kitchen. Her strong pale hands, flecked with brown, became visible at the hatch, removing the pudding plates and pushing through a wooden cheeseboard. The other three of us remained still as statues, sitting bolt upright.

'We had speculated on the reason for your visit. We had not

expected this,' Mrs Dudgeon-Stewart said as she motioned me to the Brie.

'No, well, I am sorry.'

I became aware that Mrs Dudgeon-Stewart's eyes were resting upon me with an intensity which would have made a basilisk seem shifty.

'Nell was going to come down with us,' I said. 'Thérèse wanted her to come. But she's got an abscess on her tooth.'

'An abscess,' echoed Mrs Dudgeon-Stewart.

'She's such a help, our Nell,' her husband said.

'Are we then incapable of helping ourselves?'

'No, Athy, of course not, absolutely not.'

'What is there to be helped? Nature will no doubt take her course.'

'Absolutely.'

'I wanted her to come,' Thérèse said and began to cry. The tears straggled down her cheeks, twining in and out of her damp hair, in a sad pattern of defeat. Her bent shoulders and bowed head all exhaled the melancholy of some old and intricate elegy. She pushed her chair back and, scarcely seeming to rise from it, ran from the room like a little dark animal running from its burrow. The noise of her steps on the stairs pattered through the silence.

'This is true, I take it?'

'As far as I know,' I said.

'One hears of fantasies.'

'Oh, Athene.'

'She's only nineteen.'

'No, but Tizzy isn't like —'

'It seems we do not know what she is like,' said Mrs Dudgeon-Stewart. Her strong pale hands continued to chop slivers from the wedge of Caerphilly she had dealt herself and then to chop the celery on her plate into short lengths. She pressed the slivers into the curls of celery and dispatched them with a crunch. The rest of her remained still as stone.

'We ought, I suppose, to enquire after the father.'

'We can't. We don't know who he is. Apparently she won't say.'

'No matter. I have no wish to seek him out.'

'But, Athy, perhaps if she's fond of him —'

'I am no believer in forced marriages. If she will, she will.'

'Yes, but we could at least encourage her ...'

Mrs Dudgeon-Stewart gave him a look that was far from encouraging.

' ... well, it may sound old-fashioned, but just to give the child a name, wouldn't it ...'

'I care not for the fashion. There are names a child would be better off without.'

'Yes, my dear, but ...'

'How long have you known of this?' She said, turning to me.

'Well, only since yesterday when Janey Bunsen telephoned me and asked —'

'In this house we do not stack the plates. I have told you before.' Mrs Dudgeon-Stewart's voice rose, for the first time. Her husband, already half-way to the hatch, froze with the pile of faded blue plates clasped to his cardigan.

'Oh, Athy, it's so much quicker.'

'This is not a cafeteria. I am sorry. I interrupted you.' She leant towards me, a grim smile attempting, without much luck, to force its way to her lips.

'No, well, in fact, I don't know much about the whole thing. I just heard from Janey.'

'Did you not converse in the car?'

'Not really. I think she's very tired.'

'The young are always tired.' She had regained her humour, such as it was. 'I must not interrogate you. It is not your affair.'

'It was jolly kind of you to drive her down,' her husband said.

'Oh, not at all. It's a pretty drive.'

'You came over Hangman's Hill, I presume. You remember Belloc's lines of course.'

'I'm afraid not.'

He fed the plates through the hatch, singly, while chanting:

'The hangman built his gibbet here
Because the view had pleased him so;

160

He thought to see three counties clear
Would be the nicest way to go.'

Halfway through the second line, his wife joined the chorus.

'After luncheon, Jim will take you for a walk.' His Christian name came as a shock. Indeed, there was a hint – perhaps the faintest suspicion of a pause before the utterance – that she too, after all these years, found it hard to curl her tongue round it.

'You're in for one of Jim's jaunts,' he said, stamping on some funny little round-toed boots in a damp, fungal cubby-hole under the stairs. 'Rather a speciality of the house. Keeps us out of mischief while Athene gets on with her work.'

'What is her work?'

'The early Catholic essays of Paul Claudel, jolly interesting stuff, half of them haven't been published, let alone translated. She's been at it for yonks, poor old girl.'

We climbed the steep hill behind the house. Jim Dudgeon-Stewart's boots left red slashes of mud where he slipped. The wet began to permeate the belted raincoat he had lent me. At the top of the hill we took shelter from the lashing rain in the lee of a high hedge. We could not see more than twenty yards.

'My dear old father-in-law always claimed that this was where Monmouth pitched camp two nights before Sedgemoor. Complete nonsense, I'm afraid. Chap from Exeter University wrote and told him Monmouth never came anywhere near here. Still he insisted on calling this the Monmouth Run when we went tobogganing. Such vitality. He made everything into something, you know. I still miss the harvest suppers. He'd sit at the head of the table in this old smock he'd woven himself, well mostly himself, and get the villagers to sing rounds – Hay Home and the Cuckoo's Lament and a couple of Latin ones. Marvellous fun.' He was still wheezing from the climb, and his merry round face was creased with sadness as we crouched in the brambles, the rain now coming down our coats and into our boots. 'He'd ask to have Thérèse brought in at the end of supper and he'd take her in his arms and sing a little mediaeval lullaby – Toora loora loo, you know – and then, at the end of it, he'd blow out the candles on either side of him, and the farm people would file past him one by one to say goodnight. Some of them have told me they've never forgotten those harvest homes. Well, if we sit on this bank much longer, we'll both get piles. *Andiamo.*'

At this moment, a dreadful thought struck me, so dreadful that I preferred to leave it half-formed lurking, monstrous and misshapen, at the back of the cave. Quite why it should have come to the surface at all under that rain-lashed hedge, I could not see. It seemed to have blown in by chance on the westerly gale which now blotted out the horizon all round us and the valley beneath us on either side so that we appeared to be walking on an unsupported ridge through a universe of sullen grey mist. Looking back now, I can see that it was Jim's description of the devastating energy of his father-in-law which had set up the link in my mind. Through the rain, as we walked, I fancied I could hear Thérèse's sobs. Unnerved by the clammy storm, I found my host's prattle a poor defence against despair. The air seemed to be full, not so much of ancestral ghosts of the traditional West-Country sort, but of the terrible modern events which had not yet happened.

'Do you sleep badly?' I asked for no good reason that I knew.

'No, I sleep like a top,' he said. His bushy ginger eyebrows, now glistening with rain, shot up in surprise. 'Why do you ask?'

· 'I don't know, people often do in this soft climate.'

'True, true. My pa-in-law never slept, although he lived here all his life. He used to roam the passages. But I just touch the pillow and – boom.'

That night, I felt I was on the point of suffocation. Perhaps it was the nearness of the bed to the ceiling, or the naked pink pork chops we had had for dinner, or the sound of Jim reading aloud from *Mansfield Park* after dinner – or all of these which kept my heart unquiet and thumping like an engine missing. Or perhaps it was an overpowering dislike which I had acquired for Thérèse's mother and all her lapidary certitudes. She reawakened in me a sleeping sympathy for the sloppy, the thoughtless and the wild. In my swirling head, she became confused with the priggish Fanny Price, and I felt an eager affinity with all the characters who were portrayed as bad or weak – Fanny's drunken father and her hopeless

mother, the flashy Crawfords, and the comatose Lady Bertram –
all whose lives were unfinished and open to the possibility of
failure.

I did not at first hear the mouse's tapping at my door, or perhaps
the tapping had itself brought on some Daphne du Maurier-style
dream of creaking casements and long-lost heirs prowling the
passages. When Thérèse came in, her mac over her nightdress,
she looked lost and frightened enough to have understudied the
narrator in *Rebecca*.

'Oh, Gus, I'm sorry to –'

'No, come in, I wasn't really asleep.'

'I didn't mean to let you in for all this. It's really mean, you
know.'

She hoisted herself onto the end of my bed and sat there neatly
like a child who has been told to come in and say goodnight. She
made me feel very old, also somewhat irritable as I caught from
her low, rather nasal voice some faint intimation that now, at this
particular moment in her pilgrimage of misery, although it was
not to be admitted or even consciously taken notice of, she was
enjoying herself.

'I mean, I don't want to *use* you, because it must seem like that
to you, but I just want you to know that I'm really grateful.' She
put her pale white hand on my stubby paw and bowed her head
as though she could not bear to face my gaze. Her shyness seemed
to have undergone some hidden, almost chemical transformation
in the few months I had known her. The manner was much the
same, the averted hair, the sidelong gaze, the hands nervously
plaiting the tremulous hair, the odd grateful smile, the same soft
slow speech with the nasal undertow. Yet now she seemed to use
them not so much to dodge the world and retreat from its awful
intrusions as softly to manage and divert it, or rather in this case
me.

'I must talk to someone, I mean, you have to talk to someone,
don't you? And you can see my mother's hopeless.'

'Your father then?'

'He's just as bad, only in a different way.'

'Well, I'm not much –'

'No, but you know the situation.'

'I'm not sure I do. At least I'm not sure I know what you mean.'

The wind blew the ivy tendrils against the window-pane and whistled round the corner of the house, and the rain beat upon a skylight somewhere outside the door, and no doubt the dead squeaked and gibbered in their sheets. It was the low time of the night.

'Well,' she said, 'You know Alan.'

'I do.'

'I mean, it's him.'

'Oh.'

'You didn't expect that probably?'

'No, it's a great surprise.'

'He's only fifty-nine.'

'Is he?'

'I mean, I don't mean that we're thinking of getting married or anything. It's just that he's not as old as you might think, so it's not really as surprising as all that.'

'Fifty-nine is quite old,' I said severely.

'I didn't think you'd react like that, Gus. I thought you'd be more generous. I mean, I'm not ashamed. I didn't try to get pregnant, but I'm not ashamed. I am a bit frightened, though' — and she began to weep. 'He's fond of me really,' she said. 'He talks to me about things. He treats me like a grown-up. He's interested in what I think and what I'm going to do with my life. I think he's awfully young somehow, you know, idealistic. He always has time.'

I could feel the slow stain of envy spreading over me, not so much for the love which Alan had drawn out of her — although that too reared its head — as for his careless mastery of time. Was that the right phrase? I had seen him fret for lack of time to complete his work. There were days when he seemed to be in a constant hurry, and other days when he paced about, unable to settle to anything. Yet now all these adjustments of mood and pace appeared to me to fit his needs, those unguessable desires and promptings of his undisclosed self. Both the fretting and the pacing had their place in his catalogue of pleasures, and so did his

164

talks with Thérèse. His life was, in a certain sense, conducted.

'He's the only person who's interested in me going into the theatre. I mean, everyone else is either bored stiff or says don't put your daughter on the stage, it's an overcrowded profession.' She gave an imitation of a Lady Bracknell voice, not spirited enough. 'But Alan listens, I mean, he really listens.'

'It's a great quality,' I said.

'Don't laugh at me, Gus.'

'No, it is a great quality.'

'I suppose everyone is laughing at me, most of the time probably.'

'Don't be silly.'

'I can't express it properly, but he does take me seriously. I mean, I know it's not just me. He takes Janey seriously too, and he really has these brilliant talks with her. Of course, Rob is awfully nice and kind under all that growling, but he doesn't listen to women at all.'

'No, he doesn't.'

'Janey doesn't know about me and Alan, and I'd be desperate if she discovered. I mean, she'd be so upset.'

'Well –'

'So she doesn't really know why Alan's gone away, but in fact it's because of me.'

'How do you mean, because of you?'

'Well, he said we ought to have a bit of time apart so we could think things out properly and be really clear in our minds about what we wanted to do, and if we stayed together we'd just get in each other's light. That was what he said.'

'I see. Um, where did he say –'

'No, he didn't, I expect because he didn't want me running after him, and I *respected* his privacy. But I am worried, because I don't think he's very good at coping on his own. And so I wondered if somebody shouldn't just go and see if he's all right.'

'It's a little difficult if we have no idea where he is.'

'I'm sure *you* could find him, Gus. I'm sure you'd know where to look.'

'You know that the two of us are in a bit of trouble?'

'What sort of trouble?'

I told her the *Frag* story, and something of its implications. Perhaps I told it badly. It did not seem to engage her full attention.

'Well, that's all right then if they don't give you the sack,' she said.

'Not entirely,' I said, 'I could be just quietly ruined.'

'Oh, Gus,' she said. 'But you must find Alan before he reads all about it in the papers. He'll be so upset. I mean, they couldn't arrest him, could they?'

'I don't think so, but it's not going to make him very popular.'

For another ten minutes, I resisted but eventually signed up for the quest of Alan. Thérèse would stay with her parents, and I would comb the country, doubtless pursued in my turn by the hounds of Fleet Street counting on me to lead them to their quarry. Yet as I packed her off to bed with an avuncular kiss, a curious light-headedness overcame me. It was peculiar how little over the past twenty-four hours I had reflected on my own embarrassment. Alan Breck Stewart had the ability to take you out of yourself. 'Take' is too tame a verb. He sucked you out of yourself, like a gourmet sucking some soft crustacean out of its shell.

'Sir Wilfred would be awfully glad of a word.' Awfully glad was bad.

'This *Frag* article, Gus. How can we be most helpful?' Helpful was worse.

Sir Wilfred was tall and plump, with breath as sweet as a dentist's and a smile that seemed to be tied to his neck muscles so that he could not smile without nodding and vice versa.

'This Stewart chap. An old family friend, I suppose?'

'My wife's cousin.'

'Just so. A kinsman passing through. The sort of relative we all have hidden away somewhere, one runs across him once in a blue moon at a college Gaudy or some such occasion. You probably hadn't seen him for years.'

'I'd never met him until a couple of months ago.'

'A couple of months.'

'Oddly enough, it was Guy Fawkes night, I remember.'

'Just so. And of course you knew nothing of his ... affiliations?'

'Well, by now I've heard him hold forth on just about every subject under the sun.'

'Hold forth ... exactly, a crashing bore. The trouble is so many of these bores can be so unhelpful. But there we are, one can't condemn a man because of his wife's cousins. Otherwise, where would we all be left?' Where we were left was with a strong feeling that Sir Wilfred's wife's cousins were unlikely to cause embarrassment.

'I'm not sure where he is at the moment,' I said. 'Perhaps I should try and track him down.'

'That would be most valuable. He may need some guidance ... in dealing with the media, for example.'

'Yes.'

'We of course shall continue to say nothing. We have, after all, nothing to say. You might care to take some leave perhaps ...'

'I will.'

'I'm sure it can all be sorted out, Gus.'

'I'm sure it can.'

'If you need our help in any way at all, don't hesitate.'

'I shan't. That's awfully kind.'

As the parting civilities unrolled, wavelets breaking on a gentle shore, Sir Wilfred withdrew into an almost trancelike state. The smile hovered, the eyes still twinkled, but the soul had flown. As always, I left his presence and found myself in the outer office again without any measurable physical effort. This sensation, or the absence of it, was only partly due to the thick pile of the carpet, a strange shaggy weave of violet hue, which suggested some exotic strain in Sir Wilfred's temperament normally kept well out of sight. Only as my feet hit the stone floor of the passage beyond did the realities afflict me. There were, I guessed, three days at most to explain myself and clear everything up. After that, the Department would begin, with the utmost gentleness, to detach itself from the imbroglio. An investigation would be announced, it would be said that there was no question at this stage of taking action against Mr Cotton, which meant that there was indeed a question. Once that process had begun, one was never quite the same again.

'Where will you go?' Janey said. 'How will you know where to look for him? I'm awfully worried. I really don't think he can manage on his own.'

'He's been managing on his own for fifty-nine years.'

'How did you know he was fifty-nine?'

'Thérèse told me, I think. That's what he says he is anyway.'

'He's been awfully sweet to her, you know. She hasn't got many friends, except for those acting people and I don't think they're very good for her.'

'Oh, aren't they? Why not?'

'You know what actors are like. They don't really care about people as people, and Thérèse is so vulnerable now. I just wish it wasn't Pete, I mean I'm awfully fond of him and we're friends, not a stepmother sort of thing at all, but he just isn't reponsible, and no way can you pretend he is.'

'Janey, I think I ought to say ... '

'What?'

' ... that it's probably best to keep Pete out of this as far as possible.'

'Well, he's not here either at the moment. He's gone back to St Botolph's for one of his Group weeks. I haven't talked to him about it at all.'

I did not show to advantage in this conversation. It was hard to be sure whether I flinched from telling Janey the truth because I thought she could not take it or because I could not take her not taking it. Sympathy and cowardice are near neighbours, or so I like to think. And Janey did seem bereft in her bare white house.

'There's nobody here at all, you see. Rob's gone to look for Marco.'

'What ... in the Strip?'

'Yes, or rather up in that place he goes to in the mountains. He hasn't been heard of for weeks. He was supposed to be back last month to give a talk at the Royal Geographic.'

'He didn't get mixed up in the fighting, did he?'

'Well, Robbie said there was some trouble in the hills, because the tribesmen didn't like the troops going through their holy places and eating their goats.'

'I can see they wouldn't.'

'Marco's got a special thing about goats too and how they relate to the people there.'

'Has he?'

'Well, it's hard to explain, really. Except, I did explain it to Alan, and he seemed to understand. Oh, Gus, I am worried about Alan. Where could he be?'

'He must be somewhere.'

'Mm,' she said doubtfully. 'I still think he's gone somewhere to do with his memoirs.' The mention of this enterprise cheered her up. In her ears, it had a solid ring to it. The writing of memoirs was a legitimate occupation. Indeed, the mere embarking upon it was a sign of seriousness, an undertaking to be respected in any man. And then I saw that she might well be right. Perhaps Alan was a man for whom all his past life had been but a preparation for this hour, all past experience drained, by his restlessness, of any true satisfaction and redeemable only in recollection. Like all of us no doubt in that, certainly like me, but his restlessness was so visible, so painful that he left no one in any doubt of his unhappiness. It was impossible to pretend that he was getting on all right really, that things would sort themselves out in the end, that he would come to terms with whatever it was he was so at odds with. Such comforting hopes shrivelled in the fierce heat of Alan's discontent.

But where could he be? Flown to Moscow, fled to Rome, or somewhere south and warm at any rate — a re-run of the 1930s flight path? That sounded unlikely. It was the sort of looking backwards of which Alan would have been critical. There would be nothing to be learnt from such a course. Still less did it seem probable that he would have gone north again to revisit his mother's house (to have called it his home would have been inaccurate). That had caused him pain enough when he had gone up for her funeral. There was not much else I knew of his old haunts, except for one.

'An aunt of Alan's who lived by the sea somewhere,' I asked my wife, 'does that ring a bell?'

'Oh ... yes, Cousin Edie, she lived at Herrington-on-Sea. Very dim.'

'Which, her or the place?'

'Both, I think. None of us ever went to stay.'

I liked the sound of that, and I liked the little two-coach train that curled off the main line carrying brassier pleasure-seekers to grander promenades. The ticket collector told me there was only one hotel in Herrington worth the name, right next to the tiny station. Like the station, the Skye Hotel was an enlarged orange-brick bungalow rambling along the front, sprouting verandahs and dormers and porches in peeling white wood. It was a struggle to open the heavy glass door against the wind and rain beating at the storm porch. There was a sticker on the door which said 'Welcome, the Skye's the limit!' Inside the air was warm and laden with dust and pine-scented disinfectant, and my wet feet sank into the many-coloured carpet. Across the lounge, a television set was quacking to half-a-dozen grey heads visible above chairbacks in the same pattern as the carpet. Beyond the long windows, a grey sea broke on a flat shore.

The motherly body signing me in squinted at the register through her spectacles.

'Angus, you'll be a Scot then too?'

'No,' I said, 'Aldous, not Angus. But they do call me Gus.'

'I didn't mean to be familiar. I'm Miss Macdonald. Just press this bell if you need anything.'

It was a dismal place, desolate, smelling of decay and defeat. Yet it was of places like this, so we were told, that people out East had dreamed of on black tropic nights. Perhaps there was wistfulness concealed beneath the derisive tone in which Alan had described HMS *Horncastle* and the straight-backed aunt with whom he had spent the shorter holidays to save expense, some dream of permanence, of, for want of a better word, home. And I too had begun acknowledging myself that my pursuit of him was not simply dictated by the need to save my own skin. I felt implicated in the way the papers were now hounding Alan. I had not looked after him properly. He had drawn me into a net of obligation, and as I lay on my bed looking out at the grey sea I felt in some

170

obscure way better, even if it should turn out that Alan was not within a thousand miles of this place. It seemed odd to think of him as my child when I had two of my own, but in a way nature would look after them and nature had signally failed to look after him. It was this air of neglect and mischance which so allured self-sufficient people like me and, I suppose, Janey. He was our shadow, our alter ego, the life we might have had.

The rain stopped as it does towards evening by the sea and a misty sun came out. I walked over wet pavements past villas in the Skye Hotel style, their brick and white wood faded to pink and grey in the twilight under leaden eaves: Dehra Dun, Simla, Tel-el-Kebir, Mafeking, Inkerman, Shalimar, Omdurman – victories, reliefs and pleasures all mingled in one imperial threnody. In daylight, a quaint and naked exhibition; in twilight, a sad and sweet festival of remembrance, a genteel dwindling from the first robust thrusts of empire, yet one which was in its way comforting and which called for respect. I too did not mean to be familiar.

When I got back to the hotel, the lounge was transformed. Heat, noise, laughter, pushing, jostling. The cheerful throng was overwhelming Miss Macdonald, who stood at bay behind the little bar in the corner of the room.

'Hi, Gus,' a voice called, 'come lift the elbow.'

The Cubitarians were in session. Short, chunky men in shirt-sleeves were shouting up the waistcoats of tall men with spectacles. Transatlantic fragrances drowned the wholesome pine disinfectant.

'What brings you here?' I asked.

'Couldn't get in at Cliffville, it's booked solid for the conference. Now tell us, Gus, what did *you* think of the climbdown on the syndicated loan?'

'Ah well, I've been ...' My voice faded unable to find words to explain my dislocation from the current of events. In any case, the Cubitarians swept on regardless.

'Reagan's never been the same since he dropped Chuck Smith.'

'I thought Chuck was soft on Salt ...'

'He was soft on Salt One, but he was hard as hell on Two.'

'I remember when Chuck got these two girls from Penn State ...'

171

'Chuck never went to Penn State.'

'No, the *girls* were at Penn State.'

'I tell you, nobody gave a shit about the typewriter, it was the pumpkin that finished Hiss.'

'Hiss was OK, it was Priscilla Hiss who was the Commie.'

'Hiss was not OK.'

'Well. there was Chuck, bare-assed as a ... Gus, have you met Professor Wallbang from St Andrews?'

My elegiac mood was crushed. I smiled weakly, waved at Frank Linz and ducked out of the throng along the passage leading to the stairs. As I passed the glass doors into the almost empty dining-room, I caught sight of a tall man sitting by himself at the corner table behind a cut-glass vase containing two or three spindly brownish chrysanthemums.

I opened the glass doors and put my head through. He looked up and stared at me.

'Gus. How did you find me?'

He had not shaved for a day or two. Long hairs shone a silky ginger on his chin. The overhead light was fierce in the dining-room, the red flock wallpaper fiercer still. Alan seemed very pale. He got up and we shook hands.

'I thought I had covered my spoor,' he said, with a smile which uncovered the long, yellow teeth.

'Well, we old trackers, you know. It only takes a broken twig, a crushed leaf ... '

'Ah yes, Peter Pienaar. The Bitch used to read John Buchan to us after roll-call. *Mr Standfast*, I think. She told us to read *The Pilgrim's Progress* as well to see where the characters came from, but it was dull stuff.'

'Look, are you aware that half of Fleet Street is after us, mostly after you?'

'My dear Gus, this is a pleasant backwater. I am an elderly gentleman engaged in family research. I have not told them I am writing my autobiography. They might think I was someone famous.' He gave his rasping laugh – 'Do you think I should call it *The Autobiography of a Failure*, or would that be over-egging the pudding?'

'But even here people must read the newspapers.'

'What people?' Alan said, gesturing at the empty dining-room.

'Well, there's that mob at the bar.'

'Fatuous politicians babbling away – they would have little or no interest in a retired schoolteacher. By the way, they know me here as Mr Gurney-Pollock. I am masquerading as a cousin of the Bollock. I'd be obliged if you didn't peach on me.' He emitted a giggle, also rasping.

'Do you realise – '

'Would you care for the pâté maison or the avocado mexicaine? I had the avocado last night. It was not very mexicaine. Miss Macdonald is not much of a cook.'

'You're wrong, you know,' I said. 'It's in places like this that people on the run are always identified. If there aren't many visitors about, they get looked at more closely.'

'We shall see, my dear,' he said. 'What do you think, a little bottle of Beaujolais to celebrate our meeting, though I fear it may be awfully nouveau.' This mutation into camp was now familiar, although I was still not clear how far it was an escape route and how far a sign that he had begun to enjoy himself. Was it only I who brought out this side in him? Or did others find him switch from Professor Branestawm to Anthony Blanche as the evening wore on?

'And how is Janey?' He spoke as of some mutual acquaintance whom he had not seen for years.

'Very worried about you.'

'There's nothing at all to worry about. It does no good, you know.'

'What, worrying?'

'Yes. It's a form of power mania, claiming responsibility for people you have no responsibility for. Causes a lot of trouble.'

'I think she just hopes you're all right.'

'Of course I'm all right. And I'm grateful to her for suggesting this project. I should have undertaken it years ago, when there was an outside chance that people might have listened to me. But now – '

'I think readers these days are probably more interested in the sort of people you've known ... and so on,' I said.

'Interested! It's not going to be a gossipy book, you know, not a kind of My Memories of Five Reigns by the Duchess of Dungheap. Is that what you thought?'

'No, not at all.' How odd, I did think, that he should share the same revulsion as his persecutor Clapp. Perhaps being of roughly the same age, the duchess threat seemed more real and monstrous.

'Because I did cherish a hope, a very, very faint hope, you understand, that people might actually learn something from it. Where is Miss Macdonald? I must apologise for the service here.'

'Listen, Alan, we've got to get this Selkirk Strip thing straight. What did you say when you were in Mogana?'

'Say? Nothing of the slightest consequence. One does not go to Mogana City for the conversation.'

'Oh, come on. Who did you meet? What did you talk about? You must have said something.'

'I'm afraid it would all be too technical for you, stuff about crop yields, fertiliser ratios, dietary balance, not the sort of subjects to interest a British civil servant with a classical education, ha.'

'Nothing about the military situation?'

'What military situation? There wasn't a military situation.'

'Did you talk about the British defences in Selkirk town?'

'Defences? That's a good one. A handful of beer-bellied tommies playing cards in a disused canning factory.'

'So you did talk about it?'

'My dear Gus, you don't seem to have the faintest idea what a place like Mogana is actually like, in which, if I may say so, you are splendidly typical of your Service. There is absolutely no one to talk to and nothing to talk about. So you talk to everyone about anything you can dredge up to talk about.'

'Who was the everyone? And what did you dredge up?'

'You are quite an inquisitor, Gus. You must be awfully good in committee.'

'I am. Brilliant.' A kind of weird intimacy seemed to glimmer upon us as the inquisition proceeded. Some barrier between us had at last been kicked down. 'Who did you talk to?'

'All sorts of people.'

'Who?'

'Well, among many others, there was this fellow who I used to have tea with.'

'Who was he?'

'Is, I hope. He was rather a nice man. Something to do with the Foreign Ministry. He used to have Earl Grey tea and these frightfully good little cakes, imported, like everything decent in that dismal country.'

I could see Alan sitting, angular and bony, on a heavy brocade sofa in the official's flat, perhaps hungry, having forgotten to eat for a day or two, and gobbling the little sweet cakes from a Mappin and Webb silver cake-stand, while a neat man in a dark suit with a smile made aimless conversation: eager for news of the Strip (using the British slang correctly of course), some years since he had been there ... this silly visa business. And Alan rasping in reply: ludicrous red tape ... uselessness of British Foreign Office ... place stuffed with troops now, utterly futile, must be a battalion there. So many? And still in the old canning factory? Oh, they've rigged up a make-shift gun emplacement, hopeless spot, restricted field of fire, jolly good little cakes these ... now about this literacy campaign, I wonder if ... Then the process so appallingly familiar from my own life: the report to the neat smiling man's superior – interesting conversation with a British official in one of the relief organisations – followed by the report to the superior's superior – valuable military intelligence from a British official – followed in turn by the report to the Minister – my agent, acting on my instructions, won the confidence of a highly placed British official and obtained a complete dossier of the enemy's battle dispositions – ultimately followed by the whispered boast at a diplomatic cocktail party. It is this old process of inflation, distortion and self-promotion which offers bored officials a passage to fairyland and, with luck, wafts word of their genius to Oberon's ear and translates Bottom into top.

'How many times?'

'How many times what?'

'How many times did you meet this man?'

'I don't know, two or three.'

175

'And did you talk about the military situation with anyone else?'

'Don't keep on talking in that pompous voice about the military situation. There wasn't a situation.'

'Did you talk about it with anyone else?'

'Certainly not. It was a highly tedious subject.'

'Or write about it?'

'Good God, no. I was there for FAO, not NATO.'

'So there were just these two or three conversations with this man.'

'That's right. At least they weren't quite as tedious as this conversation.'

'What was he called?'

'I can't remember.'

'Try.'

'I might have it written down upstairs. I've brought quite a few of my files with me, for the book, you see.'

'Shall we go upstairs and have a look?'

'Gus, in the middle of dinner?'

'We haven't started dinner.'

'Does it really matter?'

'Yes.'

I had to push him up the stairs. His feet seemed to stumble on the heavy red floral stair carpet, reminding me of his stumbling gait the first night we had met and Nell and I had helped him home from the Littlejohns.

His bedroom turned out to be next door to mine. The curtains were not drawn. One or two lights glimmered on the black sea. Alan's belongings had already sprawled across the neat little room. A pile of old brown exercise books teetered on top of the tea-making machine. A large cardboard box tied up with string protruded from the hanging cupboard. The bright yellows and apricots of curtains and bedspread seemed to flinch at the invasion. That sour sad old man's smell blotted out the evergreen fragrance which pervaded the hotel.

'Quite homely.'

'It suits my immediate needs. It ought to be somewhere in here, this chap's name, though quite why it matters —' He rummaged in one of the battered black exercise books. 'Yes here we are. Tea with de Silva a minor flunkey in the foreign department. A Portuguese half-caste, I suspect. Asked me to call him Teddy. A useless conversation. De S. seemed woefully ill-informed about the Strip and, after I had put him straight, there was no time left to ask him about the inoculation project. Going again next Thurs. And so on. 25th March ... more talk about the garrison ... disagreeable man from? Interior Department also present ... there's quite a bit about this tea-party. Had to explain a whole lot of military terms to them including, what's that, can't quite read it, looks like Bren gun, can't be.'

'Are these all diaries?'

'Oh yes, I've been keeping them since before the war. I used to wonder sometimes whether it was worth carting them round, but now, you see, they have turned out to be a vital source material for my work.'

'Look, I think you'll have to hide them, or better still, destroy them.'

'Never heard such nonsense. I wouldn't dream of it.'

'You don't seem to understand what's going on out there. There's a witch-hunt brewing and you're the witch.'

'Well then, you must be my familiar, ha.' The plaquey yellow teeth flashed again.

'That's exactly why I want you to destroy them.'

'I suppose I could indulge your fantasies to the extent of tearing out a few pages.'

'That would be worse than doing nothing. They would notice immediately that the pages were missing and their imaginations would run riot.'

'Well, we could salt away just the couple of volumes which deal with my experiences in the Strip.'

'Same thing. The gap in the series would stand out like an accusing finger. You'd have to choose some convincing date to stop the diary on – the year you left England, say. How many volumes have there been since?'

'A considerable number. I should say half-a-dozen.'

'Well, they'll have to go.'

'Couldn't I lodge them in a safe deposit with my lawyer or my bank?'

'No, they'll be bust open one way or another and they'd look twice as sinister when they are.'

I had begun to frighten him, and my own fear began to fade as I tasted this power.

'You really think ... I'm just an obscure old relic ... would they really want to persecute me?'

'Obscure old relics are just the people who get persecuted, because they do not know how to look after their own interests.'

'Gus, I am grateful,' he murmured and sat down on the bed.

'I am going to take them out now and get rid of them, and then I am going to have a drink and go to bed and catch the first train up in the morning. If I were you, I'd stay here for a bit and finish your researches until the heat is off.'

'Would you really? You think that would be the right thing to do?'

'I'm sure of it.'

He got up and rummaged through the pile of exercise books and handed me five of them.

'That's all, is it? There aren't any more relevant ones? Or any other documents which have anything to do with your time there?'

'Certainly not,' he snapped with a little of his old spirit. 'These absurd tea parties were utterly trivial and had nothing at all to do with my work.'

'Right, I'll put them in that carrier bag. Now I think it's best if we're not seen together again here. As I said, it's in these small places that there's the greatest risk of being noticed.'

I slipped down the back stairs through a kitchen passage smelling of fry-ups and out into the warm, wild night. Cruel exhilaration. I swung the carrier bag, striding along the crumbling asphalt of the promenade. In the distance, at the far end of the shallow bay, a curve of bright lights winked at Herrington's decay. And then, above them, clusters of smaller lights soared from resorts further along the coast and broke into the night sky, silver and gold, green and rose. The Victory fireworks. Only Herrington-on-Sea was too dispirited or too proper to celebrate. The distant fireworks dampened my spirits. A full cloak of darkness was needed for this assignment. I looked longingly at the curl of white foam breaking on the pale sand. The sea had an inconvenient way of flinging back jetsam. Nothing would be more likely to induce a retired major on a morning stroll to go straight to the police than an exercise book full of foreign names. Could I risk a dustbin? I peered into a litter bin attached to the bulbous railings. Nothing but a little orange peel and some Kleenex. Any tramp would be sure to go straight for my carrier bag. The next bin was too full. The next one was too empty. The larger bin beside the ice cream stall was made of wire. I put the carrier bag in, and then took it out again. Even in the half-light cast by a street lamp fifty yards away, it looked too inviting. I walked on down the promenade towards where the houses ended and the ground began to rise to form a low cliff. Perhaps there would be a bottomless quarry there, or a council tip. The road came to an end, and I followed a rising path through wet brambles. The other side of the rise, I came out into a wide clear space with goalposts standing out against the skyline. And there at the far end of the space was a bonfire sending flames twenty or thirty foot up into the night.

I had misjudged the place. Herrington-on-Sea knew as well as anywhere how to celebrate the nation's deliverance. I hurried across the damp grass, the accursed carrier bag knocking against my calf. Joy leapt in my heart at the thought of being parted from it. Already I could see the flames licking at it, the plastic melting, the pages curling into blessed oblivion. There is no pleasure in life to compare with the relief of riddance.

How cheerful and kindly the Herrington faces shone in the glow of the fire; there must have been thirty or forty of them in sensible coats and boots and scarves and pom-pom hats. There was an impressive determination about their celebrations. Good people, I thought, as I sauntered up and prepared, with the utmost inconspicuousness, to add my carrier bag to the patriotic flames.

'Excuse me, sir, no personal rubbish on this bonfire please.'

'Oh. It's only some old paper and stuff.'

'I'm sorry, sir. It's a council rule.'

'I only thought – every little helps.'

179

'That's right. But you see, we've had trouble in the past.'

'I quite understand.'

'It's been scientifically prepared has this bonfire.'

'Well, it's burning very nicely.'

'There's a bin down at the end of the playing field.'

'Thank you, thank you very much.'

A bespectacled man loomed out of the darkness behind the man in the council uniform.

'Hullo,' the bespectacled man said, 'there's coffee and buns in the church hall after. Just passing the word round.'

'Oh thank you.'

'Everyone welcome.'

'I'm afraid ...' I said.

'There's no need to be shy. You'll find us quite a friendly bunch.'

'Uh ...' I made a dumb show of pointing at my watch, since no words would come. And I turned back towards the path through the brambles clutching the carrier bag with mounting loathing. I found myself taking a different route back through the town, down a back street of low brick houses. I stopped at a stunted pub on the corner and stayed my hunger with an elderly pork pie and a pint of bitter. Then I crept back into the Hotel Skye, but not sneakily enough to evade a clutch of Cubitarians drinking round a low table in the lounge.

'Hi, Gus,' said Dr John Tasman Smith. 'You know Frank Linz, and this is Bert Queeg and Art Crowsnest. We were just kicking workfare around.'

'I'm a hardliner on this one,' said a man whose face and hands seemed to be entirely covered with short dark bristly hair. 'No work, no welfare. And if they don't work, throw 'em in the slammer for vagrancy.'

'Then you're supporting them, Art. When you get down to the bottom line, jail's a kind of in-house welfare.'

'Not my kind of jail,' the hirsute man laughed, showing teeth as white as snow.

'What do you think of the conference so far?' Tazzy asked.

'Ah, I haven't seen much of it yet.'

'I thought I hadn't seen you around. It's great you could come.

I could still fit you in as an interlocutor in the Options 2000 seminar.'

'Unfortunately,' I said firmly, 'I have to go back to London first thing tomorrow.'

'Too bad,' said Tazzy and gave me his marmoset smile.

'Suppose you could work your way out of jail on a voucher system. Fifty days sorting mail-bags and you get to go home for weekends. 100 days and you're home free ... '

'In fact,' I said, 'I think I'd better get an early night.'

The passage upstairs was dimly lit and quiet. Not a rustle from Alan's room. Perhaps he also had turned in early.

I lay in bed with the light off and watched the shadows thrown on the ceiling by the headlights of the occasional passing car outside. Soon the babble from downstairs drifted away, as the Cubitarians too went up to bed.

On the table by the window, I could see the outline of the carrier bag. Still, I drifted towards sleep. Strange dreams of rustling leaves and bare white feet.

It was nearly three o'clock when I sat up in bed and looked at my watch. I did not know what had waked me until there was a low groan from next door, then a louder groan, long and sonorous, like the huntsman's horn from distant woods on a foggy afternoon, and another loud groan, broken this time, and drawn out to a long dying away. The thinness of hotel walls, the loudness of one's own heart beating in the darkness, all over the world, those same groans heard by strangers crouched under the blankets, the melancholy of hotels, even the grandest, never quite deadened by the carpets and the flowers in the vase and such thoughts themselves being thought night after night by comfortless travellers, commercial and otherwise. And how iron the etiquette of solitude. Was there a hotel in the world where it was in order to knock on the next door and say 'I heard you groaning'? If such a hotel existed, would I of all people wish to stay in it?

Another groan, low and fading. I wondered how long the groaning had taken to wake me. Had it been going on for hours? And then there was no more.

My room was black and cold. The heating had gone off. The

last car had gone to its garage down in Pottersfield or up at Cliffville beyond the embers of the scientific bonfire.

When I woke again, it was six in the morning, and the cold blue twilight made me shiver as I pulled on my rumpled clothes and packed my bag to catch the first train up. As I opened the door into the passage, I hesitated. Was it better to say goodbye to Alan? Or would it be thoughtless to break into the remains of his distraught night?

I came out into the passage and my foot stumbled on something. I looked down in the dusty half-light to see a dark briefcase lying on the carpet with a white envelope on top of it. I bent down and picked it up. It was an old black government attaché case embossed with the faded royal arms. I tore open the envelope. Inside there was a single sheet of Hotel Skye writing paper headed with a fanciful drawing of the premises and the hotel motto – 'The Skye's the limit.' Underneath, in a donnish hand: 'I wanted you to have this, in the hope that you might make better use of it than your predecessors – ABS.'

Inside the case was a dog-eared orange folder. The typed paper in the folder was yellowing and the old big type had greyed with the years. There were memos from one set of initials to another set of initials, and a few drawings like the one Alan had scratched out in the dust for me. On the outside of the orange folder, Alan had written fairly recently in biro: Broomsticks – SECRET.

Now there was no doubt. The door had to be knocked on. My first knock was considerate, my second more demanding. There was no answer to either. Then I tried the handle and to my surprise the door opened.

There was no concealment in the little room. Even in the half-light, the event thrust itself at me. The sheets and blankets were thrown back, and he lay naked across the bed, one arm thrown out over the edge of it, the other up to his face, as though to ward off a blow, that gesture I had first noticed on the night we met. His knees were a little drawn up towards his stomach. The folds of the brown blankets, pale in the twilight, were like some sandy earth, a shallow pit hastily scrabbled in a poor soil by prehistoric warriors burying their dead, a defeated tribe, outnumbered, outgunned, mown down outside the gates. All the same, he did not look as uneasy as he had in life.

I put my ear down to his pale body and could hear no breathing. Then I vaguely looked around for a mirror, but this was an excuse not to look at the body. My hand brushed against his hand and it was cold. The empty pill bottle and the empty whisky bottle were on the side table. They did not interest me.

The motions had to be gone through. Miss Macdonald was already dressed and downstairs. She seemed quite at home with such events. A friend? Yes, I was catching an early train and had called in to say goodbye.

'A mistake I expect. These pills are so difficult. They shouldn't prescribe so many. I'll have to get the police.'

'I'm so sorry,' I said.

'We've never had something like this happen before. But then there's always a first time. Such a discreet gentleman Mr Gurney-Pollock.'

The two policemen were sleepy and watchful. 'Was Mr Pollock a friend of yours, sir?'

'Yes, a friend, he'd come down here for a rest. I just popped down to see he was all right.'

'And was he?'

'Well, he was a bit down. Things hadn't quite worked out for him.'

'No family?'

'No close family. My wife's a cousin of his. He was staying in London with friends of ours.'

'A lonely man, would you say?'

'Yes, lonely.' That was what I would say, what anyone would say, what all the evidence showed. A man on his own in the Skye Hotel at the age of fifty-nine must be lonely. Yet his condition would not have been cured by a wife and three children and a house in North Oxford and sherry on Sundays with colleagues and cousins. That grand discontent which lurked in him could not have been so easily appeased.

'Anyway, lucky for us you were here, sir, to sign the death certificate. We might have had quite a chase otherwise.'

'Well, it's a sad day for me. We were fond of him.'

When I told her, Nell burst into tears.

'He mustn't be buried under a false name. It's so undignified.'

'I don't see what else we can do. It would be more undignified to disclose that he had been staying in a broken-down seaside hotel under a false name. That would really make it look as if he was on the run.'

'That's a typical Civil Service reaction. Always thinking of a scandal.'

'Oh, all right then. But it's too late now unless you want me to go to jail. I've signed the certificate.'

I spent the afternoon in the garden building a bonfire for the children. At the bottom, I placed the three notebooks. The briefcase did not look as if it would burn, and I hid it in the attic.

The newspapers failed to penetrate the alias of Gurney-Pollock Deceased. And Sir Wilfred affected ennui when I managed to get in to see him and reported that a member of his department, namely myself, had made a false declaration on a death certificate.

'Gus, the fact of the matter is that the whole matter seems to have been based on a slight misunderstanding. We had our people look at it, and quite frankly there is no evidence at all that the enemy had access to any information which wasn't public knowledge. And the source of the rumour, a certain Mr De Silva, has since been hopelessly discredited as an extremely seedy character. You'll be pleased to know that we've put the word around to our friends in the media and for once they seem of a mind to accept our assurances. I'm extremely sorry to hear of Mr Stewart's death. A tragic waste. I understand he had had a distinguished career in public service.'

'He did.'

'Gus, I've been meaning to speak to you on a more personal note. I know you've been under a considerable strain these last few months. The contribution your group made to the whole operation was absolutely first-rate and, I am sure, will not pass unrecognised in the appropriate fashion. In addition, there has been this other matter and I'd like to express my own, personal, gratitude for what you've done for us in this regard. I know how difficult it has been for you, and it's only right that we should try and ease your path a little in return. What I would suggest – and it is only a suggestion – is that in your next posting you might be looking for an opportunity to recharge your batteries a little. There is a vacancy coming up at Agriculture, in the forecasting section. Oddly enough, Hilary Puttock is just going over to head the section. You'd be reporting direct to him. Does that appeal to you?'

'Oh. Yes. Fine,' I said. Dust and boredom surged up from Sir Wilfred's shag carpet. I felt a million miles away. Somewhere in the distance bells began to peal.

'Good. Splendid. And don't worry about the other matter. People forget about these things after a victory, you know. Listen.' He gestured towards the window. 'Practising for the victory service. Have they given you a decent seat?'

'Oh. I haven't been in this week.'

'No, no, of course. If there's any problem, just let Madge know. Ding-*da*-dong-ding-da. Whitlock's Triple, I fancy. I am enormously grateful to you, Gus.'

On my way out, I met a thin and hollow-eyed Riley-Jones.

'Got your see yet?' He asked.

'See what?'

'CBE, wake up, old boy, what do you think we're all here for?'

'Oh yes, sorry. Sort of, I think.'

'Sort of. I call that a pathetic response. All that "to our trusty and well-beloved Aldous, We, Elizabeth do by these presents . . ." and all you can say is sort of.'

'What about you?'

'I thought about turning it down. But the moment for that has rather passed, don't you think? I say, those bells make a bloody racket. I can't hear myself dictate. What were you seeing Wilf about?'

'You remember my friend, Alan Breck Stewart?'

'Oh yes, the superspy.'

'Well, he wasn't, it seemed. Wilf was just giving me the all-clear.'

'Another triumph for the cock-up theory of history,' said Riley-

Jones. 'Any chance of the reptiles leaving him in peace now, do you think?'

'Not much. He committed suicide last week.'

'Oh dear. Not the way to remain anonymous.'

'He left me a strange legacy. He was in the Mountbatten think-tank during the war and he left me the plans for his secret invention.'

'Which would have won the war if only – '

'Exactly. Ian, do you think you could find out about it? He said they didn't go ahead because of the aluminium shortage.'

When Riley-Jones rang me that evening, I could hear him trying to sound elated but he came over as distant and diminished.

'I've had a lovely day with an old boffin in Technical Confidential Filing who was in the Ministry of Supply at the time and claims to remember it all like it was yesterday,' he said. 'It's quite true that aluminium was in very short supply at the time, and aircraft production was naturally a priority. Still, the Broomstick would not have needed a large quantity. What happened apparently was that they carried out a test in a disused quarry somewhere in the Chilterns and the Broomstick buckled under the strain of a beefy marine corporal who broke a leg and nearly drowned in a stagnant pond. My, how the brasshats laughed. On the other hand, my friend has to admit that he was not actually present at the test and it could be a malicious fabrication. As you can imagine, all the permanent officials and the military absolutely loathed the Mountbatten people.'

'About that at least he told me the truth.'

'Well, I wouldn't take all this as gospel. I couldn't check it, because my friend in T.C.F. said all the relevant files had been destroyed and I had to take his word for it because if they hadn't been I wasn't cleared for access to them.'

The wind rustling through the beech trees above the quarry. Bright brown shoes caked with clayey Chiltern mud. Down at the bottom, Alan's bony figure rasping instructions. The beefy Marine, red and sweating, clinging to the frail aluminium cradle. The little group of brasshats peering down, trim and silent. Then the buckling, the fall, the splash, the groan of pain. Alan rushing distractedly up to the brasshats, stilling their laughter with his indignation ... indignation at what? The quality of the aluminium, the clumsiness of the corporal, the denseness of the brasshats, fate?

'Thank you,' I said, 'thanks very much, Ian, you sound like death.'

'A good guess,' he said. 'I think I've got cancer.'

'Oh,' I said. 'How do you ...'

'So does my doctor,' he said. 'But he won't admit it.'

'Perhaps he's telling the truth,' I said.

'No, he can't be. I looked it all up. It's pretty straightforward. I'm awfully modern about that sort of thing. Have it out in the open, and so on. I'm not quite sure why. It doesn't seem to do much good.'

'Whereabouts is it?'

'The colon. It's turning out to be more of a full stop.'

'Don't they just give you a bag and you immediately feel wonderful?'

'Only if you're robust and have a cheerful outlook on life. I am not one of those cases where the doctor comes out and says Mrs Riley-Jones, your husband's putting up a wonderful fight. To start with, there isn't a Mrs Riley-Jones.'

'Oh.'

'Didn't I tell you that either? How one forgets these little things in the press of great events. No, Yola's gone back to *maman* in Clermont-Ferrand.'

'I am sorry. Why ...'

'She didn't like playing second fiddle to HMG. The Strip club put the lid on it. Never home till midnight for three months running. Do you think I could ask Wilf for compensation?'

'No.'

'Nor do I. I'm rather short of compensations at the moment.'

'Come to supper, not that that would be much of a compensation.'

'Thanks very much, but I don't think I'm quite up to it yet, I find I tend to burst into tears at the wrong moment, and then get very drunk and boring, and just say fuck all the time.'

'You'd fit in perfectly.'

187

'All the same, Gus, I don't think I'm quite ready for it.'

Nell cried too when I told her about Yola going back to Clermont-Ferrand. I did not feel up to mentioning the cancer.

'But you scarcely know him, or her,' I said.

'It's just that it's happening to everyone.'

'Well then, perhaps it doesn't . . .'

'No, it's the only modern tragedy, the only thing that matters.' She spoke with force, her cheeks flushed, the lines from the side of her mouth to her chin carved like a puppet's.

'Surely when a child dies, when Undy died . . .'

'No, that is different, more terrible, *much* more terrible, but it is not a tragedy because it is a blow from God, not a failure by us.'

'Well then, a doctor who makes a mistake when drunk, say, and the child dies. Isn't that a greater tragedy?'

'No, no, you don't see at all. And it's more of a tragedy the more it happens, because it means we are all failing.'

'That must make it less of a tragedy. It's just the way of the world or the way of the twentieth century anyway.'

She looked at me. 'I can't tell whether it's that you really don't notice or that you don't care. You mean you really can't see what's happened?'

'I don't understand. You're not – '

She looked at me, more severe than ever.

'I'm not anything.'

'What do you mean then?'

'You'll see soon enough. No, I'm not going to say, because there's no point in telling you, because you're no good at pretending. You're better off ignorant.'

'My life is spent pretending.'

'Oh at work. That's a sort of game anyone can play. No, I mean serious pretending.'

'I still don't understand.'

'You're not meant to. You'd better go if you're catching the train. Tell Janey again how sorry I am I can't come, but I did promise the children I'd go to the concert.'

Inquest-bound, in inky black, we sat facing each other in the slow, rocking train to the coast. Janey wore a coat and skirt and a white shirt with a little ruff, like a woman barrister off to court. With her long head and straight back, she reminded me of a little girl in a Victorian illustration, Tenniel's Alice perhaps.

'How are the three Grubbleys?'

'Well, I couldn't think what to do with them. They've already been to the moon, and to the centre of the earth, and they've met the Queen. And then Jack said to me what do the Grubbleys eat because I always say about their clothes and who made them – like when the squirrels made them waistcoats out of oak leaves – so what do they eat? So then I thought what about a Grubbleys cookbook with really delicious recipes for children and pictures of the Grubbleys making them.'

'Oh yes, I see, what a good idea.'

'Lots of it's awfully simple like there's this sort of custardy sauce for fish fingers which is absolutely scrumptious and you can make it in no time and it really sort of transforms them from being boring into a real treat. The publishers seem to be quite pleased with the idea and Rupert, that's my agent, says that now they're owned by this food firm they might bring out some Grubbley foods at the same time, you know, Grubbley cake mix and delicious Grubbley sauces. It's just fantastically lucky that I happened to call them the Grubbleys, because of Grub.'

'Mm.'

'Alan loved the Grubbley stories. The last night he stayed with us he took *The Grubbleys Go to the Moon* to bed with him. Will it be awful, the inquest, do you think?'

'No, it will be quite quick, I'm sure. The police said it was really just a formality. You've just got to remember about Gurney-Pollock. I'm sorry about it. But there was no alternative.'

'I'll remember. I wish he hadn't died. I wish he was here still. It means we've all failed, doesn't it?'

'I think that's a rather one-sided way of looking at it,' I said primly. 'It was his responsibility as well.'

'No, but if we'd loved him properly, he wouldn't have. I keep wishing I'd never suggested about him writing his autobiography. I'm sure that depressed him. It was so silly, I only wanted to cheer

189

him up and he'd had such an interesting life.'

'He had.'

'He taught me such a lot.'

'Well, I know he was very grateful to you. He needed a home badly.'

'I need him,' she said. Tears slid from her pale eyes down her white cheeks.

'Well, at least you've got old Rob,' I said.

'Rob's left.'

'Oh, I didn't know that. I thought he'd just got back. I heard he hadn't found Marco yet. Is he — '

'No, I mean, left me.'

'Oh. What — '

'Didn't Nell tell you? She's so loyal.'

'She is.'

'We haven't been the same together since Undine died. I'm sure you realised that. I know tragedy's supposed to bring people together, but it probably only works if they're quite together to start with. If it's all a bit fragile anyway, then any shock just breaks it all up.'

'I'm terribly sorry.'

'In a way it's a relief. Rob said we could call it a trial separation. I said I'd had enough of trials. But I expect he'll call it that anyway. He doesn't like things being too definite.'

'Where is he?'

'Oh, he's got a flat in Slocock Lane. For the time being.'

'Ah.'

'I expect he'll move in with her quite soon. Rob's a terribly simple person, you know, Gus. He has very simple needs. Any woman will do really. I mean, that's why it's so awful Monica's husband going back to New Zealand.'

'Monica ...'

'Monica was his secretary. She was an awful person really, with this terrible laugh, but she was quite good for him because she didn't make any demands and she didn't want to break up the marriage. And then her husband who's a radiologist got this good job back in New Zealand.'

190

'And she's staying behind?'

Janey looked at me in amazement. In fact, the amazement was so great it brought her tired and tearstained face back to life.

'No, of course not. She's going with him. They've offered her a secretarial job at the hospital as well.'

I said nothing and looked at her knees. They showed pale and bony through her thick black stockings.

'You mean you really didn't know? But Nell knew. Why didn't she tell you?'

'She thinks it better if I don't know things. At least that's what she said to me this morning. I didn't know until then that she thought so.'

'Why not? You're awfully ... reliable, Gus.'

'No, I don't think I am really, not in this sort of thing. I expect she's quite right. I don't think I mind much anyway.'

'Yes, but you're such an old friend of Liz.'

'Liz? Yes, I suppose I am.'

Until that moment, I had not realised what a foreigner I was in this world, how alien its intimacies and desires and betrayals were to me, how meaningless to me its dropped hints and sidelong glances.

'She's a bitch really, I mean, I know she's always been my best friend and all that, but subconsciously I've always known she was a bitch.'

'What about Hector then?'

'Oh,' she said, 'haven't you seen him recently? Hector's a case, he's finished. He spends most of his time in my basement playing games with our Pete. They're both hiding from life. I have to cook them huge meals. Hector's blown up like a balloon.'

'He didn't look well the last time I saw him.'

'Gus, you have to face it, there's nothing left of him now she's finished with him. He's like something washed up on a beach, all bloated and smelly.'

Flat meadows, still half-flooded. Skeins of wire straggling from stump to slanting stump along the dull ditches, sodden hanks of wool drifting from the barbs. In the distance, cooling towers and council houses, fields of kale on the higher ground; the sky grey with the rain to come.

'I've always known about her,' Janey said, looking out of the window (so unlike Liz's direct and rosy gaze). 'Even in that nice time when you first get to know someone and you seem to know instinctively what the other one's going to say next but it isn't boring at all, and everything seems funny even when you know it isn't, I've always known.'

'Known what about her?'

'It's hard to describe exactly. There's a sort of engine inside her which is always working just for her but most of the time you forget about it, or you can't hear it, so she doesn't seem at all selfish.'

'I know what you mean,' I said, 'but in a way haven't we all?'

'Not one that works all the time. Ours has to compete with all the other things – you know, getting the children off to school and so on.'

'I suppose she can't help not having children.'

'I don't think it would make any difference to her if she had. It's an energy thing. The amazing thing is Thérèse could see it straight away. She said she thought Liz was creepy.'

'Creepy?' I said, nettled as if the accusation had been levelled at me.

'All that being so concerned, and having time to spare for everyone, and jollying people along.'

'Oh,' I said. 'How's Thérèse?'

'She's all right, she's gone down to her parents till the baby's born. She says she's very sad about Alan, but perhaps he wouldn't have been a very good father, so she's just proud to be carrying a memory of him. She's very sensible, Thérèse, basically.'

The approaching coast and the end of the line. Beyond the railway fence, disordered clumps of alder and bramble; long brick workshops with dirty windows and cracked panes; piles of timber, coils of wire, jagged mountains of metal scrap, and dull black mounds of tyres; the sea mist turning to rain on corrugated iron roofs and tarmac lorry parks; the backs of houses with scruffy patches of lawn and decaying greenhouses; at an upper window, the outline of a girl brushing her hair, half hidden by the mirror on her dressing table.

'I hate her, I do wish she was dead, I'm glad she can't have children, I hate her, Gus.'

The train slowed as the rain thickened. The brakes screamed a thin keening lament for the end of hope and trust and Alan Breck Stewart. The inquest passed off as inquests do. It surprised me how easily I lied under oath. As I was in the witness box, I thought to myself, this is the only unselfish risk I have run in my life. On the way back in the train, Janey said much the same thing, only more politely, and then I realised that it was not true. This had been an ordeal of the mediaeval sort, a trial of fidelity, well, perhaps of love, and coming through it brought the self its own peculiar satisfactions.

ENVOI

'Why didn't you tell me?'

'Tell you when?'

'Whenever you knew. When I told you about Liz being so upset when I mentioned about the secretary.'

'Oh then. I didn't know then. In fact, I hadn't even put two and two together, when Janey told me because she said she had to tell someone.'

'Well, you could have told me after that.'

'I explained to you before. I think you're better off not knowing things like that. Anyway, you were so worried about your job and Alan and everything. I didn't want to overload you.'

'You don't seem to think much of my load factor.'

'I don't understand that sort of jargon,' she said. 'You must listen to this bit.'

'From Crupper?'

'Yes ... Margery daughter to Mr Skipton married, aet. 17, Mr John Wombwell, of Devizes, but he was of a lewd and choleric temper and it was an unquiet house, and I think she counts her bruises as oft as she counts her plate, of which in truth she hath but little, since he hath sold the moiety to pay the griping Usurers. He was a low, ugly fellow who got a scar on his face in the late wars, but Mr Skipton says he got it not nobly but in an ale-house from a wench who threw a great tankard at him. They are both living, but live not together he being of an unconjugal mind.'

'I don't think I'd have liked old Crupper.'

'He's a great diarist,' Nell said.

'Or a dead gossip.'

'Same thing.'

'At least you have the grace to admit it,' I said.

'There is nothing to admit. What else is the power of speech given us for but to talk about each other?'

'Don't first-rate people talk about ideas? Your infinitely distinguished family, for example?'

'The Dudgeons only gossip,' Nell said. 'The people we gossip about may be alive or they may have been dead for three hundred years. We don't mind; we still like gossiping about them. That's the only difference between us and other people.'

Her long cardigan hung about her like a shroud. Her pink cheeks, pinker still in the cold of our sitting-room ... her long hair, negligently coiled on her long head ... how healthy she looked, like an old advertisement for female cycling, how well charted her course. The cold made me feel faint and also somehow furtive. All our preparations against disaster seemed for a moment like a conspiracy, a kind of racket to exploit the headstrong and feckless.

'If Thomas goes next term,' she was saying, 'He'll be taking his O-levels when he's still fourteen which means Oxbridge when he's not seventeen which is ridiculous. That is assuming they still have fourth term entry of course.'

'Remind me again,' I said, 'exactly what fourth term entails.' I knew perfectly well, but there was a minute pleasure to be squeezed from pretending to be a carefree person who could not be bothered with such mark-grubbing, not least because this pose annoyed Nell so.

'Oh, Gus, you know perfectly well, Dr Sproat explained it over and over again.'

'All life is a preparation for ultimate failure,' I said, 'so Thomas might as well start getting into practice.'

'Dudgeons always pass exams,' Nell said firmly. 'And where did you hear that stuff about preparation for ultimate failure? It's awfully cheap.'

It was not until after the birth of Thérèse's baby that we heard again from Liz. She and Rob had gone into that strange period of incubation which, even in our untrammelled age, is regarded as a decent minimum in such circumstances. As with some ancient menstrual taboo, time was needed to wash away the uncleanness of their coupling. Meals had to be taken in strange tavernas where they would not run into old friends, a different supermarket patronised, complicated arrangements for laundry devised, for Hector had not formally moved out of Number 43 and his dirty clothes no less than his rack of inexpensive wines had to be kept separate from Rob's. We heard that he slept nomadically, unwilling to commit himself: sometimes in his own spare room at Number 43; sometimes on the sofa in the basement flat which Pete occupied at The Laurels; sometimes begging a bed at St Botolph's after accompanying Pete to an out-patient session.

'It's a miserable existence,' Nell said.

'But you can see his point. He doesn't want to be a full-time looney. He doesn't want to lose his rights on his own house. And he certainly does not want it to look like a wife-swap because it isn't.'

'Well, he'll have to choose soon,' she said. 'He can't go on Boxing-and-Coxing for ever.'

Hector came to supper. He was so fat that his shirt strained against his shirt-buttons and you could see pale flesh underneath. For a long time, he said little or nothing and looked down at his plate. Half-way through the paella there was a silence.

'How are Berle, Hoyte and Engstrom?'

'They're all dead and I've got the boot,' Hector said. Another silence.

'Angels passing,' Nell said.

'Not over Number 43. Hacks fucking. That's all there is passing over there. Hacks putting their great red pricks —'

'Oh, Hector.'

'Nell, what you don't know is that the prick is mightier than the pen — or the sword. Much mightier.'

'Please, you mustn't —'

'I must, because at this very moment the great man is putting his great pundit's penis into darling Liz's dear little vagina, well not so little in point of fact. Not so very little. But you know in point of fact that's what's happening, because that's what's happening all the time.'

'Hec, we really know how you —'

'You don't know how I anything. What you know and what I

196

know is that at this very moment ... '

'Come on, let's go next door and talk about something else.'

'What else is there to talk about? Because you know and I know ...'

That night he slept on our sofa, vomiting in the early part of the night, moaning later on. In the morning, he said:

'I think I'll go abroad for a bit.'

'Oh *yes*.'

'The States, probably. Dallas to start with, we have connections in Dallas. Things have to be sorted out first. One must always sort things out.' One of his old low sucking laughs. In fact, his old comfortably devitalised self seemed to have returned.

We heard later that he had gone to Belgium. There was some European job, free of tax but not of tedium.

A couple of months later, Liz rang up to ask about Thérèse's baby but really to announce that she was back in circulation.

'She says will we go to dinner?' Nell said.

'No,' I said.

'Don't be prim,' she said. 'You're so prim. Marriages break up. People get divorced. You have to face these things.'

'Why?' I said.

'Because they are old friends.'

'Being old friends means you can talk freely. With Rob and Liz in their present position almost every subject is taboo.'

'That's not what being old friends means at all. It means putting up with them when they're going through a difficult time.'

'Going through a difficult time? You speak as if it was something that had just happened to them and they were not to blame for it at all. I'm on Hector's side. I won't be able to look at them without thinking of them hard at it.'

'It's Thursday and she says don't be early because of Rob not getting back until nearer nine.'

In fact, it was Rob who opened the door at the first smack of the knocker. He was trimmed out of recognition; his hair now a neat pad of wire wool; the crease on his trousers knifing his strong thighs; and he was wearing a strange little leather jacket which had ridden up his still unreformed stomach. A chastened man. He gave us an undertaker's welcome.

It was Liz who was billowing in full sail, blousy as a field of unopposed poppies. 'Darlings' and 'loves' swarmed through the air. Even the cooking smelled more exuberant. Huge tumblers of wine, good wine, were pressed into our hands as if to lose no time in dispelling memories of the miserly old régime. Another bottle. Opening it, Rob broke the sides of the corkscrew. The slivers of dark red plastic clattered onto the glass table and set the little balls of Newton's cradle (now repaired, or had Hector bought another one?) clicking faintly like the stirring of some faint memory at the back of a distracted mind.

'It won't grip now,' Rob said. 'Is there another corkscrew, darling?'

'Oh dear, I'm afraid Hector took it away with him when he took all that wine. I'm afraid he's drinking rather a lot at the moment.'

'Well, well,' said Rob, 'we've all been known to take a jar now and then.'

'But I don't think it agrees with Hector, his body can't really take it, I just don't think he's at all well. And he won't talk to anyone. I mean I can understand him not wanting to talk to me, I absolutely understand, but he won't talk to anyone since he came back from Belgium. I ring up the doctor at St Bott's and he says he can't breach his patient's confidence, so I just don't know what he says down there. Gus, does he talk to you at all?'

'Well,' I said. 'We haven't seen that much of him, recently.'

'Oh, I do wish you would see more of him, Gus. He doesn't have that many friends really and, well I know Pete's awfully nice, but he's not really a companion, and you do need someone to talk to, don't you? You see, I know he's bitter, he's got every right to be bitter – '

'Darling, is there any chance of a bite to eat?'

'I'm afraid women are more resilient really, don't you think so, Gus? We pretend we aren't, but actually basically we can cope when we have to, at least most of us, but men, most men anyway, don't have the resources. I mean, I've always known that Hector had one skin too few, that's what makes him so special, but it does make him terribly vulnerable. That's why I think it's so important that he keeps a base here so he has something to build on. But I'm very worried about when we go away. I mean, do you think you could possibly keep an eye on him, both of you, just to see he's all right, and so on?'

'Yes of course. Where are you going?'

'Oh, didn't Rob tell you? We're going out to look for Marco again, because when Rob went there the first time there was still fighting going on in the mountains, with the PGO, and so he couldn't get a visa. But this time the Embassy has promised him he will get one and I can go too and take some photographs which can help to pay for the trip. It's awfully exciting, well not exciting, because it's so desperately worrying for Rob because he hasn't had any news for months. I so hope he's all right, Marco, he's such a marvellous boy, with those blue eyes, and awfully nice, isn't he? And he's done wonderful things for the mountain people. He's such a communicator, he doesn't really need words. I mean, I know Rob says he can speak all the mountain dialects, but there's something about him that just comes across brilliantly, even when he doesn't say anything. I don't like that word sexy, and anyway he isn't that exactly, but it is a kind of magnetic sympathy. You know, I thought Thérèse was bound to fall for him, living in the same house and being the closest in age, but she's obviously one of those women who much prefers older men because of her father being so inadequate. It must be so odd, mustn't it, to go through life looking for a father figure. I'm not sure what I'm looking for, are you, Gus? I mean, my relationships, well I can't exactly see a pattern in them, although they've all meant a lot to me. I don't feel that I'm one of those people who can't form stable relationships with a person. It's just that until now the important relationships in my life have been with people who aren't terribly stable. It's just happening like that, I don't know why, but, oh Gus, of course you're extremely stable but I don't suppose you would call us a relationship. I mean, it's a friendship really isn't it, although I suppose a friendship is a relationship when you come to think about it. And anyway friendships are just as important, we know that now, don't we? Of course men have always known that, but it's one of the new things for women, being friends with women and men and keeping sex out of it, I think that's Thérèse's problem really. If she'd been older, she could have been just friends with Alan and he could still have taught her just as much and there would not have been all this infatuation and guilt and he might still be alive, because he did feel very guilty. In those last few weeks you only had to look at him, that sad face, and you could see how guilty he felt about Thérèse. Although actually I think the baby's completely transformed her, she's so steady and grown-up all of a sudden, she's really a new person. Of course it's still terribly difficult being a single parent whatever people may say. It's not only the stigma and the money worry. Thérèse will be all right for money, but it must be terrible with her mother glaring at her all the time like a basilisk, but it's just basically being so on your own that is the worst thing, being ultimately totally alone, however supportive your friends try to be. And of course you worry about the child being alone too. I do hope Alana will be one of those kids who makes friends easily. It would be marvellous if, well, I promised myself I really wouldn't say, but you know how things just pour out of me, Gus, I just can't help it, but I went to the doctor yesterday and I definitely am pregnant. There now, it was worth it just to see the expression on your face. I always wondered how you would look Gus, if something really surprised you. Nell probably told you that we always thought it was something wrong with me, a sort of kink in my tubes, that prevented me conceiving. But then, well, it was rather a strange roundabout story, but you remember the time when Hector became a friend of Pete's and used to go with him down to St Botolph's. To start with, it was out of kindness, and then he became a sort of patient himself. And he explained about us having no children, and so the doctor asked whether he had ever had a sperm count and Hector said no and so he had one, because he was in that frame of mind when he was fantastically intrigued by everything to do with himself, and it turned out that he had one of the lowest sperm counts they had ever seen, poor lamb. And of course he told me because he told me everything, even the worst things, he even told me that he had an affair with Alan. How did you know about that, Gus, you do find out about the most extraordinary things. Naturally I was terribly, terribly upset. It wasn't that I hadn't suspected about him having that side to him, because when we were first married, he was quite frank about having been bisexual in his teens, but we both thought that it was an adolescent thing which he'd outgrown. Anyway, Hector told me and I told Rob. You wouldn't believe this Gus but that was really how we got together. I hadn't properly thought of Rob in that way before although I'd always liked him very much as a person, but somehow I found that he was the person I had to confide in, because I had to confide in someone and from then on the relationship really took off, so we started from a confidence, a kind of trustful thing which must be rather unusual with an affair – what an awful word – but perhaps that is why it's such a firm thing. So you could say that poor Alan, indirectly, brought us together. Anyway, to get back to the sperm count, I told Rob about that too because things just pour out of me as I said. So he said to me very frankly, well, you're not getting any younger, charming, but would you like to try, so I said, yes I will yes.'

'Get poor Gus a drink, darling, and stop rabbiting on.'

'You see, Gus, I'm a survivor. I didn't think I was, but I am. In a way I'm rather ashamed of it when I think of people who aren't survivors but who've got so much to give, people like Alan who really live their ideals.'

'He survived long enough,' I said.

Printed in Great Britain
by Amazon

55503519R00128